Praise for *Have a Heart*

Have a Heart by António Gomes is a dazzling story of Anna, an elegant ballerina who succumbs to a heart ailment, and of Ali, the young doctor who is smitten while treating her. Anna's adherence to her Russian culture attracts and mystifies Ali, a Muslim of Pakistani and Indian parentage, while her heart ailment comes in the way of their love affair. Ultimately, Ali marries an all-American beauty, an investment analyst working in the World Trade Center. This is the setting for a beautiful tale of the human heart, both in its capacity for passion and in the precise physical details of how it works to keep us alive. Gomes writes of radiant moments in life just as he meditates wisely on its loss in death. A celebrated cardiologist, he sees the living world as a physician and feels it as a poet.

—Grace Schulman, author of six exclaimed books of poetry including, *The Broken String* and *Without A Claim* and winner of the Frost Award for Lifetime Achievement in American Poetry. Her recent memoir is *Strange Paradise*: *Portrait of a Marriage*. She is currently Distinguished Professor of English at Baruch College, C.U.N.Y.

Intoxicating and authentic, António Gomes' great gift to readers is *Have a Heart*. Gomes, a cardiologist as well as a masterful author, writes an expertly plotted and lyrically-fierce prose; a rare combination. We meet Ali, a young Muslim cardiologist, who finds himself caught between the lovely Anna, *"half-bird, half-woman; her shimmering feathers taper off in orange-speckled flames,"* a Russian ballerina who desperately needs a heart transplant, and Nancy, an all-American girl whose parents view Ali's religion as not quite suitable. Add to this a fellow doctor's theft of the fruits of Ali's research, and then the blue sky September day arrives when planes crash into the Twin Towers. Applying a breathtaking realism, Gomes beautifully describes a heart transplant, the operation almost resembling a ballet of the hands with skilled arabesques and pirouettes. We watch the donor heart engorge with blood. We wait for it to beat. *Have a Heart* is a tour de force, passionate, deeply felt, and so gripping that the midnight reader hardly notices the pages turning until dawn breaks the writer's spell.

—Stephanie Emily Dickinson, author of more than nine books including *Half Girl, Love Highway, Lust Series, Corn Goddess; Road of Five Churches; Port Authority Orchids* and founding editor of Rain Mountain Press

Dr. Gomes is a renaissance man—a physician, poet, and writer. In this, his novel about the intersection of a heart transplant surgeon's professional and love lives, he combines a fascinating, gracefully-rendered knowledge of medical technology with an understanding of the vagaries of romance. The story rests on the frail shoulders of characters who are realistic and flawed, and its overlay of cultural conflict adds a depth that is especially poignant in our times. Readable, relatable, and life-affirming—two thumbs up.

—Susan O' Neal is the author of *Don't Mean Nothing*— the first by a nurse who served in Viet Nam gives a glimpse into the war from a female perspective.

We all strive for something we can't seem to attain until that pivotal moment we finally understand what it is we truly want, then the way forward becomes clear. Ali, a successful transplant cardiologist, is in crisis—of career, of love, of faith—and each unfolding opportunity that would seem to lead him to his heart's desire only results in obstruction, frustration and eventually tragedy. But, as Ali discovers, catastrophe is often the very catalyst that forces a change of perspective by way of circumstances we never requested to set us on the path we were always meant for. Gomes' fast-paced journey through the human condition, as viewed through the fascinating world of transplant medicine, is fundamentally a love story—love of self, of others and the human journey. With an unexpected but satisfying ending *Have a Heart*, above all else, offers hope emerging from darkness that expands well beyond the pages of this novel.

—Laurin Bellg, MD, author of *Near Death in the ICU*

Have a Heart is a novel that ambitiously embraces many worlds. Ali, the protagonist, carries the layered baggage of an Asian family that has made its way to the American dream; their multiple religious and cultural affiliations play tug of war with Ali's loyalties as he goes about making sense of life, forming relationships and carving for himself a high niche in the profession of Cardiology. The novel offers us a heady sip of the intensely competitive field of medicine, where the highly specialized and noble task of saving lives goes hand in hand with research and the aggressive demands of institutional bureaucracy. We are invited to the exacting realm of ballet, as Anna is deprived of her brilliant career as a ballerina from the erstwhile Russian socialist republic when her heart plays tricks on her. Nancy, warm hearted, from the world of business, coping with her own demons, completes the love triangle as these central characters engage viscerally in matters of the heart, life and death.

The interconnected worlds of culture, religion, career, family and politics are vivid spaces that often collide in this novel. Dr. António Gomes threads confident ground as he skillfully crafts *Have A Heart*, after the well-received *The Sting of Peppercorns*. A brilliant cardiologist, he is an acknowledged novelist and writer of the literary essay.

—Dr. Isabel Santa Rita Vaz, author of *Frescoes in the Womb* and 40 plays. She is the founding member of The Mustard Seed Art Company and Guest Faculty at Goa University, India.

HAVE A HEART

A NOVEL

By

António Gomes

 SERVING
HOUSE
BOOKS

Have a Heart

Copyright © 2020 by António Gomes

All Rights Reserved

Published by Serving House Books

Copenhagen, Denmark and South Orange, NJ

www.servinghousebooks.com

ISBN: 978-1-947175-27-3

Library of Congress Control Number: 2020937399

Member of The Independent Book Publishers Association

First Serving House Books Edition 2020

Cover Design: T.Schneider Creative

Author Photograph: Big Apple Portraits

Serving House Books Logo: Barry Lereng Wilmont

This is a work of fiction. The names, characters, and incidents, are the products of the author's imagination. Any resemblance to actual events, persons, dead or alive is entirely coincidental.

DEDICATION: To my patients with defibrillators; to my wife, Margarita, and my grandchildren, Joseph, Jaden, Jonathan, Nicholas, Gabriel and Kai.

Books by António Gomes

Medicine

Signal Averaged Electrocardiography: Concepts, Methods and Applications.

Heart Rhythm Disorders: History, Mechanisms and Treatment Perspective

Poetry

Visions From Grymes Hill

Mirrored Reflection

Fiction

The Sting of Peppercorns

Nas Garras Do Destino

CONTENTS

PART

I

1998

The ballet is a purely female thing. It is a woman, a garden of beautiful flowers. — George Balanchine

CHAPTER 1

Swan Lake

The month is May, the place, Lincoln Center. Red and yellow tulips, white and yellow daffodils fill the planters, and the air is sweet from the roses in Damrosch Park. Shiny black limos and yellow taxis line the long sidewalk. Women in black, indigo, and midnight blue; some with glittering diamonds, others bare necked, knock shoulders beside their tuxedoed men as they hurry past the tall fountain. All the glitter, the *haute monde* of New York City, seems to pour into the Opera House tonight.

"Hurry up Mum, or we'll be late," says Ali, turning to his mother, graceful in her pink gold-trimmed sari, and offers her his arm.

"*Khokon*," she says, looking intently at him and using the Bengali for son, "you need a young, dashing, beautiful wife by your side, not your aging mother." He is almost 6-feet tall, lean, and handsome, of olive-brown color with brown eyes, a scruff beard, and jet-black curly hair parted on the side. Today, in a rented tux, he looks like an Indian prince in western garb.

The air of festivity permeates all around them as they hurriedly enter the Opera House. They make it into the theatre a few minutes before the doors are closed and are shown to the

front row, center. The seats belong to an American Ballet Theatre benefactor, one of Ali's patients. The house is full, with
even the standing room taken. It is the opening night of *Swan
Lake*, and Anna, the Russian ballerina, is making her American
Ballet Theatre debut as Odette/Odile. Ali vaguely remembers
her dancing several years ago after she defected from the Soviet
Union to join New York City Ballet. At that time, he was about
to leave for the Mayo Clinic in Rochester, Minnesota. That first
time he saw Anna dance, her passion and her intricate and extravagant movements infused the dance sequences right into his
own muscles, as if he, too, were a dancer. Watching her then, he
thought of the three years he'd studied ballet, so long ago, and
the loss he'd felt when his father had made him stop. He recalls
how Anna's supple, expansive technique had made her stand
apart from the Balanchine-trained dancers with their crisp, athletic speed. She was dubbed by the media the next Superstar.

"What great seats," says his smiling mother. "I'm so proud
of you—so young and already the Head of the Heart Transplant
Program at one of New York's leading hospitals!"

"Enough Mum!" says Ali, as he fidgets in his tuxedo,
straightening his bow tie and pulling forward the somewhat
loose jacket. "This rented tuxedo doesn't fit. I should have worn
my blue suit."

"You should buy your own tuxedo. You'll have many occasions to wear it." She reaches over to adjust Ali's tie when
the chandeliers grow dim and rise to the ceiling. A hush of
expectation fills the theatre. Ali straightens in his seat as the
familiar Tchaikovsky music begins and the curtain rises on a
forest glade. Beyond, on the stage, the rippling surface of a lake
shimmers in the moonlight. The royal hunting party bursts into
the clearing, astonished to see the flock of white swans gliding
serenely on the lake led by their beautiful queen. Her tiara of
diamonds refracts the moonlight over the water.

The orchestra heralds the arrival of the Prince, who quickly orders the hunting party to move quietly along the lakeside. As soon as they are gone, the Prince stretches his bow and takes aim at the gliding Swan Queen. She spreads her wings and metamorphoses into a woman with the neck and feathers of a swan. With striding steps and a grand leap, Odette, the Swan Queen: Anna makes her entrance on the stage.

Loud applause erupts in the theatre.

The Prince, stunned by the transformation, momentarily lowers his bow and arrow.

Ali pats his mother's arm. "Look at her neck, so stretched, so like a swan," he whispers. But it is her face that transfixes him. His heart misses a beat.

"The Russian ballerinas are made for this," his mother whispers back.

Bathing in the moonlight in *arabesque*, the Swan Queen shivers, as if to dry her wet body, a tendril-like tracery revealing her elegant proportions. Suddenly, as if struck by electricity, her body slips into *croisé*. Ali feels a prince-like rush to take the Swan Queen in his arms. When he took ballet lessons, he dreamt that someday he would dance Prince Siegfried, right here at Lincoln Center. He looks at his smiling mother and wonders what she is thinking. Their eyes shift to the stage.

As the Swan Queen turns, she sees the Prince approach. Terrified at the sight of him, her body trembles. Pointing to his crossbow, she cowers, her eyes full of fear. She presses her arms against her breast as she backs away moving frantically en pointe, and then she stretches her arms as if to lift herself up, to fly away. The Prince lowers the crossbow and sets it aside. She tucks her head in gratitude and rises en pointe again, gliding away in a series of rapid pas de bourrées. The Prince approaches the Swan Queen, lifts her as they circle the stage. But when he tries to embrace her, she breaks away.

Then suddenly, in a flash of lightning, a great clawed-winged creature appears upstage darkening the lakeside. The gliding swans flutter with fear. Overtaken by a sense of foreboding, the Prince goes back to his bow.

And then, the unexpected happens: *Anna—the Swan Queen—collapses.*

A collective gasp rises from the audience. Ali is on the edge of his seat. He sees her eyes roll up.

"I don't remember the Swan Queen ever collapsing!" whispers Ali's mother.

"Neither do I," Ali whispers back.

Did Anna faint? Is all this part of the new choreography? He saw her eyes roll up. He is certain she blacked out.

The Prince takes the fallen Swan Queen in his arms. She lies there, crumpled, her face hanging to the side, her limp torso contoured around his. He takes a few steps hurriedly and then runs across the stage and into the wings, still carrying the Swan Queen. He comes back with a sad look and a new Swan Queen, and the show goes on, as it must.

After the Act One curtain falls, there is a brief announcement: "We are sorry to inform you that Anna collapsed from exhaustion. The role of Odette/Odile will now be danced by Maria Bettencourt." There are loud sighs in the theatre.

While fast asleep, just before dawn, Ali enters the REM-dream state and the scene from Swan Lake repeats itself. In the dream, he is the Prince dancing with Anna, when she collapses in the middle of a dance-sequence. He is about to resuscitate her, when he wakes up, heart pounding. At about the same time the alarm clock rings. It is six in the morning. He jumps off the couch and after splashing his face with cold water and spending some time under a hot shower, he dresses for work: black trousers, white shirt, and a blue tie. He goes into the kitchen and prepares himself a cup of instant coffee. As the coffee is heating in the microwave, he takes out the prayer rug from the closet, kneels on it, facing east, and genuflects.

"In the name of God, Most Gracious, Most Merciful. Praise be to God, Lord of the Universe...

After his morning prayers, he lingers for a moment on the prayer rug, an old habit, when he thinks of the ballerina, Anna—may Allah provide sustenance to her. As he walks into the kitchen, his mother is already there, cleaning and cooking.

Seated at the kitchen table, Ali and his mother drink coffee and feast on chapattis. She had brought the ingredients with her, well knowing that the fridge would be empty or filled with half-eaten stale curries.

"I wonder how Anna is," says Ali. "I've got to check the reviews."

"I pray she's okay. What a dancer!" says his mother.

"What are your plans, Mum?" he asks.

"First clean this apartment—it's very dusty—then cook your favorite biryani—then pay a visit to Fareeda, and after that the Metropolitan Museum."

"You don't have to clean, Mum. The housekeeper will be here on Friday."

"I wish you could join Fareeda and me at the Metropolitan Museum. Her daughter, Aisha, is apparently a beauty, and she's doing her residency in medicine at New York University."

"There you go again. Have fun, Mum, and don't forget to lock the door. I'll come home to Long Island next weekend and we'll talk," he adds, not to disappoint her.

Ali gets up to leave for the hospital. A full day awaits his uninterrupted attention. He senses that his mother wants him to stay a bit longer, perhaps even raise the issue of marriage, or perhaps a forthcoming marriage proposal. He can see her reading his restlessness.

Ali walks out of his building on Seventy-second and Madison into the cool spring air. He feels strangely euphoric invigorated by a sense of optimism of being fully alive, of sleeping, working, entertaining, and contributing to this fast-paced city of teeming millions. Puzzled at his state of mind, he wonders if his elated mood has something to do with his deep sleep last night, or had it something to do with Fareeda's daughter, Aisha? And the name Aisha: the name of the child wife, the favorite wife of the Prophet Muhammad. Should he call Aisha to keep his mother happy? Her concern for him, for his bachelorhood, is distressing. The blind dates with daughters and nieces of his mother's friends and cousins had been disappointing. His personal life was in the doldrums since Ras, and he hadn't dated for a longtime. Perhaps it is time to start dating again. And Aisha is possibly a good match: a Muslim doctor for a Muslim doctor like tea for a teacup. His parents worried that he was still single at the age of thirty-eight. "Ali, better you choose a Muslim wife," his father had said in a rather provincial and serious manner when his cousin in England eloped with an English girl against his parent's wishes. And Ali partly feels that he would be letting his father down if he didn't comply with his wishes.

Immersed in these thoughts, he waits for the green light to cross the Avenue. A sanitation truck revs its motors plunging forward after emptying the litterbins. A red-haired woman in sweatpants commands loudly and flexes her muscles to take control of half-a-dozen or so dogs just before crossing the street. Madison Avenue has just come alive with skirted women and suited men waving at yellow taxicabs.

Ali crosses the street, walks a couple of blocks at a fast pace, stops to pick up a cup of Starbucks coffee, and enters the hospital through its tall, modern, Gothic arches.

As he steps into his office and is about to change into surgical scrubs, his beeper goes off. "Ali, there's a thirty-five-year-old female patient in the Coronary Care Unit I'd like your opinion as soon as you can. She's in room #4," says Dr. Mel.

A busy schedule of heart biopsies and catheterizations awaits Ali, and Dr. Mel hangs up before Ali realizes that his collegue hadn't mentioned the patient's name. He takes the elevator to the tenth floor and crosses the overpass that connects to the Coronary Care Unit, where he meets Dr. Denzel, his Fellow in training. "Hey, Denzel—busy day on our hands!"

"I'm off to get the consents for the heart biopsies," Denzel says.

"Thanks," says Ali.

Inside the Unit, he looks towards room #4. The heavy curtain is fully drawn and as usual, the chart is missing from the rack. After circling around the counters, he finally locates it with a nurse. He glances at the admitting notes for the patient in room #4. He scans the ECG and the chest X-ray, then enters room #4, and introduces himself.

"What brought you to the hospital Ms.?" he asks, searching for the name on the chart.

"I blacked out while performing at Lincoln Center," says the patient.

"Last evening?"

"Da."

"Anna?" He glances again at the name on the chart and looks intently at her, the long neck, hair still tied in a bun. The Swan Queen—pale and shaky, but still graceful as she was on the stage. Yes, of course it's Anna. He is stunned.

"What a privilege. I saw you dance last night."

"What a coincidence!" She smiles. "I don't know what happened to me," she says, and pauses for a moment and sighs. "You saw me dance last night?" She looks at him rather distraught. "When I woke up backstage, it was like a dream—all these people standing over me. I wanted to go back and dance." She fumbles for the remote control to turn off the TV.

Ali juxtaposes images of Anna: the Swan Queen dancing on

the stage; the patient, sitting on the hospital bed.

"Did you feel faint or dizzy before you blacked out?"

"No."

"Did you feel your heart beating fast?"

She takes a long time to answer. He notices her absorbing the materiality of the room: the IV pole, the defibrillator, her gaze shifting from him to the heart monitor, the running white light on the dark screen tracing the lines and waves of her heart.

"I don't remember anything," she says. "Da, I felt a fast heartbeat once or twice before, but while doing strenuous exercises to attain the grand jeté—the soaring height, I mean."

He lays his stethoscope on her chest and listens to her heart. He does it with authority—this primal contact with the patient is more reassuring than looking at a piece of paper or images of internal organs on a screen. He asks her to sit up, to take in a few deep breaths, as he listens to her lungs all the while. He uncovers the blanket hiding her feet to feel her peripheral pulses. Her feet look sore and hyper-extended, and her toe tips are flattened from the toe shoes and reddened from the ruthless pursuit of extravagant dance sequences.

"The ECG and X-Ray show some enlargement of the heart," he says. "We will have to do a few more tests and seek the opinion of Dr. Tony Grimes—the heart rhythm expert—to find out the cause of your blackout."

"When can I leave the hospital? I have performances scheduled."

"I don't have any answers yet," says Ali.

"I was thrilled with my selection," she remarks. "My dream finally fulfilled—to dance Odette/Odile in America."

"You were the best choice."

"*Swan Lake* is my favorite ballet," she says, half-tilting her head, tears forming in her dark eyes like the gathering of droplets of mist on black tulips.

"My favorite too," he says. Just yesterday for a brief moment, he had seen elegance and supple grace that were a legacy of the St. Petersburg Academy and The Mariinsky.

His pager goes off again. He goes to the nursing station and dials the Catheterization Laboratory and tells Noreen to ask Dr. Denzel to proceed. He will be there in ten minutes.

"Dr. Ali, isn't she pretty?" says a nurse

"Yes," he says, and hurries back to Anna.

"Did you see a doctor? Are you on any medications?"

"Da!" she says. "A Russian doctor in Brooklyn told me that there was nothing wrong."

"Did you see a heart doctor?"

"No. I'm afraid of doctors."

"Who isn't?"

"Is it very bad? Am I going to live?" she almost whispers and immediately turns her head away.

"You're certainly going to live and possibly even dance."

Anna smiles as Ali takes his leave. A nurse steps into the room and doles out a smile and couple of pills.

Ali smiles back somewhat regretful for the short visit. He loves to talk with his patients. With paper and pen, he draws the heart and explains it all: the diagnosis, the treatment, and the prognosis. But today he's in a rush—the nurses, Noreen and Ming, and Dr. Denzel are anxiously waiting to start on a heart biopsy.

His world is crowded from morning to night with computers and catheters, TV screens and complex modules; with pills and heart biopsies and coronary arteries coursing over the heart with blockages here and there, and reams of ECG paper showing the erratic rhythms of the heart. There are also the medical students, the residents, the fellows in training who demand a share of his precious brain cells, and the innumerable consultants in their well pressed Calvin Klein suits and silk ties, and condescending manners, seeking an opinion or a procedure right away—it must be today if at all possible. In this ultra-rapid New York culture everyone rides the bridges, the tunnels, the expressways, the hospital and corporate elevators and corridors like blood racing through a large main artery, the aorta, carrying oxygen and money and arrogance without which, seemingly, life will cease to exist. And with all this rocket-like-speed in human endeavors and ministrations, as if every element of living is a forgone emergency, life will still come to a halt; death can be postponed, but ultimately, death cannot be avoided—*death, a necessary end, will come when it will come.*

Once in the Catheterization Laboratory, as he scrubs for the procedure, Ali thinks of Anna and is struck at her composure: sitting straight up in a long pink nightgown, red lips and blush, her hair tied in a bun, as if she is about to perform; and yet, in her eyes, in her body language, the way she shifts her body constantly, rubbing her hands all the time, there is an element of fear of the future.

Ali arrives at his apartment at about eight o'clock, and as he devours his mother's saffron flavored mutton biryani, the phone rings.

"Khokon," says his mother. "I met Aisha—she's simply beautiful, what the Americans call gorgeous...perhaps not fair enough for your taste, but beautiful nonetheless with a fine nose and high cheek bones, and so intelligent. Imagine, she was on night call yesterday, and despite being tired, accompanied us to the Metropolitan."

She waits for his response, and finding none, she tells him that they were expecting him to be there at the museum. "Please, write down the phone number and call her now, the poor girl is heart-broken," she adds.

"Mum, as usual you read too much into these things. But I

will call her, Mum."

"When?"

"Not now. I have a presentation and an abstract to go over," says Ali, with a tone of irritation in his voice.

"Please Khokon, don't disappoint your mother."

"I promise I'll call her, Mum."

"When will you call her?"

"Tomorrow for sure. Goodnight, Mum, and thanks for your wonderful biryani."

Ali goes over the presentation on his laptop, and the abstract he has to send out to the Heart Failure Society meeting.

And now, since only sleep is in front of him, sleep that is often so elusive. After tossing and turning, from one thought to another, he needs a pill, a Xanax, at times something stronger, like Ambien, to alter the state of his copious neurotransmitters. He usually doesn't feel tired despite the many hours of his labors. He often thinks of his patients when in bed; however, his conscience is not troubled, for he rarely if ever misdiagnosed a condition after he became a doctor, or so he believes. His science and intuition are strong. He never leaves a stone unturned. Tonight he thinks of Anna: Anna the ballet dancer, Anna the patient. He tries to enter her mind wondering what might be going on there faced with a sudden and unexpected event like a blackout spell due to weakening of her heart that can cause a fatality from a heart arrhythmia, a chaotic electrical storm that can instantly destroy a young, beautiful, creative life like Anna's. And yet, now, he himself doesn't want to admit that there is anything seriously wrong with her. Perhaps her blackout spell was a fainting spell from dehydration and exhaustion. Surely, she herself probably thinks this way.

CHAPTER 2

Grand Rounds

Two days pass and Anna remains cloistered in a single bedded, glass enclosed room in the Coronary Care Unit—that sanc-
tum sanctorum for heart attacks and cardiac arrests where the
rhythm of the heart is constantly monitored, where the angel of
death unrepentantly hovers, and where modern medicine works
its miracles with clot dissolving, heart pumping, rhythm stabi-
lizing drugs and defibrillators.

Ali rounds on Anna daily, mostly in the morning, accompanied by an entourage of young residents and fellows. It pleases
her that he returns for a couple of minutes after the resident
doctors leave, holding her hand, providing a comforting and
reassuring smile.

On the third day of her hospitalization, a pale-skinned, silver haired, wiry sort of a tall shambling figure with a point-
ed beaky nose disproportionately sized for his sparsely haired
head, a doctor with some gravitas comes by. He is dressed in a
flashy three-piece light blue suit and a dark blue bow-tie, and
joins Ali on rounds. A starched coat hangs loosely around his
long lean body. His name and title are embroidered just above

the pocket, a distinct mark of authority that reads:

Dr. Robert Brown, MD; PhD; FACC, FAHA, FICC
Physician-in Chief and Chairman.
The Albert Livingston Professor of Medicine.

Anna feels uncomfortable when Dr. Bob Brown introduces himself and examines her, his long fingers wrapping around her left breast to feel the impulse of her heart. Her eyes move away to meet Ali's, signaling that his presence somewhat calms her raw nerves. The young doctors in training, crowd around Dr. Bob, while an intern, Dr. Tom Smith, makes a lengthy presentation of Anna's case history. At times Dr. Bob looks her way as he asks questions gesturing with his pseudopod-like arms and stepping forward in urgent strides as if he is in the process of extracting the answers from the nervous but well-prepared intern. Ali entirely defers to the visiting doctor as he asks the big questions.

"So, what do you think she has, Tom?"

"Enlargement of the heart—a cardiomyopathy. She might have fainted from dehydration with a resultant drop in blood pressure or a rapid heartbeat—a ventricular tachycardia."

"Good. What investigations are you going to order?"

"A heart catheterization, a heart biopsy, and an electrical stimulation study—the EPS."

"Excellent." Dr. Bob shakes his head in appreciation. "You agree, Ali?"

"Yes indeed, exactly the line of investigation I would follow." Ali winks at Tom, who now smiles confidently. Ali had prepared him well for the Grand Rounds with Dr. Bob.

"What about familial cardiomyopathy, Tom?"

"It's possible, but there's no family history."

"Very good indeed! Familial cardiomyopathy is a genetic disorder, related to mutations of the proteins of the sarcomere, the nuclear membrane, calcium signaling etc. Perhaps, one day soon, we'll find out more specifics," editorializes Dr. Bob in his booming voice. He then thanks them all and takes his leave charging ahead for the meeting of departmental heads. As soon as he leaves, the other interns and residents crowd around Tom, tapping him on the back congratulating him for a fine, brave, showing at the Grand Rounds.

The head doctor's visit and the presentation at Grand Rounds heightens Anna's anxiety. *Could there be something seriously wrong with my heart? Do they really know what I have? And if I die, what will happen to my five-year old daughter, Katya?*

That afternoon, seated in his academic office, Ali contemplates the mess on his desk. He is a stickler for order and perfection, but recently the patient load has been overwhelming. He is sorting out the mail when the phone rings.

"Dr. Ali, it's your mother," says Linda, his secretary.

"Khokon," says his mother, "I was expecting your call. I called you several times yesterday, but I got your answering machine."

"Sorry Mum, I have been busy."

"What's this busy-busy-business? Did you call Aisha?"

"Yes, I did, but I couldn't sort her out, Mum. And please, don't be pushy. I'll call her back in about three to four weeks when she returns from California. We can talk some more when I come home this weekend." He can sense his mother's feelings: that he is giving her the boot so to speak. He goes back sorting out the piles of paper on his desk.

He had called Aisha the night before. She seemed rather opaque and tongue-tied in the beginning, and when she finally opened up, she talked about her night calls and went about asking him what to do with a patient of hers, which she had to present on during morning rounds. And soon, Ali found himself lecturing, something he had no desire to do. Finally, when the conversation on medicine ended, and he asked her whether she wanted to go out, she told him that she was busy for the next two to three weeks with visiting friends, and a short trip to LA for a friend's wedding.

"We'll keep in touch," she said, and the conversation ended.

CHAPTER 3

Anna's Diagnosis

Over the course of the week, Anna is submitted to a battery of tests. She doesn't get the assembly-line treatment, however. The doctors and the nursing staff treat her as a celebrity. They refer to her as "the ballerina," and take time to explain each procedure. There are the nurses who dole out encouraging smiles, and the overweight orderlies who slouch around with their ample bottoms, humming all the time, anxious for a glimpse of Anna, eager to ask for her autograph to send to their daughters in the Caribbean. But at every stage, as Anna proceeds from one test to another, her anxiety mounts. When the time comes for the cardiac catheterization, and the electrophysiologic stimulation study to determine the presence of a rapid heartbeat, and a heart biopsy, she develops salvos of extra-beats that trigger the bedside alarm, which sets in deeper panic: the furrows on her forehead, her gushing tears, the incessant kneading of hands, and urgent requests to see Dr. Ali and Dr. Mel. The idea of having a piece of her heart, however tiny, removed, is like giving away small pieces of her life, her precious secrets away.

"What if you puncture my heart? What if I suffer brain damage?" she repeatedly asks and needs much reassurance from Dr. Mel, Dr. Ali and Dr. Grimes. Ali even arranges for her to speak to a sixteen-year-old girl with a heart transplant who had all these tests over and over again. But the sudden and unexpected encounter with illness plunges Anna into an unambiguous space; a space choked with uncertainty. She wants to ask the doctors to proceed slowly, to let her go home for a while, to take a break. She also wants to get it over with it, and get to the root of the problem. At other times she is in total denial, thinking that she just fainted from exhaustion.

On the night before the invasive procedures, all scheduled for the same day, and sequentially, her anxiety is palpable in her restlessness and her inability to sleep. After half-a-milligram of the sedative, Xanax, Anna finally falls asleep. She requests strong sedation or general anesthesia for the procedures, without which she refuses to sign the consent.

The next morning, when wheeled to the cardiac catheterization laboratory, she feels reassured when she sees Ali and Dr. Grimes, but even at Ali's prompting she cannot manage a smile. "Please, put me to sleep," she keeps imploring. Ali brings a CD of Tchaikovsky's Concerto # 1, and requests Elba, the nurse to insert in the CD player. "See," he says, "I even have some great music for you." Still, she cannot manage a smile. Ali holds her hand as a sedative is squirted into her vein.

She is hooked up to the monitoring machines like a fancy delicate Ferrari with a dying battery. She is barely awake when her groins are shaved, and her body is draped. In the distance she hears the beeps of her heart coming from the monitor; the cackle of the nurses and technician chatting away about the weekend, the weather, and their boyfriends. She barely takes notice of the X-ray machine hovering over her chest like a giant squid waiting to crush her, or the blurred masked faces of the nurses, Noreen, Ming, Christine, and Ann like angels keeping a close watch over her.

"How are you feeling, Anna?" Ali asks, after the heart catheterization. "The arteries are normal. The biopsy of the heart is done. All went well. In another half-an-hour it will be all over."

Dr. Grimes enters the Lab. all scrubbed. "Hi there Anna," he says. "It's me, Dr. Grimes. I'm going to stimulate your heart to see if you develop a rapid heartbeat." Anna, still dopey, barely opens her eyes. She hears faint voices, but hardly registers.

Her eyes open, her face an expression of nothingness, as she slowly wakes up as her consciousness struggles to find her place in this once promising, now uncertain world.

"It's over," says Dr. Grimes. He could initiate only ten beats of a rapid rhythm. Then Dr. Ali, the nurses and technicians, all say the same thing. Anna, now fully awake, is euphoric that the marathon procedure is behind her. It is as if her brain is bathed in happy-rejoiceful neurotransmitters.

That evening, she has many visitors from the ballet world and euphorically holds court. She speaks in English and Russian, mixing words, talking with her hands, her eyes, her eyebrows, and her wide lips, all in constant motion, as her eyes shift from the flower vases—the white, yellow and red roses; the carnations and the begonias—to the shapely men and women that crowd around her bed.

Her friend, Mary, brings her daughter, Katya, and they are still there when Ali comes by to check on her. Tiny blonde Katya, with her doll-like body, is distant and withdrawn. Ali tries to strike up a conversation with her, but when he asks her name, she slips behind Mary as if she is afraid of him. "Your Mum will be fine," he says, as he so slightly manages a smile.

Until that day, Anna was struck by Ali's calm, his coolness, his forcefulness, as he explained her condition meticulously, and unceremoniously, like an economist with statistics at his fingertips. She was surprised that he was the medical doctor in charge of the heart transplant program, expecting someone much older. But now, when he strolls in her room in his street clothes:

a tweed jacket over a light blue shirt, a dark blue tie hanging loosely around the collar, she is struck by his handsomeness. "I love ballet—the movements, the choreography—it's all so delicate," he says, as he touches her hand. "I took ballet lessons when I was ten, and if not for my father, I might have become a dancer." He pulls up a chair and sits by her bedside when Mary and Katya take their leave.

He tells Anna about his last recital, after which, his ballet teacher, a Russian, mentioned to his mother rather candidly that he was very gifted and should pursue ballet. Hearing this, his father had immediately stiffened. That evening his father had a talk with his mother and subsequently with Ali. '"Lila! What's all this nonsense about my son becoming a ballet dancer? Out of the question! Doctor, Engineer, Barrister fine! Even actor is passable, but dancer? No Never!"'

'"But he is talented...it is not as if he's going to be a professional!"' answered his mother.

'"No buts, no ifs. This is simply not part of our culture,"' said his father.

'"But..."'

'"The conversation is over. This ballet ends today."'

In the present, Ali narrates the past: "I stayed in my room without eating that day, and it was the only time I threatened to kill myself, but my parents didn't take me seriously." They both laugh.

"My mother brought me my favorite mutton biryani that I refused to eat. But I was young, and over time, I found other interests: soccer, science, and girls, not necessarily in that order."

Anna immediately senses Ali's devastation. She is surprised by Ali's enthusiasm for ballet, and by his delicately expressed feelings of his father's rejection. Undoubtedly, he is a ballet aficionado in the real sense of the word, like her friend Mary, and like her friends in her native St. Petersburg. She begins looking at him in a different way: a kind of falling-in-love way?

Finally, the day arrives, when it is time for Anna to know what exactly is wrong with her, the treatment of her condition, and its prognosis. After Drs. Mel and Ali, analyze the results of the tests, Ali approaches Anna and tells her that she has weakening of her heart muscle, a condition known as cardiomyopathy due to a viral infection of her heart. As soon as she hears this, her despair is palpable in her downcast expression. She asks no questions about her heart condition, its treatment or its prognosis. All she wants to know is whether she can dance. Ali sighs and slowly shakes his head. "Not for now, we'll see how you do." He places his hand on her shoulder.

Anna sobs. She feels as if a big bubble has formed in her stomach and bounced on her heart—her heart skips a beat, and then it skips another, and another. Panic settles in her throat, as the bedside alarm goes off. Her face contorts in pain; her eyes move rapidly from side to side.

Ali and the nurses in the Coronary Care Unit try to calm her down. They reassure her that things are not as bad as they seem, and that, she will be going home tomorrow. Their reassuring words don't work for her, her sobbing is relentless, and her restlessness is obvious in her kneading of her hands, and the constant movement of her feet. The monitor shows extra-beats, and these heighten her anxiety. Ali ends up giving her a strong dose of a sedative intravenously with which, she falls asleep. She wakes up when Mary and Katya arrive, but remains withdrawn.

"What will I do if I can't dance? How will we live?" She drops her voice to a whisper: "And what if I die?"

Mary strokes her head. "We'll find a way, don't worry. And now, look, Katya has made something for you." Mary gathers Katya close with her other arm. "Come, Katya, show Mama what you brought."

Katya, stone-faced, offers Anna a rolled-up piece of drawing paper. Anna, smiling through her tears, unrolls the paper.

"It's a bird I saw in the park. Mary said it was asleep."

Anna senses that Katya, on some level, knows that something is terribly wrong with her mother. And then she sees the careful letters beneath the bird, MAMA. Anna turns her head away, hoping Katya wouldn't see the fresh tears welling in her eyes.

But Katya has buried her head in Mary's lap.

"Anna, Anna, it will all work out." Mary's voice is calm and even confident. I love having Katya stay with me."

"But when I get home…"

"We'll find someone to help out or she can stay with me."

"Perhaps I should send her to Russia to be with her Babushka."

By the time Mary and Katya leave, a calmer Anna feels in her bones that Mary is right, she will get over her illness; it will all work out. Besides, she could send Katya to Russia to be with her mother. Mary will rescue her again, just as she did years ago, when she faced her husband, Alyosha's, infidelity. Mary had helped her file for divorce, had found a good lawyer, and had helped with little Katya. Remembering all this, Anna gives into weariness and closes her eyes.

Later, that evening, when Ali re-visits, Anna is in a more cheerful and calmer mood. Pulling a chair, and sitting by her bedside, he tells her that it was heroic of her to defect to America. He remembers reading her story in the papers.

"What a fighter you are. Wasn't it just before Glasnost?" He smiles, as if he is asking for her to smile as well. And she does. She can sense that he is tired, and yet, he speaks with confidence as if he is giving her his last ounce of energy.

"Why are you asking about my defection now?" she says. She expects him to discuss her illness. He doesn't answer; he just smiles.

"Are you in the process of breaking the ice, of parting the waters so to speak, to tell me to fight, da?" She says. He shakes his head.

"I must say—the way you approach me, the way you strike a conversation about personal matters rather than my illness, all to make me feel relaxed. Da?"

"You must be optimistic, Anna." Again, he gets her to smile.

"Are you a master at giving bad news, knowing just how to make it softer, more bearable?" she says.

"Your heart is enlarged, Anna. But it's not all that bad. Your condition might get better; the cardiomyopathy might regress. It's known to happen."

"There you go again: sweet and sour at the same time, Da?" she says.

She is listening, but is she registering? When the news is bad, perhaps there are chemical barriers that surround the frontal cortex at one's will, one's demand?

"Your heart function is around thirty-five percent; the normal being over fifty-five percent," he says. "Dr. Grimes feels you need a defibrillator, but we are not entirely sure whether you blacked out because of a rapid heartbeat. I have decided to wait and see how your heart function does over time. Let's give it three months."

"And what if my heart doesn't improve with the drugs?"

"I will keep a close eye on you. You should enlist for the cardiac rehabilitation program in the hospital—it will help you recuperate." His eyes travel to the bedside table, and the photo of Katya. "What a pretty daughter you have. Will she be a ballerina?"

"Maybe," says Anna, and smiles.

The next morning, as Anna begins packing to leave the hospital, she wonders what all of this means for her career, and to her daughter Katya. It must have been the mushrooms, she thinks, those poisoned mushroom she had eaten with the good ones when she last went to Russia. Her mother had taken her deep within the military preserve northeast of St. Petersburg, a great place to find wild mushrooms. She remembers the odor of soil and rot, and the wafting fragrance of wild sautéed mushrooms from a nearby dacha. It had made her mouth water. She was sure that among the mushrooms they collected that day a few of the little brown ones were poisonous. But with all the commotion that followed, she had forgotten to throw the poisonous ones away. It is a very Russian sport—*hodit po gribi*—to gather mushrooms, but neither had exercised this sport for some time.

As they made their way among the birch trees and pines that day, her mother had suddenly stopped. "They would bring them to the trenches," she said. "They made them dig their own graves and shot them in cold blood. It is here they killed your grandfather during Stalin's Great Terror."

Later that night, distracted after such an emotional day, Anna ate the sautéed mushrooms and fell sick. She began retching and vomiting and had a temperature, but she refused to go to a hospital.

She wonders if the poison still lingers in her system after all these years. Had it affected her heart?

CHAPTER 4

Anna's Heart Mending

In a flash, summer is upon New York City. And Anna is home, relieved, contented, after the nightmare she'd gone through. But soon, the euphoria of survival, the slices of cheerfulness crumble like the quick shriveling of summer peony flowers. She broods about her illness, and the loss, temporary or permanent, of her art and her livelihood. She locks herself in her room and refuses to open the door. Katya's Russian nanny, Victoria, calls Mary in a panic.

"Come on Anna, open the door," says Mary, repeatedly banging the door. "Katya will be home soon." After hearing Katya's name, she finally opens the door. Her eyes are blood shot. Mary holds her in her arms until the crying stops.

"You are depressed Anna," says Mary. "Why don't you venture out, take walks in Central Park, and see a therapist? It is not easy to cope with what you have gone through."

"I'm not depressed!" she snaps. "I don't need a therapist!"

When Katya is around, she manages to control herself. Sometimes, she feels that the crying helps to ease her anxiety.

Finally, with Mary's coaxing she begins attending the cardiac rehabilitation program at the hospital three times a week. It positively affects her mood and her physical condition improves. Gradually, over a course of several weeks, in an up-swing mood, she occupies herself with reading, playing Chopin on the piano, and listening to Beethoven's and Wagner's symphonies.

On the day when Anna has an appointment with Ali around three in the afternoon, she wakes up in a chipper mood, and hurriedly attends to Katya, proceeds with some stretches, and sits down for breakfast of a muffin, marmalade and coffee, after which she looks in the closet for something nice to wear. She has many dressy clothes, but nothing for a visit to the doctor. After Victoria arrives, she takes a taxi ride to Bloomingdale's. She walks around the store, looking for something on sale and affordable, trying out clothes, when it strikes her that she is no longer short of breath. She emits a deep sigh of relief. She finally settles on a light pink suit.

On her way back to her apartment, she stops at a café and orders an espresso. From her window seat she looks at the colorful busy summer city world: men and women casually dressed, happily sauntering the streets, entering and exiting shops, chatting away, relishing hot dogs and quenching their thirst on Gatorades, ice teas and Colas—she savors life, the human element passing by. Her health now means more to her than ever before, and the improvement in her breathing gives her added hope and optimism.

Anna takes a cab home, and tries to rest, but as afternoon arrives, she feels a rising anxiety, and the worries and questions she has about her heart, about her future, keep recurring in her mind like some drumbeat. She is looking forward to meeting with Ali, her doctor, the doctor she likes as a person, a doctor she feels attracted to, but at the same time she feels anxious not knowing what he will say.

A visit to a doctor, a heart specialist, is always heart wrenching.

A little before three, she leaves her apartment in a taxi for a three-thirty appointment at the hospital. While entering the out-patient office, she feels the thump in her chest, and anxiety surges like heat on a summer night. She hyperventilates; her hands feel cold, and she feels nauseated. She leans against the wall and takes several deep breaths, and finally sits down in the waiting area and absorbs herself in a New York Magazine; gradually, she finds herself relaxing. She digs into her bag for her pocket mirror and applies lipstick and blush. The other patients, all much older, perhaps in their sixties and seventies, stare at her as if to say: Lady, you don't belong here.

The wait seems long, and the waiting room is emptying out. Finally, at four o'clock, Anna is called into the small, cold, examining room. She undresses down to her bra and lace panties, puts on the hospital gown, fumbles with the ties until she gets them right, and hops on the table. She closes her eyes against the glare of fluorescent ceiling light when Ali walks in.

"I'm sorry for the wait. I was called to the lab. There was an emergency. How do you feel?" he asks, as he slips his hand beneath her breast to feel her heart. She can feel it beating hard as if it wants to jump out of her chest. Before she can answer, she feels the cold of the stethoscope. She has goose bumps.

"I felt a thump in my chest as I walked into the clinic," she says.

"That's not unexpected with your condition," says Ali. "You can sit up now and take in deep breaths. Go on, keep breathing."

"Sounds good, Anna. I want the tech. to take an ECG. I'll see you in the office after that."

After the ECG, she hurriedly dresses and checks her hair and makeup in the mirror. His words of "sounds good," are reassuring, and by the time Anna enters his office, her anxiety is gone.

"Come in Anna, have a seat." Ali smiles.

"How do you find me?"

"Great! I see no evidence of heart failure. But I want you to have an echocardiogram to see objectively whether the heart function has improved. The heart failure drugs are doing their job. I'm content with your progress."

"May I take class? At least the barre?"

"A gentle barre only; but no jumps, no weights, nothing too strenuous for now."

She goes home overtly reassured with the progress she'd made, and the recent past already seems like an illusion. But the following day, Anna becomes petulant. She cannot perform professionally. She has blown her last chance for renewed fame, lost a singular opportunity to become a ballerina assoluta, of achieving the fame and status of her countrymen Nureyev and Baryshnikov. It dawns on her that once again fate has been cruel to her. And if that is not enough, the next day Katya's nanny, Victoria, gives notice that she will be leaving in early July. Anna decides to send Katya to Russia to spend the rest of the summer with her mother.

A little more than three months have passed since Anna's blackout on stage. She is seeing Ali professionally, at least once a month. One Friday evening, after he examines her and finds her well and improving, she, the last patient on his list, they spent time talking about ballet and her life in the Soviet Union. She tells him about the parts she played, how she once danced for the Soviet Politburo and for the many dignitaries that visited the USSR. She can see that he is interested and impressed. They talk about the origins of ballet, the Russian Academies in St. Petersburg and Moscow, and the Mariinsky Theater. She is surprised that he knows about Petipa, Diaghilev, the Ballet Russes, and Balanchine.

"I didn't always like Balanchine's modern plotless ballets," she adds. "But I wish I had worked with him. He died soon after I came to America." She tells him about the ballerinas Pavlova, Danillova, Ekatrina, Tamara Geva, and Ulanova Galina whom she admires, and proudly proclaims that America owes its ballet entirely to Balanchine and Russia.

"I majored in Eastern European and Russian history," says Ali. "In the past I even idealized with the socialist system. I felt anguish over the suffering of the Russians after the fall of Soviet Communism—that Godless Empire doomed to failure."

"Da, history has been cruel to us Russians, but it was our Russian character of suffering that nurtured our great music, the wonderful art, our poets and writers."

"Yes, there is an element of the East in the Russian character," he opines.

She had never thought of it that way; nonetheless, his knowledge and sensitivity astonishes her. She had not met anyone in America with such an understanding of her culture and history, and as she rises to leave, feeling emotional and somewhat overwhelmed, she quickly kisses him on the cheek, as if in gratitude.

"Some evening when I'm free, we should go out for coffee, and talk some more," he says.

The following day she calls him to tell him that she felt some extra-beats. She sounds distant and in some distress.

"Can I see you now?"

"Calm down Anna. Don't panic. I want you to wear a monitor for twenty-four hours. Let me put on my secretary to give you an appointment for the monitor. I'll see you after I get the report. Here, take down my cell number and call me if you feel worse."

She calls him back in an hour or so to tell him that she feels better.

A few weeks later, when he sees Anna in the clinic, Ali tells her that the monitor was good—there were extra-beats, but less than ten an hour. He can sense her contentment in her broad smile. She gets off the chair and assumes a pose. Is she seducing him with a pas de bourrée? She then stands in the fourth position with arms raised and slightly rounded en couronne. Catching hold of his arm, she invites him to join her, and goes about adjusting his arms and coaching him. She pulls out Katya's letter from Russia with a snapshot of her mother and Katya in front of the Bolshoi. "I miss her so much," she says, and her eyes well-up with tears.

"I'm sure things will work out and she'll be back with you soon." Ali embraces her and wipes her tears. She kisses him lightly on the lips.

As soon as Anna leaves, Ali cradles his head in his hands. He must stop these office flirtations. What if things go too far, or somebody sees them and complains, or she herself accuses him of improper behavior should the relationship sour? It had happened to a friend's husband, a gastroenterologist, who was accused of sexual harassment. In our litigious society anything can happen, but he thinks that Anna is not the type. At the same time, he debates whether he should ask her out. He is already attached to her. What if he falls in love with her? He had made the mistake of giving her his cell number, assuring her that she can call him at all hours of the day or night.

In Anna, he senses a deep pathos unlike anything he has seen in his other patients. But then, he is not involved in a personal way with any of his other patients. Mysterious, captivating Anna! He feels a need to protect her. He is at a loss, unable to bridge his feelings towards her, and her medical issues. There is a strong chemistry between them. But he is her doctor. He deeply regrets her illness, wishing her heart's recovery—it is known to happen. But right now, it seems to him that they are circling each other in a kind of courtly dance—a patient and her doctor—a doctor and his patient—each uncertain how or where to proceed.

Anna's health continues to improve. She is able to work out on the barre and even to do a few jumps. She is getting acclimatized to the new reality: that her days of performing are probably over. Perhaps time, that healer of healers will play its act. She begins giving private ballet lessons and applies for a teaching position at the Julliard.

In November, Mary convinces her to join her and her husband, Brad, on a trip to the Grand Canyon. They bring along a friend, a widowed businessman. Mary tries to fix her up like friends often do, but Anna tells Mary that she has no interest in Mr. Goodbar. It is the scent of Ali, like aftershave, that lingers.

The day after she gets back to New York, Anna has an ultrasound examination of her heart. She feels trepidation when she goes for the examination: What if her heart function hasn't improved or has gotten worse?

She is relieved and ecstatic when Margarita, the technician, an immigrant from Minsk, tells her that it has improved significantly from thirty-five percent to forty-nine percent. She cries. Margarita, cups her face in her hands and tries to console her, telling her repeatedly that it all looks good, that she is almost cured. But Anna cries when things are too good, as well as when things are bad. After the crying, she laughs, and now it is the turn of Margarita to cry. Russian immigrants in this brave new world, they embrace each other for a long time, and Anna feels she has made a new friend.

She rushes out of the laboratory and almost runs to Ali's office. It is six in the evening, and Ali is about to finish with his last patient. The nurses and assistants have already left for the day. As soon as the patient leaves, Anna burst into his office and gives him the good news.

"I'm so happy for you, Anna," he says.

"Thanks to you, my great doctor," she says, and he responds to her buttery words with an embarrassed smile. But now Anna is animatedly describing in detail her walks in the Grand Canyon, Brad's music echoing in the Canyon walls, and Mary's friend Joey, the hedge fund manager who tried to impress her with his wealth.

"Did you miss me?" she asks.

"Yes," he says, hesitatingly.

Is he feeding her a slice of hope, as if now the past is behind them and a door has opened, however slightly?

"Would you like to go out for dinner?" he says, abruptly.

It surprises and thrills her at the same time, and she does a pirouette. It is the best news she has had for a long time: her heart healing, and now the opportunity to go out with this great doctor. Suddenly, it seems like the morning after the ice storm when the sun plays on icicles, spreading diamonds and sapphires.

"We'll celebrate my cure with champagne and caviar," she adds with a coquettish smile. "I'm going to call my mother and ask her to send Katya back."

"No, wait another month or two to give me time to reconfirm the echo findings," he says. "Where shall we go for dinner?"

"Have you been to Café des Artistes?" she asks on the run with her body almost out the door, as if fearful he will change his mind.

"I will make reservations for this Friday."

Ali stands up in the empty office and looks out of the window. Outside, the autumn chilly night is upon the city: a world of rising concrete, a glass-enclosed world lit up. The office and the patient suites are deserted: the nurses, the techs, the patients have all gone home. Suddenly his mood plummets. For reasons he cannot fathom, today, he feels alone in this empty, lonely landscape of a doctor's world. He has nowhere to go. He longs for female companionship: to be with Anna. And then it strikes him: *My God, what have I done? Am I doing the right thing dating my patient? Wouldn't it cloud my judgment in handling her care in the future? Her heart function has improved, but she is far from cured. What if she has a relapse?* His ambivalence is palpable. And yet, he longs to know the woman in Anna, to take the relationship to another level, to bask in her personality and her artistry. Hadn't he wished all along that she would recover? We live our lives, don't we? So why hold back? Falling in love with Anna wouldn't be a problem were she not his patient. He decides to turn her care back to her primary physician, Dr. Mel. That is the obvious solution; yet, Ali dreads telling her, knowing how emotional she could be.

CHAPTER 5

The Woman in the Mirror

When Ali goes to her apartment on Eigthty-second Street and Madison Avenue, he is ushered by the doorman to the waiting lounge. He straightens his yellow-striped tie, thinking he should have worn a suit instead of the blue blazer. When he looks into the mirror in the lounge, he is not sure of the tie either. Perhaps it is too gaudy? He should have gone for light blue, and the knot, not the samosa his father had taught him, but more a kabab on a stick. He undoes it and tries it again and again. Finally, it is a near perfect triangular samosa, or so it seems. Unlike his father, Ali is clumsy with his dressing; besides, he has come on the run. There are always last moment surprises, emergency consultations on Friday evenings, and this Friday is no different. As he ruminates on the color of the tie, now that the knot is perfected, he sees a woman in the mirror as he is woken from his reverie by a gentle tap on his shoulder. He turns around. It is Anna.

"Wow! You look stunning," he says. She smiles. "Let's go, the car is parked just outside the building."

Ali cannot take his eyes off Anna: a black dress hangs loosely over her body, a platinum pendant with emeralds and diamonds

sparkles against her long bare neck, and on her head, a red hat
with an orange feather. What captivates him the most is not the
dress or the jewelry or the length of her long neck or her breathtaking beauty. It is the hat. He has never been with a woman who
wore hats; and this one with the flame-colored orange feather, is
classy, is singular—is Anna. The other women he had admired
for their beauty, their stature, complexion, body line—all pale in
front of this woman who is standing next to him.

As soon as she is seated in the car, bubbling with optimism,
he tells her that she doesn't have to see him professionally any
longer, and can simply continue her care with Dr. Mel from now
on. She smiles. He is not dating his patient, is he? He is absolved
from his scruples.

The maître'd shows them to a table in the Christy Room
under Howard Chandler's painting of the Christy Girl, flanked
by his other voluptuous murals. But the stares and smiles from
the diners are all on Anna as the waiter pulls out her chair.

She knows what she wants, quickly ordering escargot on
crispy risotto cakes for appetizer. He is unsure—she suggests
a steak tartare, followed by ossobuco. She orders quail with
chanterelles.

They toast each other: she with champagne, and he with
Perrier.

She eats coquettishly and seductively between bites, slowly
and purposefully, as she tastes every forkful. Ali finishes eating
well before she does.

"What was it like defecting?" he asks.

She shrugs, and after several sighs in-between snippets of
food, puts down the fork. "Defecting was my mother's idea. I
was very happy in the Kirov. If not for the KGB man, I would
have never left."

"KGB man?" Ali asks.

"Da, he was in love with me." Anna stops there expectantly,
as if waiting for Ali to react.

"A KGB man, hum!"

"Da, he harassed me with phone calls, swore his love, promised a great future with him— da, boasting that with his influence I would soon become prima ballerina. It was only to get away from him that I finally consented to defect during my USA tour.

"I aspired to be prima ballerina assoluta someday," she says, proudly lifting her head, speaking at a frenzied pace, her eyes narrowing, then opening; at once looking down, then up.

"So, what happened? Ali asks.

"On the opening night of the American tour, when I played the part of Kitri in *Don Quixote*, a short, bearded man holding a long-stemmed orange-flame rose stopped me backstage on my way into the dressing room. Da, it was like my mother had told me and rehearsed over and over again. It was my mother's dream that I defect to America." Anna pauses. She lifts her thin eyebrows; her face turns serious.

"Da, he said the electrifying words," she says.

"'I am Igor. The firebird has shed her feather, come this way and hurry up.'"—words, fateful words that were chosen by my mother from the ballet *Firebird*."

Ali reaches across the table and gently touches the jaunty feather.

"Now I get it, the orange flame-feather—*t*he firebird is your leitmotif."

"We quickly left through the back door. A man posted in front of the dressing room followed us until a wall of Igor's men blocked him. We slipped into a waiting black car that took off and was lost in the Broadway traffic. I was shaking, crying. Igor, a total stranger had his arms around me. He took me to the Canadian Consulate where I slept that night from sheer exhaustion. The next day, I asked for political asylum in America."

"Perfect script! Perfect execution!" Ali gives a hearty laugh.

She pauses to sip champagne, this Russian Exile, and looks at him briefly.

"Da, dizzying attention and adulation from the paparazzi," she says at a fast pace as if from memory. She frowns.

"So, what went wrong?" he asks.

She is trembling now. Momentarily she closes her eyes. After a long silence, she continues in a softer voice, the excitement dying down, eyes still on the table, her long fingers toying with the saltshaker. "I never felt quite right. I grew anxious, paranoid. It is hard for you to understand. You haven't lived in Communist Russia."

There is a change in her expression, the gathering of furrows underneath her eyelids, and tiny droplets of sweat on her temple, as if she is overtaken by an element of fear. Ali has seen such an expression in his patients just as they are being wheeled for a complex procedure.

"I would like some vodka. Do you mind?" she says.

The waiter comes with chilled Grey Goose. She takes a long draught.

"I started looking at the people on the street," she says. "Was I being followed? Would they get my mother? I was afraid the KGB would hunt me down." She pauses for a sip of Perrier.

"I felt like a traitor to my country, da—a great—what is that word the media uses? Excuse my English, please. Yes: a photo-prop for Capitalist propaganda."

"Your English is great!"

"I knew nothing about politics. Freedom didn't mean much to me. As a ballerina, I was insulated—totally blind to the Communist regime."

"Why did your mother want you to leave the Soviet Union?"

"It's very complicated, Dr. Ali."

"You don't have to call me Dr. Ali. Just Ali, please."

"Thanks," she whispers: "Ali." They both smile. The connection is finally severed between the doctor and his patient.

"My mother's family were aristocrats from the town of Tsarskoye Selo, and the 1917 October Revolution was not kind to them—da, my grandfather was executed," she says. "And when Rudolf Nureyev—the virtuoso of the Kirov ballet—won rave reviews in Paris for his performance as Solar in *The Kingdom of the Shades,* and as the Prince in *Sleeping Beauty,* and sought artistic asylum in France, my mother decided that I should do the same."

"She wanted a better life for you."

"Da! I got close to my mother during my recent visit to Russia. She told me about the poet Akhmatova, and their visits to the Stray Dog, a bar where the dissident writers met in the later part of Stalin's era. She was arrested as she walked the steps to the underground."

"Do you have any of your mother's poetry?"

"No, I have nothing. I never knew she was one of the dissident writers. These things were not talked about, even among family members. Only during my last visit, she opened up to me." Ali looks at her intently, much surprised and bewildered.

"The day the Soviet Union collapsed, my mother wrote to me: "*I drink to my father's ruined house, to my broken life, to the world that was brutal and coarse, and to you Anna, I raise my glass that God has finally saved us all.*'"

"Has God saved us all with the downfall of Communism?" she asks. Ali hears a twinge of sarcasm in her voice.

"Maybe, maybe your mother was right—the downfall of Communism was an act of God."

She laughs and twists her hand above her head, rather sarcastically.

Like Ronald Reagan, Ali believed that the Soviet Union, that godless nation, was an evil empire.

"God has no part in my life," she says, as she looks in the pocket mirror and presses her lips together to evenly spread the lipstick she has just applied. She is animated now—the vodka has calmed her raw nerves.

Ali looks at the outline of her red lips on the vodka tumbler and feels like pressing his own to the rim. His gaze shifts from Howard Chandler's nudes on the wall, back to the lipstick marks and before he knows what is happening, he is aroused.

"Ali, are you upset because I am faithless?"

The mention of faith abruptly quenches the spark. "I'm not upset with you. Don't you think God and religion are important? Don't we need something greater than ourselves to lean on?"

She shrugs and takes another sip of vodka, and several long gulps of Perrier.

"Religion? What good has it done to the world?" she says.

"It's not for us to judge," he says. "I was brought up in two faiths: Islam and Christianity, and sometimes I feel confused, but yes, I am a believer."

He is distressed by Anna's atheism or is it Godlessness? He remembers Rasa, the Muslim Iranian doctor he had dated who had lost her religion, but Anna is different. God is a foreign element to her, like a Martian. He has to approach the subject gingerly, or she will reject it outright like a rebellious teenager. As Ali contemplates what to say, she speaks softly, almost in a whisper.

"I got a job at the New York City Ballet, but I was unhappy—I didn't like their repertoire. I didn't know anyone, and I hardly spoke any English. I was very lonely."

"Your defection seems like a James Bond movie," says Ali. "And how do you feel now, twelve years later?"

"I don't know. In America they say it's not over until it's over. If not for my mother, I would have never defected. Communism had been good to me—it had made me a classical ballerina." She stares at the mural on the wall.

"It must have been difficult for you being all by yourself," he says.

"Da, very difficult still! I met some not so good people, and now with this heart problem and a daughter to take care off.

HAVE A HEART 53

I also met some wonderful people in America, like Mary, and now you."

Ali smiles, and places his hand on hers.

"I miss my daughter," she says, and begins to cry.

He stretches his hand and touches her face. She gets up and goes to the powder room. There is a sparkle in her eyes when she returns; tiny droplets of tears like pearls still cling to her eyelashes. She looks more beautiful than ever.

"Did you ever think of going back to Russia?" he asks, to break the silence.

"Yes, after Katya was born. Mama said life in Russia was hard, but I decided to go and see for myself. Communism was over. Maybe I could remake a life there. So many painful memories here." She chokes on the words, and Ali wonders what those painful memories are.

"St. Petersburg was in decay—the buildings run down, weed had replaced grass, and the people were cold and unfriendly. Not that all this was terribly worse than when I left the country, but now the contrast was clear like black and white," she says.

"I thought St. Petersburg was beautiful, like Paris," says Ali.

"Not now. One day, when things change for me, and if we are together, I will take you there." She looks down as tears flush into her eyes, as if the words, "if we are together," were premature, far-fetched, and in bad taste. He offers her his handkerchief. Even in tears, her beauty astonishes him.

"There was no way I could live in Russia," she says. "It was all so depressing: the shabbiness of the city, the decay, the lifeless faces, and the building where we lived and where I grew up with its two rooms on Liteiny Avenue, that were shared with another couple, was run down, unpainted for years, the walls crumbling, the foyer dark and damp, and the plumbing leaked a greenish-brown liquid of rust. And to top it all, I had my purse with its precious dollars and its credit cards stolen.

"At night a chill would come over me, a fear of being locked in there, of never being able to leave." She pauses, thinking.

"I felt an urgency to leave for America, for New York—it had a different meaning now—Freedom." She stares with a blank expression as if she has lost the trend of thoughts into the distant past. She looks pale and distraught.

"After I returned from Russia, it was Katya who kept me going," she says. "I felt at home in New York: decorating the apartment, enjoying the streaks of morning sunlight, walks in Central Park with my baby, some summers in the Hampton's with Mary and Brad, English classes. I earned some good money teaching ballet to the children of rich Americans and a few Russian immigrants."

"What about your ex-husband? Does Katya spend time with him?"

"No, I have sole custody of Katya. I don't want to talk about my ex-husband—not now," she says, raising her voice.

When the waiter appears, they both ask for Cappuccino and decide to skip the dessert. And then, on second thought, Anna asks for the dessert menu and orders a chocolate soufflé and entices Ali to order one as well.

"Well, okay, and why not—cholesterol binge today!" Ali takes her hand. "You need to be careful about what you eat and what you drink." He wishes he hadn't sounded so paternal.

"You don't understand," she says, her voice rising. "I eat today—tomorrow I starve. We ballerinas are starving all the time to keep our weight down."

As the waiter leaves with the dessert menu, she falls silent. He sees tear filled eyes again, but this time the tears roll down her cheek. "I want to see my daughter." The words sound like a sob. She begins to cry.

"The divorce—the child—now my heart," she says.

Ali feels uncomfortable. There are people looking their way, older people. He immediately wonders what they are thinking: Are they fighting? Is he ditching her? He touches her face, asks her why she is crying. He finds himself looking down, then up, towards the bathing nymphs. One of them looks so much like Anna. Perhaps prodding her to talk will stop her crying.

"Anna, things will work out," the words pour out of his mouth. "Your heart function has nearly normalized—the cardiomyopathy has regressed—soon you'll be reunited with Katya." But his attempts to reassure her make no difference.

"Would you like to leave?" he asks in a low, nervous voice. She doesn't answer. Suddenly she has closed down tight like a clam.

Ali doesn't know what to say. A doctor with a homely Asian upbringing, he knows how to control his emotions. This is something he is not prepared for. People keep looking their way. He sees a young couple at a nearby table whispering.

"We should leave!" he says, with a commanding finality.

Without nodding her head, she rises and strides to the lady's room. When she comes back, she is ready to leave, her make-up perfect.

In the car, she doesn't say a word. She is withdrawn and distant, as if her aristocratic self is entitled to silent misfortune. The ride across Central Park seems unusually long despite the lack of traffic. Ali thinks she wants nothing to do with him. He is at a loss; he doesn't know what to say. The silence sits between them like the eerie silence in a desolate park. He feels relieved when he sees the lighted buildings on the East Side, on Ninty-sixth Street, standing tall and welcoming. As the car comes to a stop in front of her building, she takes her time, rummaging in her bag for the keys. Ali isn't sure whether to hug her or give her a parting kiss as he stands on the sidewalk waiting for her to step out of the car. He thanks her for the evening and promises to call. And Anna suddenly exudes calm in her confident smile; and yet, underneath it lurks an element of sodden buried distress. She barely says goodnight as she closes the car door, and then she turns around and says, "Thank you." She abruptly kisses him on the lips, rapidly makes half-a-turn, and walks into the building sure-footed, her head held high.

CHAPTER 6

The Ashura Celebration

After Ali arrives at his apartment, he feels nauseated. He lies on his bed, thinking; his pants and shirt still on, tie loosened. Is it Anna's uncontrollable tears that provoked anxiety, a queasiness in his stomach, or was it the rich, fatty food that gave him reflux?

The nausea attains a crescendo. He retches. He runs to the bathroom and pukes a little of what he ate that night. He undresses, gets into his shorts and goes to bed. He gets up again, thirsty, and looks for something to drink in the fridge. He takes a few sips of Coca-Cola with an anti-acid and goes back to bed. As he starts feeling better, he ruminates on Anna's problems uncertain whether he can digest them. He empathizes with her loneliness and the difficulties of being a single working mother in New York City with a heart problem. The things she told him about her family, her links to the Russian aristocracy, the Stalin years, her grandfather's execution, her mother's association with dissident writers, her defection to America—these things have all the ingredients of mystery, of desolation and sorrow, of lives in flux, where the *terra firma* is rattled by many earth-

quakes, leaving fault lines and shattered lives. He thinks of his
parents, their disownment, and his father's family's uprooting
after the Partition of India, the slaughter of Muslims and Hin-
dus as they crossed the Hindu Kush, and it all seems to ring a
resounding bell.

He wonders what Anna really means to him. He loves her
glamour, her beauty, and the way she seems to trust him and
rely on him. He even feels a little responsible for letting the evening end on a rather sad note, for losing control of the situation.
Perhaps he shouldn't have asked her about the past; *for some
the past is a dance of shadows on deserted desert floors; each
with its pain and its rebirth.* Undoubtedly, she's a woman to
reckon with, a ballerina, a celebrity, but her emotional instability upsets him viscerally; but then again, her reactions seem entirely justified. And the way she looks, the purity of her skin, the
way she dresses and carries herself, and even her vulnerability,
qualities that are so seductive, and yet, there is something in her
he cannot fathom. Perhaps, there lies her appeal, the mystery of
it all. He wonders whether Anna in some way nourishes his own
artistic inclinations so summarily killed by his father years ago.
Is that the attraction, or is there more? Should he let it simmer
for a while?

He lies in bed questioning: is he looking for a girlfriend or
a wife?

He thinks of Aisha: sweet, petit, gorgeous Aisha, the one
his mother pestered him about. Perhaps, an ideal woman for
him: same culture, same religion, and a doctor. When he met
her for dinner, toward the end, she had reluctantly confessed
that she has a boyfriend—a final year medical student. "But
please, Ali, don't tell your mother. You see, Steve is Jewish, and
your mother might spill it out to my mother." Would Steve's
mother accept a Muslim daughter-in-law? And would her parents accept a Jewish son-in-law? She seemed to be in a terrible
bind, and asked Ali's advice. Ali didn't know what to say. He

wonders why she even bothered to go out with him; perhaps to satisfy her parents? He had wished her good luck. The next time his mother asked him whether there was anything cooking, like thick butter chicken curry between him and Aisha, Ali simply told her that they had not clicked. His mother was upset and visibly sad. But when he had broken up with Rasa, the Iranian doctor they called Ras, his mother was devastated. She cried.

Born in Teheran and raised in America, Ras, seemed tailor made for him: A leopard-eyed beauty with long curly black hair, skin the color of milky tea, and a full tall body. Wealthy and vaguely aristocratic, she blazed away in her BMW Coupé. Ras smoked and loved Apple Martinis, but he thought that this was a passing playful phase in her life, and that she could be redeemed, and he gladly rose to the task. Anything that was not easily attainable challenged him, made him work harder, like in his professional career. In the foyer of Ras's spacious home on the Long Island Sound, Ali had seen a portrait of the late Shah Muhammad Reza Pahlavi— the King of Kings. In the living room there were photographs of her father with the Shah, and their Swiss style chalet in the rich suburb of Elahiyeh, now appropriated by the regime of the Mullahs Another photograph had been taken in the lobby of the opulent Shah Abbas, drinking and smoking cigars with tall reddened American oil men and arms dealers in Stetson hats. When Ali asked Ras the whereabouts of her parents that evening, she said, Washington. "They are meeting with Congressmen, lobbying to bring back the monarchy in Iran." She flung her head back, as if she herself belonged to the Pahlavi dynasty. Ali had been against the Shah's regime. And now, this opulent house on Long Island Sound with its carved furniture, the movie theatre, the poolroom, and all the photographs made him uncomfortable and uneasy. And then, matter-of-factly, he had found himself in her parent's opulent master bedroom with a gold-plated Jacuzzi and a canopied bed, where she abruptly undressed him and performed oral sex. She wouldn't allow him to undress her, let alone touch her breasts or her sex. He had felt oddly confused by the mechanics of their sex act; she was a virgin, he was certain of it, and she would only give herself to the man she married—it was a cultural thing not uncommon among western minded Iranian and Pakistani women in America.

As they sped west on the Long Island Expressway in her BMW, with the wind on their faces, Ali had felt for a moment like a King of Kings himself.

He had invited the Iranian rebel (as he called her, to her amusement) to meet his parents. She seemed a good match, this beautiful, rich Muslim doctor. And once they were married, she would settle down and fall into the rut of having children and taking care of the household just like his cousin's wife in Washington. He had advised Ras to be composed and respectful in the presence of his parents, particularly his father, but Ras flirted with Ali. She kissed him and squeezed his butt, when his parents were around, not necessarily watching, and then laughed at his discomfort. And then, she had the audacity to light a cigarette in his very home. Ali had abruptly pulled it out of her mouth and inserted it into his glass of Coca-Cola as his father had walked in, but his father had taken notice of it. His mother was attracted to her, perhaps for her beauty and the fact she was a doctor, but his father didn't like her. "To me she looks like an Iranian slut," he said. "We have such sluts in the Pakistani community as well. They are rich, some of them very rich, and think of themselves as European royalty!"

When Ali subsequently met her at a party, she cornered him. "You know what your problem is, Ali?" she said. "You are too much of a prig with your holier than thou attitude! Have a couple of Martinis! Let yourself loose!" Ali had walked away, deeply insulted. Later, he felt sorry for her. It was all a charade. It was naïve of him to think she could find redemption. That was when Ali decided to stop dating and think things through.

Now thinking about it, he wonders whether he himself is living a deception. Did he live like an American, think like one and live like one? Is he like them all—sons and daughters of Asian immigrants—American Born Confused Deshis, or AB-CD's? The word *desi*, meaning 'countrymen,' is used to reflect people from the Indian Subcontinent, but Ali is not Indian, neither is he Pakistani in the true sense of the word. Not really. But his parents are, and always will be. When he was ten years old his mother had taken him to Mumbai to meet her sister who had moved there with her husband; and when he was twelve, his father had taken him to Karachi to meet his family. Besides the fussing and the kissing, the squeezing and the eating, and the endless amount of people on the streets, these visits in his youth didn't make a mark on his character; never had a lasting presence in his mind.

He is confused about a lot of things, like most young people are. However, he doesn't see himself as an ABCD. He knew a few Indians and one Pakistani in Medical School and during his Residency and Fellowship, but he cannot label them as close friends, not like his high school buddy, Jerry Cohen. It was only in London during his visiting fellowship at the Hammersmith, that he was exposed to many Indian, Pakistani, and Middle Eastern doctors, and they had a substantial impact on his political views; additionally, he had taken a liking to Indo-Pakistani-Bangladeshi cooking.

Now Anna seems a welcome change. But will his parents accept a divorced godless woman? The night, dark and hot, suddenly chills. *We don't live our lives, do we? We live the life of others!* He feels a rush of sleep encroaching. He turns to lie on his side, then again onto his stomach, and the acid reflux begins acting up. He feels bloated and gassy.

He goes to the fridge; it is empty except for a paratha and a can of Coca-Cola. He eats the buttered paratha, after which he pops a Nexium capsule. If he had a wife, the fridge and his stomach would always be full.

He goes back to bed but sleep escapes him now. He begins thinking of his trip to Pakistan four years ago, the land of his forefathers, a world he remembers little about. His father's family was wealthy and without his knowledge, at his father's coaxing, his paternal aunt, the matchmaker of Karachi, had prepared an album of young eligible Pakistani women for Ali to pursue. It turned out that Ali was more interested in the social fabric and the politics in Pakistan than an arranged bride to take back home to America. The idea that he could choose a woman without knowing her well seemed strange to him. Perhaps it was his mother's influence and his Western upbringing. His mother didn't object, but neither did she applaud Ali's cross-cultural dating, but his father, although a post-modern Muslim via England, didn't like the idea. After all, Dr. Khan, despite the objection of his family—most having settled in Karachi after the Partition of India—had married a Hindu who had rebelliously converted to Catholicism. They had met at the Calcutta Medical College and after obtaining their degrees, they migrated to London where they worked for the British National Health Service, and from there, to America.

Ali feels that his parents are not entirely honest with him; indeed, he feels that they are somewhat hypocritical. While a teenager, Ali had once spotted his father together with his doctor friends indulging in the forbidden Scottish brown in his study, which he then thought of as some fancy ritual tea. He had thought that when he came of age, he would be part of this ritual among his father's doctor friends. Years later, when in college, he realized that it was not tea but the forbidden whisky. His father kept a bottle of Johnny Walker Black well concealed in his study behind all the books, which Ali had accidentally found while looking for a surgical textbook.

In college, in medical school, and subsequently during his residency training and fellowship, Ali hadn't strictly observed the rigors of the Islamic faith or for that matter, the Catholic faith either. He said his daily prayers and sometimes attended the Mosque (with his father) and the Church (with his mother) when he came home on holidays. The simultaneous forays into two Abrahamic faiths—Islam and Christianity—was the source of much guilt and confusion, an inner struggle against oneself.

And now, as he lies in bed awake, he remembers that day of the *Ashura* celebration. The mourning procession had already gathered in Fishtar Park, when Ali, in black jeans and a white shirt had positioned himself by the replica of the Shrine of Imam Husayn. A white horse, Zuljinah, the horse of Imam Husayn, all decked with a Golden saddle, a crest on his forehead, stood calmly and steadily among the crowd of mourners and observers. And then the procession had begun: the mourners marched in time to a base drum, naked from the waist up, performing *Matam*—the mourning for Imam Husayn. Some carried iron standards and some held sharp objects like knifes and flagellated their raw backs, a strike for every beat of the drum; others beat their chests, their tremulous lips invoking the names of Imam Hussein and Imam Ali. Ali's intention was to simply observe the ritual, but soon, it was as if he was overtaken by an infectious enthusiasm permeating through the hoi polloi, and Ali was engulfed by the mass hysteria. He found himself joining the mourners, beating his breast, often losing the tempo, unsure what he was doing. A rickety old man by his side, his bony rib cage visible through his flimsy *kurta-pajama*, a young boy perhaps a grandson holding his hand, kept uttering the name of Husayn. Ali was perplexed by the chaotic scene and felt he lacked the intensity and faith of the mourners, but soon thereafter, he fell into the rhythm. He suddenly felt exhilarated, as if there was an outpouring of endorphins, something he usually felt while running the last hundred meters of his ten-mile run in Central Park. But this was entirely different, more powerful than anything he had felt before: a mass celebration of death and martyrdom from whose ashes the Shi'a faith lived on. He beat his breast ever so harder, wishing he had chains so that he might bleed and suffer more pain for his faithlessness.

Suddenly, one of the mourners in front of him, a young man probably in his early twenties, collapsed. Blood gushed from a deep gash in his neck, bright red blood. Ali immediately ran to the man and placed his hand on the wound. But the carotid artery kept pumping. Ali removed his shirt and tried to bandage his neck, to stop the bleeding; a few bystanders looked on, but the procession continued. Faint sounds of "Husayn… Husayn…" kept coming from the dying man, as he rolled his eyes. By now Ali was cradling his head.

"Ambulance! Call an ambulance!" Ali shouted several times. The old man, his face serious and intense, and yet in anguish and pain as if witnessing a loved one's death, responded: "He is a Martyr—he's dying for Imam Husayn. Soon he will be with Allah in heaven." Just as Ali, his pants soaked with blood, slowly placed the young man's exsanguinated body on the ground, there was a loud sound, like a bomb blast, and all pandemonium broke loose. Ali remembers running towards the mosque, where limbs and guts and charred bodies lay shattered amid mangled cars and carts, smashed watermelons, and blood. A bomb had gone off at the very entrance to the mosque. Ali had tried to help the injured, but there was not much he could do in the pandemonium. Some of the injured were taken to the mosque, while others were taken to the hospital in ambulances and private cars. At least twenty people died, and more were injured. Fortunately, a truck nearby took the brunt of the blast, or there would have been many more casualties.

The symbolic ritual of flagellation and the chaos of the bombing left Ali confused and unsettled. He wanted to feel the

emotions; the sadness of the martyrdom of the Imam, the tragedy of the unknown man he had held in his arms, but his faith
wavered and weakened after the bombing. In an instant, his in-
tellectual mastery of his surroundings, the civility and humanity
of the human condition was shattered, leaving in its aftermath
apparitions of panic and death. How could Muslims kill each
other so indiscriminately? How could they relish such sectarian
hatred?

For, it is said in the fourth Surah: "If a man kills a Believer
intentionally, his recompense is Hell to abide therein forever."

For the first time in his life, Ali felt exposed to two dispa-
rate worlds: the world he was coming from, the world he was
born in and raised, a world that was ordered, a world where
people mowed their lawns, watched television and soap operas
and movies, a world indulging in and usurping the community
of the screen as their own; a world where they planned holidays,
enjoyed meals, and counted their money; a world that had already fought its wars of class and culture, and now fought wars
in other lands, bombing other countries but immune from being
bombed themselves. And there was this other world, a distant
world, a sodden world, an underground world that he had barely begun to taste, but the taste, the scent of this other world was
so powerful like the scent of the spiced curry that lingers on
permeating the very clothes and walls and corridors of apartment buildings and homes; a world that would perhaps shape
him in many different ways, or a world that he would distance
himself from, tear it apart and discard like wet-sticky clothing
and ultimately forget. This world was a frantic, chaotic world, a
world wracked in poverty where people fought hundreds of daily mutinies, small wars and vendettas. This was a world where
tradition, loyalties, religion and customs were deeply rooted,
tied down by centuries old history.

He kept dreaming about the events and saw himself as the
young man dying in the arms of a stranger; but he didn't want

to die. He was no dreamer, he was not destined for martyrdom, and he fought to live. His mission in life was to provide life and hope and cure for the ailing, the physically sick humanity. When he woke up from the nightmare, he would feel for his body, for the neck, to confirm that he was still alive, and would soon be on his way back to New York. He had lost interest in the album of brides. This was no place for brides. It was a place for martyrs.

He now wonders whether he has lost his faith altogether. Had the trip drained whatever passion he had felt for his religion or any religion for that matter? He still prays doesn't he? Is it just mechanical with him—the ritual of prayer tattooed on his frontal cortex? Or is it guilt or fear of the Almighty? He is a nomad wandering aimlessly in the desert, who badly needs an anchor.

He realizes that he has strayed in his thoughts; he has more urgent maters to consider, personal matters. No, Anna is not the right woman for him. It is best that he maintain a doctor patient relationship with her. The flirtation has to stop. Thinking, he lies in the bed wide-awake. He looks at his bedside clock. It is almost one-thirty. He pops a Xanax and sets the alarm for seven-thirty. He has an important meeting with his Chairman, Dr. Bob, at eight-thirty in the morning. He desperately tries to talk himself to sleep but keeps tossing and turning.

CHAPTER 7

Ali's Dexterity

When Ali walks into Dr. Bob's spacious office at eight-thirty in the morning, he finds him seated behind his mahogany desk, intensely absorbed in the *New England Journal of Medicine.* Ali cannot but notice the trophies and certificates, the memberships of prestigious organizations around the globe that Dr. Bob belongs to, and that hang on the walls proclaiming his many accomplishments, his tour de force. Someday, he would like to occupy an office like Dr. Bob's—a Chairman's office.

Dr. Bob reluctantly sets the journal aside and turns to Ali. "Now what can I do for you?"

"The service is extremely busy," says Ali, wishing Dr. Bob didn't seem so eager to get back to his reading.

"Excellent," says Dr. Bob.

"Thanks, but it has become so busy that I badly need help— Dr. Denzel, my Fellow, is super—I want to hire him after he finishes his fellowship. I also need to recruit a PhD. It's impossible to get National Institutes of Health funding without basic science collaboration. You had promised..."

"Well, well, I'll do what I can," Dr. Bob abruptly cuts in.

"Why don't you send me a document outlining your needs? And as far as an associate, take a look at Dr. Feingold. He's about to complete his heart failure fellowship at the Mass General Hospital. I'll ask him to give you a call." Dr. Bob looks at his watch. "I'm sorry Ali. I have to interview a candidate for an administrative position at 8:45," he says. Rising, and placing his hand on Ali's shoulder, he escorts him to the door.

Ali is disappointed. He had scheduled the meeting weeks ago, and yet Dr. Bob rushed him through, as if he was a representative of a drug company. He gave him no time to discuss the issues, no time to talk about a raise. And who is this Dr. Feingold Bob is pushing? He wants to hire Dr. Denzel, and that is what he is going to do.

When Ali joined the Medical Center two years earlier as head doctor of the transplant program, Dr. Bob had promised him additional staff and also said that he would hire a PhD to help with his research program. Ali's ambition was not only to excel clinically but in research as well—the only way to climb the academic ladder.

He admires Dr. Bob, who serves as his role model and was instrumental in his recruitment. He feels that Bob had all the right connections that catapulted his meteoric rise to Chairman, and if he himself deals the right cards, he has a lot to gain from him. Now, he is frustrated that Dr. Bob was somewhat short on delivery. Recently, he was spread thin and flaunted his dealings not by bold administrative acts, but by pompous honking. Ali however feels a certain kinship with Dr. Bob for giving him the opportunity to further his academic career but he is growing increasingly impatient with his stalling techniques: sending in another proposal means waiting a few more months to review, then a meeting with the administrator who will suggest a business proposal, and it can go on for another full year. Nonetheless, Ali's determination is not to be deterred; on the whole, things are going rather well for him. Besides, the move to New

York has markedly improved his social lifestyle, replete it seems with adventure in the air, unlike in cold frosty winds of Rochester, Minnesota. He is determined to find a way to continue with his research no matter how arduous the road. He intends to apply for a National Institute Grant even if Dr. Bob reneges on the seed money to hire a PhD.

After Ali leaves Dr. Bob's office, he rushes to the Catheterization Laboratory. There are many hearts to biopsy.

While Ali is taking a tiny bite of the heart of Mr. Cobb, with a biopsy probe, Ali's beeper goes off. He asks Ming to answer it.

"Dr. Ali, a woman, Anna, would like to speak to you."

"Tell her I'll call back," he says.

The sound system in the lab is playing Eric Clampton: "*Leyla, I'm begging, darling please. Leyla, darling won't you ease my worried mind…*"

At that very instant, Mr. Cobb complains of chest pain and shortness of breath. The blood pressure keeps dropping. "We have a problem," says Ali. "Get an ECG—call for a stat echo and administer fluids. Please, turn off the music!"

"Denzel, prepare for a pericardial tap."

"Mr. Cobb," says Ali. "We have a slight problem. There is fluid accumulation around your heart. I'll need to insert a needle to remove the fluid. But don't you worry Mr. Cobb, all is under control."

"Ok doc', do what you must," says Mr. Cobb.

It turns out that the biopsy needle has punctured Mr. Cobb's heart. The ultrasound examination confirms that blood has leaked around the heart, which is now flopping and tumbling in a pool of its own blood. Signs of heart compression are setting in. The blood pressure registers at 70/40.

"Call additional help," says Ali.

Nurse Anne arrives from the other labs, and Dr. Miller, the anesthesiologist rushes in. There is tension in the laboratory that accompanies any emergency, and yet, everyone is calmly going about his or her work as if all this is routine.

"Go ahead Denzel," says Ali.

"Pass me the needle," says Denzel.

Ali helps Denzel insert the long needle through the chest wall under ultrasound guidance into the sac around the heart and evacuates the blood with a syringe. Immediately the blood pressure recovers. It is one of those complications from a procedure that if not recognized and treated urgently can prove to be fatal.

"We got this one going," says Ali to Ming. "Get a bed in the CCU and call the next patient."

At six that evening, after performing six additional heart biopsies, and attending to his in-patients, Ali finally steps into his academic office. He still has letters to dictate to the referral doctors, and, if time permits, and he is not overwhelmed with sheer exhaustion, he'll work on his research protocol on the mechanism of heart rhythm abnormalities in patients with heart failure whose hearts are removed before transplantation. He is still at his desk at eight o'clock, munching a tuna fish sandwich, when his phone rings. It is Anna again.

"I'm terribly sorry, Anna," he says. "I had an emergency and a busy day. I was going to call you before I retired to bed."

"I'm the one who's sorry about yesterday. I got carried away. I wanted to tell you what I've been through."

"For now, be optimistic. Tomorrow will bring a better day."

"Da, I already feel better. You have such an effect on me," says Anna. "What are you doing this weekend?"

"I leave for Las Vegas on Friday for an important meeting,"

he says. I need time to work—to finalize a research protocol."

Anna calls him a couple of days later to tell him that Brad, Mary's husband will be performing in Las Vegas and Mary has asked her to accompany them. "See, you can't get rid of me." He doesn't know what to say. He laughs an uncomfortable laugh.

"You are not happy that I'll be there?"

"Oh no, that's great," he says, reluctantly. He had concluded that Anna was not the right woman for him. But at the end, the desire to be with her, to absorb her beauty, her sexuality, the drama of her stories, her mannerisms, and her French tinged accent gets the upper hand.

They make plans to meet in Las Vegas.

CHAPTER 8

Dinner in Las Vegas

In Las Vegas, Ali's research meeting has been arranged by a pharmaceutical company, Superior Medical Labs. Inc. Dr. Bob, a consultant to the company, is to Chair the meeting. When Ali checks into the Venetian, he spots Dr. Bob in the bar with Carmensita, his administrative secretary. Dr. Bob asks him to join them for a drink, but Ali begs to be excused.

At the meeting, however, Ali is bewildered when he notices Dr. Bob's name, and not his, listed as the Principal Investigator on the Project at the Medical Center to study the effects of a new drug, Cardiospeed in heart failure.

"I believe there's been a mistake," Ali says.

"My name will facilitate the Institution getting the project," says Dr. Bob. "Besides, my friend, ours is a symbiotic relationship. It is up to you to recruit the patients and write the manuscript."

Ali nods, silently.

"I assure you, you'll get due credit," Bob declares authoritatively.

Ali is flushed with anger but can do nothing about it. Clearly, Dr. Bob's administrator will work out the budget, Dr. Bob will draw a salary from the project, and the Institution will credit Dr. Bob, and not Ali, for getting the Project, when all along it was his idea. Ali had approached the Head of Research and Development at the drug Company through Dr. Bob, spelling out the details of the study, but Dr. Bob, who knew the Head of R&D well, must have projected it as his own idea.

"That son of a bitch," Ali grounds the words and swallows them hard. He'll get him for this when it's time to recruit patients for the study.

Ali now wonders at Dr. Bob's agenda; most certainly he would use the funds to accomplish his own goals while Ali did all the work. The man was a master at self-promotion and had a large following with a powerful agenda: a biology Institute a la Howard Hughes, a Bob Brown Society, a Bob Brown Chaired Professorship, a Bob Brown Featured Lecture, a lobby to push his ambitious agenda to the Board of Trustees, and a Bob Brown building for which he was collecting money from his generous patient donors for construction. There was a rumor that he had cajoled some of his most devoted members of the society, and his many wealthy patients to write letters to the Swedish Academy that he should be considered for the Nobel. Within the last few years, accolades had poured from all over the world; he was the recipient of all the awards, so that medical societies and associations hurriedly had to create several new ones for him. He had achieved the highest honors in his short life, most of which are often the realm of the dead. His smarts, combined with subtle insecurities and paranoia, were attributes not unusual in high achievers. He knew how to manipulate power to his advantage, and like the current President and Vice President, he was a smart fundraiser. At one of the staff meetings he had pronounced unabashedly that patients should be sized up for donations. He had become big and powerful and like most powerful people who control the lives of others, the man seemed to have lost all sense of reality.

That evening, there is a message waiting for Ali from Anna to meet him at the bar at six 'oclock. Ali is still fuming about Dr. Bob, and somewhat conflicted about meeting with Anna, but hearing her voice on the recording, he instantly drops Dr. Bob out of his mind. As he showers and dresses, he begins to look forward to Anna's company. He wonders what she will look like, and what pleasures the evening will bring. He is kept waiting at the bar for more than twenty minutes, and again Dr. Bob's treachery comes to mind. He constantly shifts his position from sitting on the bar stool to standing as he sips his soda.

He is about to call Anna's room, when he sees her coming toward him. She kisses him gently on the lips, and he places his arms around her. Her warmth elevates his mood, and once more he forgets Dr. Bob. They hop into a cab to Caesars Palace, where they meet Mary and attend Brad's show, after which they dine. Anna eats only a salad and when Ali asks her why she isn't eating real food, she answers that she is on a diet.

They take a walk in the make-believe Venice, and some photographs at the tacky San Marco Square, and Anna coaxes Ali to go with her to the casino.

Anna plays the slot machines, while Ali watches the reels spinning, the lights flashing, the quarters clanging as they drop feverishly into the tray, twenty dollars the prize of one, and Anna jumps up and down. For the next five tries the machine eats all her money like a starved creature. A sparsely clad waitress with bouncing boobs, balancing a whisky soda, a beer, and a martini on a tray, asks Ali if he cares for a drink. Ali politely shakes his head. Anna tries to entice him to try his luck at the slot machine, but he refuses, smilingly. There are loud noises, shrill clanging sounds; a siren buzzes aloud—someone nearby has hit the jackpot.

After Anna loses some more dollars at the black jack table, they go for a walk on the Strip and watch the dancing fountains at the Bellagio. When the fountain display is over, and the city lights come on, as day turns to dusk, she leans against him, and he kisses her on the lips with intensity. A voice suddenly awakens them from the brief moment of intimacy.

"Anna, Anna!" She is startled and almost loses her balance. As she turns, a man approaches. They speak briefly in Russian.

"This is Alyosha, my ex-husband," she says. They shake hands.

His boyish face looks pale and gaunt, and his eyes are bloodshot. Anna continues talking to him in Russian for a few more minutes, and then, rather abruptly, takes hold of Ali's hand and extends the other towards Alyosha. He takes his leave in a shuffle after shaking hands with both of them. Ali notices his weak handshake.

"Does he live in Las Vegas?" Ali asks. She just shrugs as if she doesn't care. He asks her if she would like to go for a coffee. "No," she says. "It's late."

They walk back to the hotel. He notices a mood change like at the Café des Artistes. Her hand in his, feels limp, detached, cold, and bloodless like a phantom limb.

"Do you want to come to my room?" he asks. "The night is still young." He had fantasized spending time with her alone in his room, of making love to her; and if there was no sex, to touch her, to feel her body on his.

"I'm tired, she says. I'll see you tomorrow for dinner." She plants a lingering kiss on his lips.

The kiss sort of momentarily takes the edge off his frustrations. But when he goes to his room, he feels restless. He paces the floor. He wonders about her ex-husband and what their marriage was like. He wants to ask her about it after the sudden and unexpected encounter, but feels she is closed tight like a clam. He questions her ways: the sudden mood changes, her insouciance, the quick retraction into an impenetrable cocoon. Is it, utter selfishness on his part to expect more? Is all this part of her culture or is it her personality? Is this the price he has to pay for her beauty and celebrity?

He lies in bed, thinking. Sleep doesn't come. He pops an Ambien and turns on the TV.

At seven the next evening, a limo picks up Ali and Anna, and takes them for dinner with the drug company executives and researchers. Anna's elegance in a low-cut purple dress, a dome-shaped black hat with an orange feather, and a necklace of pearls on her swan neck, creates a stir as she floats with a ballerina's stride into the restaurant. Like a model on a catwalk in a Parisian fashion show. She holds her head high as if acknowledging her breathless audience. Ali is relieved that she is in a better mood, and it is rather singularly ostentatious to have such a stunningly beautiful woman on his arm.

There are twenty people for the private dinner in a large, dimly lit room designed to look like a wine cellar, with wine barrels for walls. The fruity oak fragrance of aging wines gives it the unique character of another time, another place, perhaps in a Chateau in southern France.

The introduction made, Dr. Bob, who is at the head end of the table, offers Anna a seat on his right, followed by Ali, and to Ali's right is the blonde and beautiful Leigh, a representative of the company. Ali and Anna are relieved that Dr. Bob doesn't remember Anna, who, he had met briefly during rounds when she was in the Coronary Care Unit in the medical center. When Anna tells Dr. Bob that she is a Russian ballerina, he goes on expounding on his trip to Moscow and asks Anna about her defection. He praises her beauty and courage. Anna is utterly impressed with the place and tells her defection story with drama and theatricality. Ali wonders if he is imagining that her accent becomes more pronounced, and more Russian words pepper her speech. The story incites curiosity and a sense of mystery. Clearly, she takes center stage. The way Bob looks at both of them, Ali can sense an element of jealousy on the part of Bob.

Ali watches Dr. Bob indulge himself and Anna, with many glasses of Chateau Laffite Rothschild that he orders (the company spares no expense). Quite high on the wine, Dr. Bob announces several times that he will get front row seats to see Anna dance at the Metropolitan. Ali feels embarrassed, and to Anna's frowning, tells Dr. Bob that she doesn't dance professionally any longer, but Dr. Bob pays no attention. To Ali's irritation, Dr. Bob and Anna insist that he taste the excellent Bordeaux, but he meets their pleas with refusal.

He feels out of place like a drowning pea in a soggy salad. He is somewhat comforted when the words from the second Surah ring loud in his mind: "When they ask you about wine and gambling say: "In them is great sin, and some profit for men; but the sin is greater than the profit." But how can he quote the Qur'an to these unbelievers? They will only laugh at him. Ali puts his arm around Anna and hugs her mostly to remind Bob that she belongs to him. And then to incite some jealousy, he strikes a lengthy conversation with Leigh on the drug protocol.

As the dinner comes to an end, everyone is under the influence of the *riche* Bordeaux, except Ali. Out of the blue, Dr. Bob unexpectedly poses a question: "Ali, are you contemplating marriage with Anna?"

"It's a bit early to tell," he says, a flush rising to his cheeks.

Dr. Bob backs his chair, gets up, and places his arms around Ali and Anna.

"Hey, you guys should get married soon, when the going is good. I bet you can't wait to rush the honeymoon." Anna begins tearing with laughter, while Ali puzzled, shakes his head. He thinks Dr. Bob is gaga with alcoholic intoxication.

"What's so funny?" he asks.

Anna and Leigh cannot stop laughing; Dr. Bob joins in, then everyone else does too.

Dr. Bob cannot take his eyes off Anna, and Anna flirts, reveling in his attention. Ali cannot wait to leave—the drinking, the decadence, the laughter, the obstreperousness, are beyond the pale. He feels like a lion lost on a busy highway.

"Here ye, hear ye," Dr. Bob says, a bit wobbly and flushed: "This is a great meeting and thanks to Dr. Marchetti from R & D and to Mr. Fusco from marketing, and Ms. Leigh for being generous hosts. The wine, the food, and the ambience was great. I think we have a great drug on our hands that will go a long way toward improving the *quality of life* of our patients with heart failure. And how can I end without toasting this elegant lady—the ballerina, Anna—for her beauty, her charm, and the graciousness of her presence." He takes Anna's hand in his, bends down almost to his knees, kissing it, and lurches forward. He loses his balance and falls on her. There is a roar of laughter and applause from around the table.

Ali stiffly looks down. On the way back to the hotel, Ali remains silent.

"Your boss is funny and full of life," says Anna.

"Unlike me, right?"

"You are stiff, Ali, and inhibited. I myself need a drink to loosen up. Your boss is like Russian men, wild and boisterous when they drink. He means no harm."

"You like to be the center of attention, don't you?"

"By the way, you should have tasted the wine. Just tasted, I mean. Do you know that each bottle costs over a thousand dollars?" she says.

Ali doesn't respond. He can see that she is flustered. It is obvious to him that she expects him to be impressed.

But instead, Ali feels dejected. She is right—he's too uptight, a social misfit. He isn't her type. Perhaps the Iranian rebel was right all along, and his father was probably right as well. He should look for a doctor, and a Muslim one at that, or he should make a radical change. At that moment, something comes over him—a desire to reject himself, to do something drastic, something shocking, a makeover; for once to shed his reservations as he had done in college when he asked for a cigarette and a Budweiser and made out with his date in the back seat of the car just to show his friends he was one of them.

They were in the hotel lobby when he suddenly turns towards Anna. "Let's go to the bar," he says. "I'd love to have a drink."

"Ali, you don't have to because of what I said," says Anna, seemingly remorseful. She places her hand on his arm and pulls him close to her. But Ali insists. They go to the bar.

He orders a whisky-soda; she a club soda, and they sit sipping. He relates to her how he had seen his father drink the forbidden Scottish-brown. He asks for another whisky-soda, and when he gulps that down, he switches to an Apple Martini. He raises the glass: "To the Iranian Rebel!"

"To whom?" she asks.

"Never mind," he says, and burst out laughing as if at that moment he sheds his inhibitions and embraces a world of play and fun—a world of indulgence. "Fuck it," he says. He attempts to get off the bar stool and almost falls. He is all over Anna in the elevator, kissing her face, touching her, swearing his love for her, while Anna laughs hysterically. Ali cannot place the keycard into the slot to open the room. She does it for him.

"Come in my love," he says, bowing low in front of her, and falls. Anna helps him get on his feet.

"Come in, my Tsarina Anna," he says.

"You are drunk, Ali. You have an early flight to catch. And I'm off early in the morning to the Grand Canyon with Mary and Brad. Go to sleep," she says, and sets off to her own room.

"When will you be back in New York?" He calls after her.

"In two weeks. Will call."

"I love you Tsarina Anna," he shouts, as an elderly couple passing in the corridor stares. He crashes on the bed with his clothes on.

He wakes up at three in the morning with a severe headache and throws up all over the bathroom sink; he has never done this before and swears he will never touch alcohol again. He wonders what had come over him. He remembers the words of the Imam that the world is a difficult place plagued by Devils, forever tempting the indulgence of the senses, to make the good, the straight, and the faithful, crooked and unsightly. What Devils were at work? At that moment he feels utterly embarrassed and depressed. His mental store, the synapses rich in lipids, glucose, and serotonin, crash.

At the airport, Ali spots Carmensita at the ticket counter. "Carmensita?" he gently taps her on the back.

"Dr. Ali!"

"Are you on the 10:15 to New York?" Carmensita nods.

Ali remembers Carmensita and Dr. Bob at the bar, and wonders whether there is something sizzling between them, but when she meets his stare, he looks away. Carmensita is a big woman, carrying a strikingly beautiful mulatto face, with dirty blond, curly hair. Her breasts are generous, her hips shapely, and large. But he prefers slim women, fair skinned, like Anna.

"Sir, Counter # 4," orders the attendant twice, interrupting his thoughts.

"See you in New York." They wave.

Ali settles in his seat, wondering why he had drunk so much. What was he trying to prove? And Anna, did she enjoy seeing him vulnerable, so out-of-control?

"Hey Dr. Ali, I think you are in my seat. Never mind, I will take the aisle," says Carmensita.

Ali would have preferred to be alone, what with the hang-over and the pounding headache. When the attendant comes around offering drinks, Carmensita orders a Bloody Mary and Ali a Pepsi. She goes on jabbering away about Dr. Bob and their close relationship.

"He confides in me...even seeks my advice," she says.

"Can you prompt him to give me a raise?" Ali laughs. And then without really meaning to, he tells Carmensita that he is a teetotaler, and about last night's alcoholic binge, and his split-ting headache.

Carmensita promptly assures him that she can get rid of his headache in an instant. She takes out a white powder from her bag, and despite his protest, pours it into the Pepsi, assuring him that it is herbal, and that no harm will come to the brilliant doctor. "Take this," she says, and so slightly pinches his thigh.

"What's in it?" he asks. "It's not cocaine, right?"

"It's a herbal powder—it'll get rid of your headache," she says.

The headache is unbearable. Ali drinks the cup of Pepsi with the powder, and within about fifteen minutes or so, his headache disappears. He is totally impressed that Carmensita's powder ac-complished what two Excedrin's and two Tylenols couldn't. And he begins feeling good, very good; a sort of dopamine rush comes over him, and before he realizes, an involuntary swelling in his groin. He doesn't have the presence of mind to ask her what's in the powder; its effect makes him relaxed and laid back.

"Feeling better?" she asks, with a sly smile.

"Where are you originally from, Carmensita?" he asks. He always wants to know where people come from, where they be-long, to what religion, to what community. He often asks his patients such questions: their past histories, family histories, per-sonal histories; almost two-thirds of his patients in New York are born elsewhere in the world, not in the place called America.

It almost seems that his question to Carmensita is the open-ing she was looking for. By now she's on her second Bloody

Mary. She goes animatedly, her hands in constant motion, touching him, relating that her parents left Cuba after Castro's rise to power, and simply followed their rich master Señor Mendez, with links to the New York and Las Vegas Mafia, but after his death, they had to fend for themselves. Her family members were no Cuban aristocrats who read El Diario and the Bergen Record, and loved Richard Nixon and Ronald Reagan. Her grandmother, Consuela, and subsequently her mother, Carmela, worked as maids in Miami Beach hotels; but in Cuba Libre before Castro came to power, they had been Priestesses of Santeria in the barrios of Habana. Their ancestors were peasants, descendants of the original slaves, the Yoruba people, and plenty of Spanish blood flowed in their veins. She proudly claims ancestral linkage to Mexican indigenous people, an Aztec, a great-grandson of Juan Chichiton, a servant of the Dominican friar Diego de Calderon who traveled Central America spreading the word of Christ from the Uplands of Mexico to the shores of Cuba. When she mentions that Diego de Calderon died of Chagas disease then known by some as "la fiebre del mato grosso," Ali says. "I have published a paper on Chagas disease. It is acquired through the bite of the Ruduviidae bug. And years later it manifests as heart failure and heart arrhythmias."

He wants to tell her more about the disease, its management and prognosis, but she cuts him short and continues with her story. She boasts that she had learned the art of the *curandeira* from her old grandmother and is well versed in the power of healing herbs. Undoubtedly, Ali is impressed.

He barely hears her ask if he knows anything about herbal medicine. By now, he is too sleepy to respond. He doesn't wake up until the plane lands at La Guardia. When he bends over to tie his shoes, he sees a wide blotch around his crotch.

CHAPTER 9

The Birthday Party

It is a Friday evening when New York City expectantly slows down; a fast trickle of weary feet line up at the beer bars, wine bars, martini bars, and restaurants.

In the twelfth-floor apartment, on East Sixty-Seventh Street, Dr. Denzel's birthday party is in full swing. To Brubeck's *Take Five*, Ali and Cindy, Dr. Denzel's wife, sway in the living room amid loud chatter that at times drowns the sax emanating from the Bose stereo system. Ali has to shout to tell Cindy how great her husband is and what a difference he'll make to the heart transplant team. Their attention abruptly turns towards the doorway as the booming voice of Dr. Bob drowns all.

"What a swell party! Hey, happy birthday, Denzel."

The tall, dark-skinned, black-eyed, and handsome Denzel, dressed in white slacks, a black shirt wide-open at the collar in a silk white jacket, slightly taller than the lanky Dr. Bob, vigorously shakes his outstretched hand. But Dr. Bob steps forward and embraces Denzel, heartily tapping him on the back.

"Where's my wife? Cindy, Cindy?" yells Denzel.

"Here, Ali, why don't you dance with Nancy? Says Cindy.

"Nancy, this is Ali—The Dr. Ali I told you about."

While Cindy, the dark-brown Caribbean-beauty with a braided afro in a brown jump-suit rushes to meet Dr. Bob, Ali stares at Nancy, who is staring at Denzel. He sees a tall woman with a fine nose and a roundish face—a woman of considerable beauty—this Nancy. Her golden-blond hair is soft, shiny and curly, and falls in braids to her shoulders. She wears a dark blue low-cut jersey that highlights her midriff and her sapphire eyes. Her black pants cling tight to her ample buttocks and hips. His subsequent thoughts are: is this woman single? Is she divorced? Is she a model? The latter seems unlikely however; she isn't slim and anorectic and too tall to be a model. In fact, she is a bit on the heavy side. He likes slim women, like Anna, but is immediately taken by her laughter as she flirtatiously turns towards him.

"What did she say about me?" he asks, wondering if it is another fix-up.

"I expected the head of the Heart Transplant Program to be short and fat and bald, and old and be-spectacled, like my long-ago pediatrician in Staten Island."

He laughs.

"You're exactly as Cindy said, Cool!" They both laugh.

"You're gorgeous," he says.

"Thanks. But not as gorgeous as Cindy, right? She braided my hair. "

"You are both stunning," says Ali, and adds: "Are you single?"

"The right man hasn't come my way," she says. "And what about you?"

"The right woman is out there somewhere." They laugh.

"How do you know Denzel and Cindy?" he asks.

"I met Cindy in *Port au Prince*. Denzel was my classmate at Stuyvesant; now I invest their money."

"Maybe you can invest mine. Not that I have much to invest."

He places his arms around her and starts to take a step when the music comes to a sudden stop.

"Please! I would like to say a few words," shouts Denzel, center stage in the living room. "Thanks for coming guys. It's also a celebration of my new job—I'm a little nervous to step into the white coat of an Attending. I know I can do it. Boy, am I kidding myself? Thanks to Dr. Bob for offering me the job. Thanks to Ali for teaching me all I know. Have a wonderful time and enjoy yourselves. Carmensita has offered to concoct her delicious fragrant and fiery punch. Oh, I almost forgot—sorry, Cindy—thanks for your love and support. I wasn't supposed to announce this—we are going to have a baby." There was loud applause.

With Nancy by his side, Ali is thinking that it is he and not Dr. Bob who gave Denzel the job. Well, Denzel is being politically correct, a trait he hadn't previously realized Denzel possessed.

"Dr. Bob would like to say a few words," says Denzel from the far corner of the room.

"I would like to wish Dr. Denzel a happy birthday and extend my welcome into the faculty," says Dr. Bob. "Ah, we had great candidates for the job, but lemme' tell you, Denzel was the best. Right Ali? Congratulations, Cindy, you make a lovely couple." And he embraces Cindy and plants a kiss on her cheek.

"There he goes again, stealing center stage," Ali mumbles.

"Happy birthday to you, happy birthday ..." sings Cindy, and the others join in. When the hullabaloo dies down, Nancy tells Ali that she is an investment analyst specializing in biotechnology companies. She goes on rattling animatedly about bio-engineered pig hearts, pig livers, and kidneys for future transplants.

"You should have been a doctor," Ali says.

"Medicine fascinates me," she says. "I was pre-med in college. I couldn't keep up with the grades. My father was disappointed. He wanted me to be a doctor or an engineer like him."

"My father too."

Nancy launches into how she invested in the British PPL–Therapeutic stock that created Dolly, the cloned lamb and other biotech companies like Celera and Human Genomics, and how she had made a killing for her clients.

"With so few transplant donors, the future belongs to genetically engineered and mechanical hearts," she adds. Ali is hardly listening (investments and finances aren't his cup of tea), absorbing instead the tilt of her head, her wide-open laughter, the golden blonde hair, the milky-white skin, the mildly exposed midriff. But when she refers to the totipotent stem cell, and the Godly promise it holds, Ali is flabbergasted!

"I am dying for a drink." Nancy pulls him to the make-shift bar, where Carmensita is preparing her punch; Dr. Bob, the master taster, by her side.

"Dr. Ali, you've got to taste my punch," says Carmensita. She takes out a vial with a reddish ingredient and sprinkles it liberally into the mixture.

"One of your herbs?" says Ali. He turns to Nancy: "When I was flying back from Vegas, Carmensita added a herbal powder to my drink that got rid of a splitting headache and put me to sleep."

"Here, try some. I spiced it a bit."

"Ali doesn't drink," says Dr. Bob.

"Okay, I'll try some." Ali wishes he didn't sound so defiant.

"Change of heart Ali?" Dr. Bob cuffs him lightly on the shoulder.

"Just for today."

"Nancy, would you like some?" asks Ali.

"A glass of Chardonnay," says Nancy. "On second thought, that looks, delish."

As they are sipping the punch, Dr. Bob places his arm around Ali and says softly: "New girlfriend? What happened to the Russian ballerina?"

Ali is startled at the mention of Anna. He is surprised that Bob remembers her.

Ali introduces Nancy to Dr. Bob. Again, Dr. Bob takes him aside. "I'd hold on to this one," he advises. "She's a knock-out, man."

"And what's this about herbs?" Dr. Bob turns to Carmensita.

She loudly pronounces that she has cholesterol-lowering herbs, heart muscle restoration herbs, and *Paraiso*.

"Did you spike my drink with *Paraiso*?" asks Ali.

"That's a secret, Lovey," she says. Turning towards Bob she continues: "Did I mention *Yerba de Diablo*....my...my!" She gives a hearty laugh and twists her hand in the stuffy air as if to highlight the importance of her words, to show that she is not only an administrative secretary, but also a doctor of a different sort. Nancy and Ali listen with amusement. Ali sees Dr. Bob's eyes pop out; his interest heightens.

"This punch is great—it tingles the tongue. Can I have the recipe?" asks Nancy.

"For you honey! Well—if you are with this cutie—maybe, but without the secret spice," and she pinches Ali's cheek.

"What was the last herb you mentioned?" Dr. Bob asks.

"*Yerba de Diablo?*" she says, pushing her chest forward. "The devils curse, Dr. Bob," and she swings her hips, and stomps her foot, as if to lay one.

Ali looks at Nancy, hoping to catch her eye and takes a step away from Dr. Bob and Carmensita and her punch. But Nancy's eyes are on Dr. Bob.

"How do you know so much about herbs?" Dr. Bob asks, his mouth close to Carmensita's.

"I told you. We Arrube people have a long tradition of *Curandaria*. Do you know what that is?"

Dr. Bob shakes his head.

"Some other time. Drink your punch, pappy."

"Lemme tell you—the National Institutes of Health has recently announced their plans to offer grants to study the effects of herbal medicine for the cure of heart disease and cancer," proclaims Dr. Bob, taking a step towards Ali and Nancy.

"Can you get me some of your herbs for experimentation?" says Dr. Bob.

And who would be ideally qualified to apply for these grants if not the great Dr. Bob? Ali sees it coming—Dr. Bob will gather his troops and preach from the pulpit: "'This is it—this is the future—herbs for cholesterol, heart function, heart arrhythmias, heart failure etc. Wasn't it the foxglove that gave us digitalis?'"

Ali laughs at Dr. Bob's proposition when he promptly lectures him about a colleague of his, a graduate of Columbia, who had written a paper during his Harvard Doctoral Fellowship of his amazing discovery of the use of the sodium channel blocker, tetradotoxin (TTX) in the practice of zombism in Haiti.

"Lemme tell you—there is something in these herbs, some ingredients yet to be discovered for the benefit of mankind," Dr. Bob says, as if he can peep into the distant future, the unearthing of a powerful drug that could dissolve a cholesterol plaque and earn him universal accolades and the Nobel.

"I want to experiment on some of your herbs," repeats Dr. Bob to Carmensita.

Ali feels a bit woozy. The room is too noisy and stuffy. He looks at his empty glass, wishing for some fresh air.

"Let's go to the verandah?" He places his hand on the small of Nancy's back as she refills her glass before guiding her to the porch door, while Carmensita pulls Dr. Bob to dance the salsa.

Ali points to the East River. A tugboat leisurely passes by.

"That Carmensita—she's some character isn't she?" says Nancy.

"Indeed!" says Ali.

"She has the hots for you."

"She's not my type."

"And Dr. Bob—he's so presumptuous and flashy in his velvet suit and the red bow-tie! Is he your boss?"

"He's everyone's boss—The Big Chief—rather erratic and prone to drinking since he lost his wife from cancer. I think there is something going on between him and Carmensita."

Ali notices Nancy looking at him curiously with her caressing blue eyes. He turns his face away, and points to the sixty-foot fancy yacht of some multi-millionaire cruising the East River.

"I'm amazed the way Carmensita talks to Dr. Bob," Nancy says.

"They're already a bit drunk." Ali looks away. "I'm a bit drunk myself—I have a low tolerance to alcohol." Ali sighs wishing his head would clear. "Yes, where was I? Dr. Bob—I'm told he is a jolly good recipient of his newfound freedom after his wife's death. His father-in-law was the Editor-in-Chief of the prestigious *New Medical Journal* where he published his seminal articles and proposed that rupture of cholesterol plaques results in heart attacks."

"Wow!" Nancy is impressed. "He seems a flamboyant character, very colorful and somewhat obstreperous." She turns to Ali. "I always thought doctors were boring and stuck up."

"There are many of those, too," says Ali, quietly.

Their gaze shifts to the living room, where Dr. Bob is holding court with the resident doctors and nurses from the Coronary Unit.

The air outside is stuffy; an intermittent breeze cools Ali's damp skin. The night sky of New York is starless with streaks of bright red, orange, green, and yellow. Below, the trees lining the sidewalk are a dark green. In-between the trees, a kaleidoscopic view: yellow taxi roofs, a black limo, a blue BMW with lights like laser beams; colorful pedestrians crisscrossing between cars in great hurry. In one corner of the street below, a young man in jeans kisses a business suited woman; two men holding hands briefly zip along on roller skates. Suddenly an ambulance whizzes past with blazing sirens.

"Perhaps, some unlucky man had a heart attack," Nancy says with a hint of humor adding. "You may be wanted, doctor." They both laugh.

"New York is lovely at night from up above," says Ali, intently looking into her big sapphire eyes.

"Have you seen the view from the World Trade Center? You should go there sometime."

"Will you take me?"

"Sure."

She tells him about her recent trip to India: the noisy and chaotic streets of Mumbai, and her visit to the Taj Mahal: of how she was accosted by a monkey who slapped her behind while another almost ran away with her stuffed paratha. They both laugh out loud. She recites the names of Mogul Emperors: Shah Jahan, Akbar, and Aurangzeb. "Did you know that when the Taj Mahal was finished, the emperor Shah Jahan had the hands of the workers chopped off, and the architects blinded?" she says.

"How barbaric; I'm no Shah Jahan; I only steal hearts." They both laugh.

With all the talk about Mogul Emperors, Ali mentions his own origins. "One night in London's North End, a group of punks called me Paki, and I snapped back. "I am not a Paki—I'm an American! And the punks shut up."

She asks him about his travels, his family, and his work at the medical center, drawing him out, her dark blue eyes holding his gaze.

He feels like the center of their universe, feeding her slices of himself.

"My mother was a Hindu woman from Calcutta, who converted to Catholicism under the auspices of Mother Teresa and married my Muslim father against the wishes of her family," he adds. He can sense that Nancy is impressed. "When she married my father, she was looked upon as a double traitor who had betrayed not only her religion, but the constraints of her orthodox Brahmin culture."

"I'm not surprised," says Nancy. "And you? Do you take to your mother's or father's religion?"

"I consider myself a Muslim…but, not a practicing one—not really."

The differences between Nancy and Anna were striking. Although she is into finances, Nancy's interest in biotechnology and pharmacological products captivates Ali. There seem no hidden mysteries in her. Her demeanor suggests she is an open book whose pages turn easily and pleasantly. He is also amazed at her knowledge and fascination for the East and its social fabric. He is likewise impressed with her interest in him, his life. Anna has no such interest; she is entirely self-absorbed.

It is almost eleven. The city lights shimmer in the waters of the East River. The moon has slowly made its ascent and, for a brief moment, seems to bathe them both in its radiant glow, its magnetic hold. Is the moon signaling the beginning of something new: each other's world together?

Back in the living room, the lights are dim. Some people slouch on the couch; others cling to each other, dancing to the rhythm and jazz of Miles Davis. Ali sees Carmensita dancing with Linda Rivera. Dr. Denzel in the distant corner of the living room, flirts with Julie while Cindy wraps up the leftovers in the kitchen. Ali takes Nancy in his arms. They dance the last dance, holding each other tight. He feels her breath on his neck, the smell of peppermint and punch. When at last they draw apart,

Ali feels he has to see her again.

"Would you like to go out for dinner sometime?"

"Sure, baby. But I'm out of town for a month or so. I leave for Acapulco on Sunday with my friend Nalini, and after that for job related training to London and Mumbai. Our company is opening offices there."

"That's exiting! Will you call me after you return?"

"Sure, baby. Here, let me give you my number." She writes her number on the back of her card and passes it on to him. He fumbles in his coat pocket for his card and hands it to her.

On the drive home, Ali feels the testosterone high of a pubertal boy, and a certain excitement—the excitement one feels when something adultish happens unexpectedly. Nancy is someone he would like to see again and in bed. All this, because he hasn't had sex for a long time since Dianne in Minnesota? But, didn't she seem too perfect? Is this a sort of a random ordering?

When Anna crosses his mind, his mood grows somber. He wonders whether she is having a good time with Mary and Brad, or whether she is lonely and sad. The very thought of Anna feels as if he is wearing a guilt-ridden tie around his collar. But why? Is Anna worth it after all? Will anything develop? Will there be an unfolding story? He thinks of calling her to allay his guilt; but then, he thinks of Nancy.

Nancy is taken up with Ali—his poise, and the self-confidence are qualities she admires in a man. Like him, she is looking for a husband; anxious that her ovaries will stop spluttering their eggs as she approaches her thirty-fifth birthday, and life's adventure will abruptly end. Recently, she had browsed over and answered singles ads in *New York* magazine. She had wondered whether she should place an ad herself, and worked on it on her Laptop: Seeking an extraordinary Man. (No—too corny!) Pretty Lady or Lady in Red. (Sounds desperate.) No, Lady looking for her Man (but why the Lady bit?). I'm 35 (what about 30? Just a little cheating will do?), slim, blonde, blue eyed, sexy, funny, spontaneous, passionate for life and living. (That's a cliché—got to reword it.) Love the theatre, museums, jazz; walks in the Park, fall foliage (that's catchy), eating out, and traveling to the East. Looking for a handsome professional man, doctor or lawyer or financial consultant preferred (too limiting! Upper-east-side bitch!); preferably, over 5' 10" and athletic; willing to share my world: for love, commitment and marriage (a must? Another cliché—got to cut it out!). Promise—we will not only have laughs—as an investor, I will make money work for us (that's too tacky!). Send photo, phone number, and a note. Her ad was too long, expensive and somewhat predictable. She hit the save button. She decided to shorten it some other day.

There were arranged blind dates by friends that were some-times silly and at other times capricious. So, when Ali asked her out, she was more than thrilled, but when she sobered and began thinking about it, his Muslim background unsettled her. How will she act? Will he mind if she has an extra glass of wine or if she has an occasional smoke? Well, he didn't have any problem with the punch; he drank the whole glass. In the pres-ence of a cardiologist, she couldn't smoke—that would be out of line, bordering on criminal. But the cultural and religious dif-ferences might ruin the relationship. Besides, she's isn't looking for a boyfriend. She is looking for a husband. It will not work out. But wait a moment—he is so handsome, so intelligent, and a doctor besides. Not any doctor, the head of Heart Transplant. She has to give it a try. And yet, she panics and hurriedly calls her friend, Nalini, a doctor, a young brilliant breast cancer spe-cialist, whose interest, like Ali's, is in academic medicine, and with whom Nancy had taken several trips to Asia.

In Acapulco, Nalini at first tells Nancy point blankly that if it were she, she wouldn't get involved with a Muslim. "They are too religious—stuck up with all sorts of societal restraints and religious constraints." When Nancy goes on and on raving about Ali, and that his mother is Indian, a Bengali, a Hindu, converted to Catholicism, and that he is not a "practicing" Muslim, Nalini has a change of heart. "Go out with him, Nan, and be bold, be bad, really bad—order a bottle of wine, and swear with a flare. And if you get a good laugh—he's your man."

CHAPTER 10
Anna's Revelations

Several days after returning from Las Vegas, Anna calls Ali and animatedly describes her visit to the Grand Canyon: the Granite Gorges, the crystalline rocks, and the flaming sunsets. She speaks about Mary's husband, Brad, blowing his trumpet, its sounds echoing amid the canyon walls.

"And, I have a surprise for you," she adds: "Tickets for Don Quixote!"

They meet for a brief dinner beforehand at the Josephina expectantly waiting for the performance by the visiting Kirov. He feels her excitement, as she enthusiastically describes the Kirov, how it is the best, the most original ballet troupe. Ali hears a yearning in her voice to dance again.

During intermission she tells him wistfully that watching the performance reminds her of her days with the troupe, and her stellar dancing then. "Oh Ali, I miss it so much." He sees tears form in her eyes. He feels sorry for her, wondering what he himself might have felt if he were not able to practice the profession of medicine. He holds Anna's hand tight, fearing that her mood will change color and spoil their evening. "Of course you miss it," he says.

Anna doesn't reply, lost in her own thoughts. He offers her a glass of champagne. Tonight, he is willing to do anything for her; he will cross any boundaries, climb any fences to make her happy. She coaxes him to have a sip of champagne as she nudges close to him. He takes a few sips to make her happy.

After the performance, they hop into a cab, clinging to each other. It is a cold, windy November night. When they step out of the taxi, Anna suddenly disengages from him, and pressing her arms against her breast, she backs away moving frantically *en pointe*, and then, she stretches her arms as if to lift herself up, to fly away. The few leaves still remaining on branches of balding trees fall all around her. The arousing scent of Anna's perfume mixed with the sweat-pungent odor of decaying autumn makes Ali giddy. Her spontaneous burst of energy takes him by surprise. Like a nenuphar, she can bloom and shrivel in an instant.

Suddenly, she stops, out of breath. She sits down on the steps of a brownstone, and coughs, a dry hacking cough. He gives her a mint.

After she regains her breath, they walk a couple of blocks at a subdued pace to her apartment. At the doorstep of her building they embrace, and their lips find each other, intensity mounting between them. All of a sudden a loud ring from his cellphone awakens them from their amorous reverie. He gingerly disengages from her while she hangs on to his shoulder.

He snaps the cellular shut. "I've got to leave, Anna. I have an Emergency!"

He kisses her and runs down the steps. At the bottom he turns around. "I'm so sorry Anna. I'll call you soon," he says, and vanishes into the night.

Anna is stunned. She hoped he would come in.

She had set out salmon roe and Russian salad, and blini

with caviar—expensive Beluga caviar she had purchased at Zabars. Now, she has to eat it all, but after the first fork full she finds her appetite in ruins.

What sort of an emergency was this? He wasn't even on call. Couldn't it be handled by Dr. Denzel or one of his many Fellows in training?

She smashes the dish on the kitchen floor. She had smashed things before—her favorite Czechoslovakian crystal glass, purchased in Karlovy Vary when she didn't get cast as Swanhilde in New York City Ballet's Coppelia. After this outburst, Anna adjusts to her plight as she usually does, knowing that she is always the best of them all: the perfectionist.

It is entirely his fault, she thinks, looking at the kitchen floor. She gulps down a half-glass of Chardonnay, chilling in the fridge. After venting her anger on the china, the caviar and the blini, she feels drained, and lies on the bed. Did Ali have any idea of her feelings? Did he realize how much she loved him? Was he capable of love? And then she remembers the kiss, savors it, feels the sudden passion in it, and all her questions vanish. A feeling of calm settles over her like the aftermath of a snowstorm.

On his way to the hospital, Ali is smitten with guilt; he has broken the very commitment he had made to himself, that today he would go all the way to make Anna happy. He remembers her dry hacking cough. It had bothered him. Has her heart function worsened? Is she having a relapse of the cardiomyopathy? He hasn't seen her professionally for some time, and wonders if she has stopped her heart medications.

He wonders whether he should go back to her apartment after he tackles the emergency. He could sense her hurt in her expression as he left. He had no choice but to go to the hospital.

One of his patients, a Trustee, had a cardiac arrest.

Is he falling in love with Anna? Infatuation, yes! But love? He's isn't sure. And even if he did, is there any future for them? On a personal level, he still cannot see her as his wife. Suddenly, the words from the *Surah* ring in his mind: "Do not believe unbelieving women, until they believe: a slave woman who believes is better than an unbelieving woman, even though she allure you." But who is he to point an accusing finger? Isn't he a Muslim only by name, and a rather faithless one?

At the very instant Ali enters the hospital parking garage, he has another call. His patient just died. He is no longer needed. He calls the patient's wife and offers his condolences. The wife takes it well; Ali feels relieved. The old man had terminal heart failure, had suffered enough. They all had given their very best.

What should he do now? He is again struck with guilt for leaving Anna precipitously. He owes her the evening. He stops at a flower shop on Lexington Avenue and buys a dozen red roses. He makes his way to her apartment. He rings her doorbell. He rings it a second time.

"Who's it?" she asks in a tremolo.

"It's me, Ali. Can I come in?" There is no answer for some time, and then he hears the buzzer. She is visibly surprised to see him. Her eyes are red and teary. He embraces her and holds her for a long time, so long, that he feels the crush and the smell of his roses. He pulls back and hands them to her. He apologizes, explaining to her that the life of a doctor, particularly that of a cardiologist, is fraught with emergencies. "I never know when I will be called, and the demands are many. If you needed me, if you had an emergency, wouldn't you expect me to be there on the spur of the moment?" Anna looks at him attentively but doesn't answer his question.

He walks around the living room, the kitchen-cum-dining area closely examining every artifact, every painting on the wall. "Great apartment! Very artsy," he says, as he examines

Hockney's modern art in the living room, and an icon of the last supper in the dining area. But it is the latter that catches his eyes. He thinks of his own apartment, its bare artless walls.

"Is this Russian?"

"Da, very old, an antique I bought in St. Petersburg. Come let me show you the one in the bedroom. It is an icon of Christ. My mother gave it to me. It apparently came from the palace of the Czar in Tsarskoye Selo."

The religious images reassure him. Perhaps one day she will find salvation?

Anna turns away from Ali and goes to the CD player; turning up the volume to Tchaikovsky's music, she begins dancing the Dance Vertige. Her movements are frenzied. She takes hold of his hand and pulls him to the floor. All along he has imagined dancing with her. Now he feels exhilarated. He is finally fulfilling the artistic inclinations crushed by his father, albeit with nobody watching. He is dancing ballet with Anna—the fallen Russian ballerina.

She suddenly pirouettes. He lifts her. She is light as a feather, and for an instant, he holds her above his head. When he lowers her down, her body grazes his face, and for a moment he nuzzles her crotch. She stays in the split, her torso held up by his trembling hands. He notices her breathing; he wants to kiss her but holds back. She wraps her neck around his, and as suddenly, she falls back as if in an eternal swoon. His movements are crude and when he attempts a jêté, he almost bangs into the piano. Like Prince Désiré, he bends down and kisses her slightly on the lips, then lifts her in his arms and lays her on the sofa. Slowly, she stirs back to life. She tilts her head back, and her chest rises. He holds her small breasts with his eyes. She laughs out loud. Her sudden burst of energy overpowers him. She has prepared it all for him, a miniature Sleeping Beauty.

She gets up quickly and changes the CD; the sound of a sax fills the living room. She pulls him toward her and they dance, swaying to the slow, voluptuous rhythm of Stan Getz's "Corcovado." She leads him, and he easily follows. He nestles his cheek against hers; their lips brush. He can see pearls of sweat on her forehead. Her body radiates pheromones, arousing him. He senses she feels his erection as her body briefly flutters, like that of a swan. He encircles her wide-open mouth with his.

The music plays. The dance slows. They drift into the bedroom.

They lie on the bed in each other's arms. Pulling away for an instant, he sees tears form in her eyes, or is he imagining, fearful that it will all suddenly end in tears? His voice cracks: "Why do you cry?"

"I'm not crying." She smiles.

She undoes her chignon, and her hair falls over her shoulders and down her back like a curtain. He starts to unzip the back of her dress, but she resists, and instead unbuttons his shirt. He slips the straps of her dress off her shoulders, revealing her breasts like white peaches. Their milky silkiness and her pink nipples have a virginal quality of a young girl. She sighs deeply. He takes her hand and places it on his crotch and slides his own beneath her dress. She holds his hand tight.

"Please, go slow Ali," she whispers. He cups her face in his hands and looks deeply in her eyes. "Ya tebya lyublyu," she adds dreamily.

He unzips his pants, and she helps him remove them. She briefly stretches her swan neck and roams her wide eyes over his naked geography. His body is long and lean; his skin, a mixture of olive and brown.

A deep moan of pleasure comes out of him. He pulls her mouth away into his. He cannot hold back any longer. He slips her dress over her head. Her beautiful calves are molded as if by Michelangelo; her buttocks are round and small, like a boy's. His hand inches fast on her thighs as he so slightly and gingerly spreads them.

"It's been a long, long time..." she whispers.

Her eyes are shut and her mouth wide open. He kisses her. She opens her eyes as he holds their moistness, their glaze, with his own....

Then suddenly, she pulls free. "I'm sorry...I can't do it," she says, as she abruptly jumps of the bed, and rushes towards the bathroom.

"Why? What happened?" he asks with a tone of frustration. She shuts the door to the bathroom. As he is putting on his trousers, she appears in her bathrobe with a distressed expression.

"What's wrong?" he asks.

"It was too fast, too quick," she says.

"We have gone out for some time now, Anna." His irritation shows. He is fully dressed now; anxious to leave.

"Please, don't leave Ali," she says. "Lie down, relax. Let's talk."

He hesitates, and then says: "Okay."

"Sex without love is wrong," she says, as she lies by his side.

"But I love you," he blurts out.

"You didn't say so."

He freezes and doesn't answer.

"I'm sorry Ali. I didn't mean it that way. I haven't been with a man since my divorce, and even before that there wasn't much between me and my husband. I'm afraid of relationships. I love you and yet, I don't know if it will work out. Sometimes I feel you're so different. I'm afraid of disappointment and hurt. I'm not convinced you love me."

"Are you taking your medications? Did you see Dr. Mel?" he asks, thinking that she has had a relapse. She doesn't answer. She feels his question is misplaced. She wasn't talking about her illness, but about their relationship. There is an element of foreboding and angst in her look as if their near-lovemaking has opened old scars and turned them into fresh wounds—as if she knows that something is wrong, that tomorrow another reality will take center stage.

He embraces her, and as always says the same words: "You'll be OK Anna, things will sort themselves out."

"I don't want to hear that stupid statement," she says. "It is as if I'm a machine, your hopelessly tragic patient. You are not my father. Not my husband. I never had either one."

"I'm sorry Anna," he barely whispers. She knows it is mechanical with him: you'll be okay. He says it to his patients, young and old.

"What do you mean never having a father or a husband?" he asks.

She goes to the kitchen and returns with a glass of Chardonnay.

"Anna, you didn't answer my question."

Her mouth twitches. She closes her eyes. Her lips move over each other. Her eyes open wide. She takes a sip of the Chardonnay, and in a rush the words pour out.

She tells him that it was many years ago, in the spring of 1992 after her performance as Titania in *Midsummer Night's Dream*, when she had walked out of Lincoln Center. A man had approached and handed her a bouquet of red roses. She thanked him and hurried on. When she got home, she opened the card that accompanied the bouquet. There was a short congratulatory note written in Russian, his name, Alyosha, and a phone number. She hesitated to call him. "But in the end, I did." Anna sighs. "It reminded me of the time when my father had appeared out of the blue and offered me a bouquet of roses after my performance in Moscow." All that she remembered was her father's military uniform and the arguments he had with her mother when he returned from his foreign postings. From the day she left for the Academy until she danced in Moscow, for the Politburo, she never saw him. Then he appeared in her dressing room with flowers. He commented on her beauty and her dancing and apologized for his negligence. She became stiff, and then a sudden surge of anger, like fever, came over her. She hurled his flowers at his face. And she ran. "We never met again."

"Your reaction is understandable," says Ali.

"My father was a member of the Communist Party. He belonged to the proletariat and rose to the rank of Major. My mother despised him for his cheap taste and his addiction to vodka and women. He ultimately met his end in a Mujahedeen ambush at the Khyber Pass in Afghanistan."

"I'm so sorry Anna," he says.

"Da, where was I? I had no friends, so I decided to call Alyosha," she says. "He too was a dancer and had overstayed his visitor's visa like so many Russians after the fall of Communism. We began seeing each other and soon he moved in with me."

She takes a sip of wine, and says rather dreamily: "Da...in the beginning it was wonderful with Alyosha. He massaged and stroked my sore dancing feet, as if they were made of porcelain. He had no job, and soon, he started drinking." She looks away towards the window and continues: "He was physical, but not sexual. It was as if he didn't want to make love. In the beginning it suited me fine. Later, I wondered if I was inadequate and inexperienced. Were my breasts too small? Was I too thin? Not sexy enough?"

"Your body is beautiful!" says Ali.

"You really think so?"

"Truly!"

"Ours was a co-dependency. Alyosha depended on me for his self-confidence, financial support, and shelter, while I liked his company, his attention and his caresses, when he offered them."

"So, what happened?" Ali asks.

"He wanted to marry me. I said no."

She jumps out of bed to go to the bathroom. Perhaps all this is difficult for her—it shows in the sharp edge of her voice.

"There were constant threats of break-up," she says. "And so, I decided to get married. I mistakenly thought that things would get better after marriage, but they got worse. Alyosha drank more and more. He was abusive and insulting when he drank. He would walk out of the house and disappear for days.

"Finally, he joined a tango company and began dancing tango professionally, but after a couple of months had a falling out with the manager of the company and left. He started drinking again and began acting out. I could not take the stress and the temper tantrums. Gradually it began affecting my work. After about a year, I became pregnant. I wasn't keen to carry the pregnancy.

"Ballerinas don't have children. I protested—it would be the end of my career. After all, it was Balanchine who said: '"Any woman can become a mother, but not every woman can become a ballerina!"'

Sitting propped up on the bed, Ali listens without a word at Anna's story. She pauses for a deep breath, for many deep breaths and then a long silence like during the intermission of a play, when she abruptly leaves the room to go to the bathroom and the kitchen. When she comes back, her features are somewhat roughed up in lipstick and smudged up rouge. She must have been crying in the bathroom.

She continues animated again, as if rewired, as if she is enjoying telling her story. Anna is best when telling her stories, every detail, with gestures, and tears, and always, she is the victim.

"Later, I would succumb to Alyosha's jealousy. You are not the jealous type, are you?"

She seems more relaxed now. She laughs and tickles him all over his body. The scent of perfume and Chardonnay mixed with the lingering after-burn of foreplay arouses him. He reaches for her; she gently backs away.

"He couldn't make a career in ballet," she says. "I wondered whether he plotted to destroy mine. Mary convinced me that once Katya was born, I could always go back to ballet."

Anna again moves closer to Ali on the bed. Her warm thigh is next to his. The desire to make love resurfaces in Ali. But she continues talking. She tells him that she was an only child, a lonely child who had spent her adolescent years away from home at the Academy, and always dreamed of a child to dote upon, and she finally decided to keep the pregnancy. Her friend, Mary, agreed: "'No matter what Balanchine said, to have a baby is a passing rite of every woman,'" she said.

"After the baby was born, Jack came into our lives, and everything changed," Anna says. "He was a tall, older, wealthy man with a big family Trust, who Alyosha met in a bar in the West Village. They seemed to know each other for some time. He was very kind to me, often helping with Katya, picking me up from rehearsals with his Jaguar, and showering us with gifts. He had become a father figure, an anchor between the two of us. He had a positive effect on Alyosha who stopped drinking. Sometimes, Alyosha and Jack would go out by themselves."

"Isn't that strange?" says Ali

"Da, but I didn't think of it that way. It was Friday evening. I wasn't expected home before seven, but I was hungry and stricken with a slight headache—luckily it wasn't a migraine. They were becoming more frequent—the pressure of rehearsals, ballet instructions, and Katya, were taking their toll. I swallowed two Excedrin tablets, and left the rehearsal early, longing for a bubble bath and maybe some champagne and caviar before I picked Katya from daycare. There was lots of champagne, a whole case of Dom Perignon, a gift from Jack. The music was loud when I entered the apartment, and when I opened the door to the bedroom, there they were: Jack on top of Alyosha. Alyosha had a black gown on—my gown—it was thrown over his head. Jack was in a pin stripped suit. Half-naked. His pants wrapped around his high-heeled boots... I threw them out of my apartment," she says.

Her body tenses and blood rushes to her face. She gets off the bed and paces up and down. Ali stands up and takes her hand pulling her towards him, but she resists as if she doesn't need his sympathy. He remembers Alyosha, the encounter in Las Vegas, and Anna's reaction.

"I was devastated," she says. "I wondered whether this was a new or suppressed self-discovery in the Land of Freedom and Honey, or was I so naïve, not to have realized it?"

"Didn't you have any hints of his homosexuality or bisexuality?" Ali asks.

"How could I have known? I never had a lover. Premarital sex was taboo in Communist Russia. But when I looked back at his sexuality: his almost feminine caresses, the tenderness, the excessive foreplay that rarely culminated in sex, it all added up."

Ali listened attentively, at a loss for words.

"When I realized how Alyosha had used me, I felt betrayed. I hated him. I carried the hatred like a cancer."

"It must have come as a shock. You poor thing!" Ali jumps off the bed and embraces her. She pulls away, and paces the floor. He sits back down on the bed.

"Several months later," she says, "Alyosha called to apologize. I hung up on him. Soon thereafter, Jack called and asked for a meeting. I reluctantly agreed. I had a soft spot for him. When we parted, Jack handed me an envelope. When I opened it at home, there was a handsome check. He begged of me in a note to accept it. I used part of it as a down payment for the apartment, the rest Mary's father invested in the stock market. One year later, we were officially divorced. By the way, you remember when we met Alyosha in Vegas? I was very upset because he told me that Jack had died."

"That's hard to take. How did you manage?" asks Ali.

"I disposed Alyosha from my mind. I occupied myself with my work and gave entirely to my daughter. Inside of me something died. The things you have waited for all your life—poof—just vanished. It might as well. My husband, he was a non-entity, if you know what I mean. Over time I felt a sense of relief. I checked myself: I was HIV negative. I could move on with my life. Buying an apartment and decorating it was exciting, it gave me a sense of belonging. But *men*, I couldn't stand them, I didn't trust them, didn't see the need for one."

"I'm terribly sorry, Anna, for all you had to put up with," says Ali.

"By the way, my mother and Katya are coming from Russia for Christmas. I'm so happy. I will have a dinner party for her. Will you come?" She is animated again.

"I would love to meet your mother."

It is almost two in the morning. Ali wants to stay the night with Anna, but he has many cases lined up, starting at 7 am. Her story was shocking and unsettling. He had encountered bisexual men in the past, during his residency training: married men who fucked other men. However, he had never met a woman whose husband was gay, and the woman was entirely ignorant of the fact. On his way home, he wonders whether he had been delicate enough, suave enough, with Anna. He regrets they didn't make love. She isn't some woman with tits and a cunt that a man might want to fuck; she is different. His and hers cannot be labeled as fucking, but lovemaking. He knows that's the way she sees it; that's the way he sees it too. She is still traumatized from the divorce and her husband's homosexuality or bisexuality. Perhaps sex is not her cup of tea, at least not now, not so soon. Above all, she's lost trust in men. She needs to gain trust in him; she needs time, and he needs to be patient. He hasn't had sex for a long time; they are both rusty. He sensed disappointment and chagrin in her eyes when he said goodbye.

He wishes he had stayed the night with her. But above all, he is overwhelmed with misgivings, as well as concern for Anna. She is still raw, and entirely self-absorbed.

PART

II

In three words I can sum up everything I've learned about life. It goes on. —Robert Frost

CHAPTER 11

The Musical Soirée

Ali returns to New York after speaking engagements in Europe and South America. His recently published paper on the survival of heart failure patients with assist devices is widely praised. He is suddenly a much sought-after speaker, rapidly gaining national and international stature.

A few days after his return, he has a meeting with Dr. Bob, and it has to do with his overdue promotion to Associate Professor, and a raise in salary. But Ali senses that Dr. Bob had not taken it well when he went ahead and hired Denzel as his associate. He had his own candidate that he had tried to push on Ali. Like nudging a son to take a chosen bride. But Ali had ignored his wish and they hadn't met privately since.

When they meet in his office, Dr. Bob immediately congratulates him on the publication of his article.

"A very good paper," he says. "I hope it influences the Promotions Committee. Send me your updated CV. If only you had an NIH Grant. But I'll do my best. As for a raise...." he shook his head. "There have been extensive cuts in reimbursement. The Transplant Program is running on a deficit. We get almost no reimbursement from Medicaid, which account for more than thirty percent of your service."

"Well I'm not entirely sure about that," Ali counters. "The bottom line is that we provide the service: Medicaid, Medicare, private insurance, HMO's—I didn't become a doctor to solely bring in money. You should confront the hospital administration to split the pie the hospital collects. They make a killing on Medicaid patients, and you well know it."

Blood rushes to Dr. Bob's face. His cheek starts twitching violently like that of Chief Inspector Crusoe in The Pink Panther. He holds the palm of his hand to his cheek to steady it.

"Times are tough," he says, raising his voice. "No one got a raise last year. In fact, many had their salaries cut."

"Indeed, I was one of them," says Ali. "But there were others who got a raise. My biopsy numbers, cardiac catheterizations, and clinic visits have gone up by over twenty percent."

Dr. Bob shakes his head in acknowledgement, but otherwise doesn't respond.

Ali is furious. Everyone knows that Dr. Bob got a raise when most salaries in the department were cut.

"Well, I've made my case. I'll leave it to you to decide." says Ali, defiantly, and leaves.

He didn't relish personal confrontation, but the moment has come when he has to stand his ground, to assert, to fight for what is right, for much is at stake, including his professional pride. Inadvertently, but categorically, he has sent a message that he is unhappy, and he well knows that Dr. Bob has let him know that he, Ali, is no longer the favorite son, and certainly, no longer his protégée. Perhaps it is time to look for a new job. Overpowered by the weight of injustice, he summarily loses faith in the system. It leaves a bad taste in his mouth.

What happened to honesty and integrity and personal accountability?

As he leaves Dr. Bob's office, he passes Carmensita's desk.

She asks him about the headaches. "Not one since Las Vegas," he says.

He is despondent as he steps out of the hospital for a coffee. His secretary, Linda, has given notice that she will be leaving to join Dr. Bob's secretarial staff. He re-enters the hospital and his academic office. He sits on his chair and contemplates on his personal and professional life. The meeting with Dr. Bob was unsettling. He wonders why Dr. Bob gave him a hard time. Is it because he hired his own man? Or is he jealous of his accomplishments?

And his personal life is at a standstill.

Suddenly, he feels empty, as if his holdings have slipped out of his pocket. If only his heart were of wood, hard dry wood. It is rare for him to feel this way. His life needs to be balanced, to be on an even keel: If the personal is not so good, or nothing to speak about, then it has to be counter-balanced with the professional and vice-versa, but if both aspects of life are rocky, incongruous, one feels a sense of paralysis, and life itself becomes an afterthought.

Is there any hope for him and Anna?

He looks at his watch and realizes that he is late for the dinner party. Should he call Anna and cancel? But he feels drawn to her. He wants to see her again and meet her mother. But what about Nancy? They haven't met since Denzel's party. He stops at the neighborhood liquor store, something he has never done before, and just stands in the store like a lost animal in the middle of the highway, gazing at the racks and racks of bottles. He asks the approaching clerk if he carries a bottle of vodka.

"Any special Brand, Sir?"

"Russian," says Ali.

When Anna opens the door, Ali hands her a bouquet of red

roses and a bottle of Stolichnaya. They stand at the threshold, looking at each other, near lovers of yesterday, unsure how to proceed, as if a kiss, a hug, might rekindle the hidden or dormant passion frozen in time.

Finally, she stretches out her arms, hugging him. She introduces him to her mother, Natalie. Anna re-introduces him to Mary and Brad, and asks him if he wants to eat some biryani she specially ordered for him from an Indian restaurant, or if he prefers to try some of the Russian delicacies. Ali is overwhelmed by her thoughtfulness. Anna seems relaxed and happy, so unlike their last encounter. He immediately forgets his trials and tribulations at the medical center.

She goes over all the gastronomic delights at the dinner table with its plates of Russian salad, salmon, black caviar, blintzes, and dumplings. A bottle of vodka, a bottle of Chardonnay, tequila, and a bottle of champagne in a silver ice bucket rests on an adjoining side table. In the middle sits a large flower vase with white and red orchids. He tries a bit of caviar on a cracker; the fishy-salty tang on the tip of his tongue feels like fresh seaweed in his mouth. He wraps the cracker in a napkin and pockets it ever so slyly. He thanks her for the mutton biryani and fills his plate with it.

Ali often meets Natalie's intense penetrating gaze. He sizes up her tall slim figure: the prominent cheekbones and the long straight nose with its bony protrusion in the middle that gives her an egotistical aristocratic air. He sees the soft resemblance to Anna. He wants to talk with her but doesn't know how to break the ice.

He notices Katya, with her striking blonde curls, now taller and prettier than he last saw her in the hospital. She is playing with Anna's friend's daughter, Annika, who is also her age. He hears Annika boasting of her two homes—one in the city, another in the woods upstate—and how she chased a rabbit and made birds out of clay with her mother, but Katya doesn't seem interested in her stories. She stares at Ali and gives him a sudden smile. He goes to her, lifts her off the floor, throws her up and catches her in mid-air. She squeals with pleasure, and soon Annika demands a turn. Ali tosses each of them in turn, until Anna pulls him away.

He looks across the room, where Mary and Brad are the odd couple. Brad, who reminds Ali of Wayne Newton, has his silver-tinged black hair tied in a ponytail. The cowboy hat and the leather vest, and the small puckered scar over his right cheek, gives him the air of a country musician. Mary, on the other hand, with her blonde straight hair and a glow of self-confidence mingled with gentle manners, exhibits a very proper New England chic. What, Ali wonders, could they ever have in common?

The musical soiree begins when Anna sits at the piano, and plays softly, like ripples over moss-laden pebbles. When she finishes they all clap.

"Rachmaninov's Prelude in G-sharp Minor," she says, bowing. "He is my favorite Russian composer; his Russianness comes from the heart." She gestures towards her mother. "If not for the insistence of my mother, I would have become a concert pianist."

"Indeed, and if not for the insistence of my father, I would have become a ballet dancer," says Ali.

"Believe me Ali, you are better off being a doctor, especially with your qualities," Anna, says. "You should thank your father."

Natalie has put on some lively Balalaika music, and she takes hold of Anna, and they both begin a Russian folk dance. Ali watches, as mother and daughter circle around with subtle doll-like gestures. They stop, exhausted when the music ends.

Now it is Brad's turn. He has an upcoming performance at the Blue Note. Only after Anna wheedles, he condescends to play. He purses his lips on the mouthpiece of the sax and when he blows on it, his cheeks puff like balloons, the scar on his face stretches out like a scimitar, and the room fills with the rhythm and sound of jazz. Ali stares at Brad, mesmerized by the minor keys, the sudden lows and highs. Ali is elated that he is among such talented musicians, but he wishes that he, too, had something to present.

Brad places the sax in its case, takes a long drought of tequila, and wishes them goodnight. Katya's friend leaves, and Katya is put to bed. The living room suddenly feels empty and quiet.

Mary questions Ali about his work and his family. She relates to him how she met Anna after her performance at the Lincoln Center. "I handed her a bouquet of roses and expressed an interest in writing an article about her."

"Interesting!" he says.

"We met again the following week for dinner."

Anna is lucky to have such a friend, thinks Ali. He was impressed with Mary before, though he didn't know her well. Tonight, he takes a liking to her, finding her genuine and honest.

Suddenly, Mary turns towards Ali and says, "Ali, Anna will make a superb wife for the right man."

Ali nods in agreement wondering whether the remark was meant for him. He tries to shift the conversation to Russia, boasting that he had majored in Russian history. He tries a gulp of straight chilled vodka and finds himself barely able to breathe, prompting much laughter from Anna and Natalie.

"Vodka is not for you. Try some wine if you must," says Anna.

After the coughing spell subsides, Ali tells Natalie that Anna had mentioned the difficult times her family endured under Stalin. He speaks slowly, as if he is chewing on every word, a diction he often used while lecturing to stress the point he is making. She shrugs and stiffens, as if she doesn't want to get into that part of her life. It is then that Anna cuts in. "Ali, I'm sorry, my mother doesn't speak fluent English. She understands, but has some difficulty expressing." She and her mother begin speaking to each other in rapid Russian. Her mother's voice has a resounding quality, so different from Anna's soft French-like accent.

"Look, look, it's snowing," says Natalie, pointing to the window. She has a broad smile on her face and her eyes light up in her aristocratic face. Anna runs to the window. Thick clumps of snow with a purple hue fall like cotton balls. She opens the window and collects snowflakes in her hands. She inhales the fresh air and sighs in ecstasy. She catches hold of her mother, and they circle around as if in some ritual; exhausted, they fall on the sofa. Ali looks at them in puzzlement.

"It's the snow Ali. It makes us Russians happy," says Anna.

A quiet abstractedness settles over the room while the outside world turns white.

Then, as if the heavens have opened up, Natalie begins to speak in an unsteady but highly cultivated voice: "It was horrible time for Russia—for my city—my Petersburg. Stalin had killed all the writers. Only Akhmatova was left, and that horrible man had silenced her by arresting her son." Her voice rises: "I was her *poklonnik*. What is *poklonnik*, Anna?"

"Fan, Mama," says Anna.

"Da, I was her fan—she was my *Musa*. I had attended her poetry readings at *The Stray Dog*." She pauses for a long draught of vodka. It is as if the snowfall has triggered emotions that pour out of Natalie like an aged unclogged fountain spouting water: sad, decades old water.

For a moment, there is silence in the room as if to honor all the nameless dead that Natalie speaks about that none of them knew but feel the strange omnipotence of the moment. Then, Natalie tells them that she had gone to the Fountain House to show Akhmatova her long poem, and Akhmatova had shown her work, *Poem without a Hero*, dedicated to her friend, the poet Mandelstam. A man had followed her after she left Akhmatova's apartment, the loose manuscript in her hand. When she arrived home, she set her manuscript on fire—all of it. She knew they were watching her—they would soon come and get her.

"Mama you should start writing again," says Anna. Natalie doesn't respond. Her complexion changes. She looks pale and tired.

Ali listens quietly, feeling the immensity of the moment, of history itself. These ruminations of a vast country in decay, a country subjected to repeated totalitarian repression, and the magnitude of human sufferings, of lives ripped apart, made many things, like living in a free country, the mission of a doctor, worth it all the more.

"How horrible," says Mary, and embraces Natalie who is now devoid of any emotion. Her demeanor changes, as if a large wound is opened. She stares straight ahead. Perhaps, thinks Ali, she is having a vision; perhaps, she is seeing all those dead poets.

"You will not understand me," Natalie bursts out, as if scolding them, belittling them. "Here poetry means nothing. In Russia, poetry was everything. Even Stalin was afraid of it. Poetry was the soul, the silent power. Poets were the moral emblems—the torch of justice and truth."

"I would like to read your poetry, Natalie," Ali says. "Perhaps Anna can translate?"

She stares ahead with a blank expression as if nobody is in the room. Ali notices the skin below her eyes, its darkness and pouches with their many gathers and fussy lines.

She cleans the table and leaves for Katya's bedroom.

"She's very tired," Anna says. "It is difficult for her. Sometimes she has this blank look on her face...."

"She is such a noble woman," says Mary.

It is already past midnight when both Ali and Mary simultaneously get up to leave.

"Anna, please keep your appointment for the tests," Ali says.

In the elevator, Ali tells Mary that Anna is still in denial of her heart ailment.

"She's such a talented dancer, such a wonderful teacher. I will make sure she has the tests you ordered," Mary says.

"Anna is lucky to have you as a friend," says Ali.

She gives him a parting kiss on the cheek and takes his hand in hers. "I'm so glad that Anna has such a wonderful doctor." Giving his hand a squeeze, she turns to go when they hear Anna's voice.

"Wait for me," says Anna, as they both turn around. "It's so beautiful. Let's walk in the Park." Ali has a busy day coming up tomorrow, but Anna's enthusiasm is contagious.

Fifth Avenue is deserted. The snowflakes fall in thick spangles, shimmering on the way down. Anna and Mary walk hand in hand. The street is aglow with tinges of yellow and purple, and skeletal trees on the sidewalk rise like pillars of fluffy white.

"Like Nevsky Prospect," says Anna. "I can almost hear the jingles of St. Petersburg sleigh bells in the distance."

Ali breathes in deeply the fresh cold air filtering through the snowflakes. They saunter into Central Park, where the trees are covered with white blossoms that stick to the thinnest of branches. The park is like the floor of a vast white palace, with walls of crystal glass. Anna picks up some snow and she pats it to make a snowball. She throws it at Ali and it lands on his face. He quickly makes his own snowball, and soon the air is filled with snowballs and laughter, and snowflakes blow in the wind like diamond dust. In this fantasy world, they are children in a snow-white night.

CHAPTER 12

The Unsettling Ferry Ride

The day before Ali is to go to London for a speaking engagement, he and Anna go out for dinner, after which he invites her to his apartment.

She has nothing to say about his dwelling. It is as if its drabness, simplicity, without any paintings on the walls, no artsy artifacts, is a turn-off. A bachelor's pad fit only for sleep and not to entertain. Like a hunter's cabin in the woods.

He senses her insouciance when he attempts to lead her into the bedroom. "I'm not in the mood," she says.

Her iciness irritates him, but he lets it pass. He wonders whether she will ever be in the mood.

After he returned from Europe, there was a letter waiting for him. In it, Anna lamented about her status: the loss of her profession with no hope of dancing again; the difficulties of raising a child without a father; many of the same things he had heard before. She was troubled with his busy schedule, particularly the lecturing trips out-of-town. She confessed that their diverging interests, including his unflinching dedication to doctoring and ambition to excel and shine in his professional and academic career, and his background made her wonder whether they were meant for each other. She was just an after-thought in his scheme of things. It was as if she sliced through their lives, their personalities, like a knife through meat and butter. Ali understood her concerns. They seemed to be on different planets, different stages of life. Her shades of life were grey and black; his, yellow and green. He had called her and requested they meet to talk about it.

It is a balmy winter Sunday afternoon. Ali arrives late, held up in the hospital. "I'm so sorry, Anna," he says. She shrugs her shoulders. He suggests an Indian restaurant downtown. Anna isn't keen for Indian food.

"The food's great! You'll love it," he says.

She reluctantly gives in.

Ali is in a bouncy mood—a prestigious medical journal had accepted his manuscript for publication. As they drive downtown, Ali gives her the good news, and the impact the publication could have on his career. Anna quietly listens. He is supposed to talk about their relationship not his career.

The restaurant is packed and noisy. They are seated at a table near the kitchen. The sight of kebabs, tandoori chicken, mutton biryani, and vegetables floating in creamy spicy sauce with coriander, and golden-brown parathas, set his mouth watering. A group of girls, second generation Indians, probably students at NYU, in tight jeans, tank tops, and red lipstick, stroll in, cackling in perfect American English. A dark-skinned man in kurta-pajama, perhaps a taxi-driver, sits nearby eating with his hands, slurping away, and licking his fingers. Anna stares at her plate.

"The food is too spicy," she says. "I'll try a paratha with chickpeas."

"Here, mix the chickpeas with raita," he says. "it will take-away the spicy bite."

The atmosphere in the restaurant is stuffy; the air dense with curry smells.

He regrets bringing her to this restaurant; perhaps an upscale one might have been a lot different. He wants to introduce her to Indo-Pakistani food; in the past it had always been French or Italian, her preference, and sometimes, he had gone with it to please her. Here the food is good and tasty like the Indian food in East London, on Brick Lane. Anna's apprehension is unsettling and leaves him no choice but to gobble up what is on his plate at a fast pace. His stomach feels bloated when they leave. He pops a Nexium capsule for acid reflux that he carries with him these days.

He asks her if she has ever taken the Staten Island Ferry.

"No, I haven't," she says.

As the ferry glides away towards Staten Island, the temperature plummets. He holds her close, as she munches on a hot dog and some chips. They watch the skyline recede in the crisp winter evening; in the far-off-distance, the World Trade Center Towers shimmer in the golden sunset.

On the way back from Staten Island, they marvel at the downtown skyline lit up, like an extraterrestrial universe. He thinks of all the shadows of their short affair. He so yearns for her, but she seems to elude him. At that moment he wants to believe they are made for each other—all the while knowing they are not. It is as if each is overwhelmed by the other's culture, and past experiences; overwhelmed, and yet drawn to them. They turn towards each other as the ferry approaches the dock and hold each other's gaze, one last moment before they disembark. And then she closes her eyes. Is saying nothing the contemporary etiquette for farewell? Ali wonders.

"Ali," she says, finally. "I don't think that it will work out between us. I said it all in my letter. You are totally immersed in your career, mine is dead!" He shakes his head and they fall silent again. He looks down, as if he sees the dwindling of life, and tears well up in his eyes.

"Besides," she says, "I don't feel well. Sometimes I wake up at night short of breath." Her words shake him out of his lassitude. He gathers her in his arms.

Is her heart condition deteriorating?

"For how long has this been going on? Why didn't you call and tell me?"

"You are not my doctor. I didn't want to bother you." He shakes his head and looks away. Guilty. He was in his world entirely. Like a turtle in its shell.

She now sobs on his shoulders. "Don't cry," he says wiping her tears. The tears settle his doubts. Anna never cries unless her feelings are strong. Her emotions are powerful, sometimes childish like that of a girl in a woman's body, but they are real.

He is about to say, "Thing's will work out," but manages to hold his tongue. Perhaps there is a lot to talk about. Oceans to fill. But they hardly speak a word. The mind agonizes in silence. Unfulfilled and confused, he senses she is drifting away unlike the ferryboat that finds its destination. They walk away holding hands, clinging to each other.

He asks her to see him in the hospital, and the following day he tells his secretary to give her an appointment. He genuinely feels responsible and concern for her.

Anna doesn't keep the appointment.

He calls her and tells her that she should at least go back to Dr. Mel. But Anna makes no promises.

Ali sees her in the office three weeks later. She looks tired and a bit puffy around the eyelids. He isn't surprised to find her in mild heart failure. He orders an echocardiogram and a monitor and asks her to see Dr. Grimes.

"Are you taking your medications?"

Anna looks down. After a long silence she confesses that she has stopped all medications for some time and is taking vitamins, Echinacea and St. John's wart.

He is upset but manages to control himself.

"I'm your patient now. Your hopeless patient, Ali," she says. He has surmised that something like this could happen.

"I want to hand over your care to Dr. Denzel. It's best." He says it with authority. The authority of a doctor.

"No, No! I would rather die of heart failure." She begins to cry. "You—you are my doctor now."

He stands up and goes to her. Cupping her face in his hands, he kisses her on the forehead as if parting with some of his own energy to heal her many wounds, to let her know that he will be there for her. He notices her moist eyes as she leaves. He is certain that she is having a relapse of the heart failure, and it overwhelms him with anxiety, and guilt.

He is suddenly overtaken by a desire to pray. He closes the office door, kneels on the floor facing the East, his hands on his knees, his head bowed, he recites the words from Qur'an 7:143: *"To Thee I turn in repentance…"*

CHAPTER 13

Union Square Café

After Nancy returns from her trips, she expects to hear from Ali and keeps on checking her messages. She wonders whether she should call him to find out about their date but keeps procrastinating. She feels depressed—perhaps it is a down phase after the Acapulco and Mumbai highs. In college, she was diagnosed with a mild bipolar condition. It was hard for her to maintain relationships, but more recently with Paxil, she found a new balance: the ups are not as high, but the downs are not as low. If not for Paxil she would have been in the dumps now, thinking of death.

She had given up on him when late one evening, her phone rings.

"Hey, it's me—Ali. My apologies for not calling you earlier. I've been getting home late these last few days. Dr. Denzel met with a skiing accident."

"I know, I heard from Cindy. I thought you would never call."

"I so want to see you again," he says. "I was meaning to call you to tell you how much I enjoyed your company at the party—you're terrific, a great conversationalist, and gorgeous."

"Thanks for the flattery."

"I'm serious. Can I see you this Saturday?"

"I have a wedding in Boston. My cousin's getting married."

"Why don't I call you after you return from the wedding?"

"Sure. We'll just have a lot to catch up," she says.

As soon as they hang up, Nancy wonders at Ali's life of endless doctoring and no play. Is he even worth a date? He seems to have climbed up the ladder so fast, and in our capitalist culture, and in New York of all places, one can do it only with hard work. Had he not mentioned ballets and operas, besides movies? He had come across as a man of the world, had he not? She remembers what her friend Nalini said: *Don't you forget it Nancy—he's a Muslim. Don't live an illusion. Don't set yourself up for another disappointment.* She remember Nalini's words: *'"Be bad, real bad—order a bottle of wine and swear with a flare! And if you get a good laugh, he's your man."'* That was funny and at the same time cryptic. She hadn't seen Nalini for over a week. Maybe she should go out with her for dinner before she goes out with this hard working MD.

Ali finally takes Nancy on their first date to Union Square Café. The maître d is one of Ali's patients, and treats them like royalty. They are barely seated when Nancy relates that she is moving back to the city. She'd rented an apartment on Sixtieth between Columbus and Amsterdam. "That's great," says Ali. "It's only a couple of blocks from Lincoln Center, Time Warner, and Central Park." He can sense her happiness with the move. He passes the wine list. "Please Nancy, it's okay! I'll have a sip too. Just because I'm a Muslim doesn't mean I don't drink at all." He tells her how he had seen his father and his Muslim friends drink scotch secretly. Tossing back her hair, she burst out laughing.

"I'd love a champagne cocktail," she says. He likes her bubbly-like-champagne mood. She asks him about the transplant business. He hesitates to talk about work. She looks at him expectantly.

"We did one heart transplant last week, and one twelve weeks before that," he finally volunteers.

"Isn't that's slow?"

"Hearts are hard to come by."

"You don't like talking about work do you?"

After some hesitation, he relates that things were not upbeat for doctors lately.

"There have been cuts in reimbursement. I haven't gotten a raise for the last three years. We only collect thirty percent of what is billed, and sixty percent of that goes to overhead costs. Besides, like everybody else in the medical center, I'm under pressure to increase the numbers."

"That's horrible," she says with a frown. "Does that mean that they want you to do procedures that are not indicated?"

"Well, they don't say it that way. Over my dead body—I'll not do tests and procedure that are not indicated."

"I'm sure...."

"I don't want to bother you with all this. It's been on my mind—I just came from an ugly meeting with the administrator.

"Capitalism gone awry!" he says. "It's hard to get a straight answer from the administrators. The monies go to over-inflated overheads. There is no accountability in the system. One of these days the whole health care system is going to crash." He feels he has said enough; he doesn't want to burden Nancy with such depressing talk on their first date.

"What's going on in the financial business?" he asks.

"Times have been great for us."

"Bill Clinton has been good for the economy," he asserts.

"Oh well...I like Clinton," Nancy says, and then adds, "I hate his morals."

"Surely you aren't upset over the Monica Lewinsky scandal?"

"Would you let yourself be seduced in your office by your patient?"

"No, not really—well, there was a patient, a *former* patient that I was involved with." Ali wishes that the conversation hadn't taken a sudden unexpected turn. He curses in his mind for his honesty.

"Were you lovers?"

Ali catches his breath, astonished that this woman he has only met once would ask such a bold question. But this is New York. Not Minnesota.

"No," he says. "If its sex you mean, no, there was no sex."

"Is she giving you trouble now?"

"Absolutely not."

He is saved from the cross examination by the waiter, who comes with a sizzling duck for her, and seared tuna for him. He is anxious to shift the conversation back to her.

"Well, what's a pretty woman like you doing single?" he says.

"My mother keeps reminding me about her overdue grand-motherhood."

"Welcome to the club."

"What's an eligible bachelor like you doing single?" she asks.

"Well, you haven't given me your answer."

"I was going out with a Wall Street broker, a bond trader. He really wasn't my type, but we related to each other professionally, and that seemed a good start. We met for dinner, mostly at Italian restaurants downtown. He wasn't interested in exotic cuisine like Indian, Thai, Malaysian—he was allergic to spices. He was into baseball, wrestling and bodybuilding. In the beginning he was a novelty, but as time went by it bothered me that our interests clashed. And when the fifth date approached, in a phone conversation, he brought up sex. But why should sex be brought up?" She pauses with a serious, yet captivating look.

"The New York single scene is like a bullfight," she says, "and like the bull it's usually the woman who ends up getting killed." She takes a sip of the Crème de Cassis champagne. "Sex should happen naturally—don't you think?" she says. "I detest the whole New York single scene when it comes to sex. You know what I mean: after the second, or the third, or the... etc."

"Agreed," he says with a sharp tone to his voice and a serious expression on his face. For a moment Ali wonders about her past experiences with men. Is she no different than the others—the thirty-something New York single women—playing the game, not giving in until the very last moment, when all the cards are on the table? Would she ask him to produce proof that he is negative for HIV, hepatitis, Herpes? It happened to his friend Dr. Grimes when he went on a blind date with a lawyer. But patience is on his side. He had no interest in bedding her right away. It seems to him that every woman he goes out in New York, unlike in Minnesota and London, has a problem with sex.

"You don't want to know what happened?" she asks.

"Yes, yes."

"It ended. And what about you?" she asks.

"Not much to tell." She looks at him, waiting for an answer. He mentions about dates with female doctors, and how boring they turned out, like job interviews. Nancy cannot stop laughing.

"My last girlfriend...well, she wasn't a girlfriend really if you know what I mean. She was a ballerina, a Russian—who was my patient. She was different. We went out a few times."

Nancy's lips tighten. "What do you mean different?"

"She was exotic, moody, and entirely unpredictable."

"Are you still in love with her?"

"I'm not sure if I was ever in love with her. Infatuated, yes!"

"Do you still see her?" she asks, as she toys with her napkin.

Her facial muscles tense. *Watch out man. Don't make her too jealous.* "Only as a patient at the Medical Center," he says. "I feel a lot of pressure from my parents to marry. They are always trying to arrange one match after another."

"The same goes here. The pressure comes from my mother. My father is a man of few words. Besides, I want children and my biological clock is ticking away fast."

"Any dessert ma'am? And you, sir? Some dessert wine or brandy perhaps?" asks the waiter.

"Some ice cream will do. I'm stuffed," says Nancy.

"Oh yes, would you like some dessert wine, a glass of Château d'Yquem perhaps?" says Ali. "They serve it by the glass here—the elixir is meant for goddesses like you."

"You seem to have done your homework."

"It's the doctor in me. We are an organized lot. And our professional life does rub into the personal."

"Do get a glass for the lady," he says to the waiter.

A representative of a pharmaceutical company anxious to peddle what seemed a promising new drug for heart failure once brought Ali's group here for dinner and went about ordering expensive French reds and whites and this Château d'Yquem. The Château, he was told, was harvested only under special climatic conditions, sometimes once in a few years.

"Academic doctors have perks too and are wined and dined by drug and device companies?" asks Nancy.

"Yes, indeed," he says. "Excuse me—I need to use the bathroom."

On the way to the Men's Room, Ali sees Carmensita with Dr. Bob and Mr. Fusco of Medical Labs. Inc. at a corner table in the next room; unnoticed, he immediately turns his head and darts into the bathroom. He is in no mood to face them. He wonders what Dr. Bob is doing with Mr. Fusco. Are they talking about the study? If so, why wasn't he asked to join them for dinner? Thinking about it, he hadn't recruited any patient for the study as of yet. Well, what the hell, he thinks; after all he is not even the Principal Investigator. On his way back, he's careful to turn his head away from their table. Nancy watches him cross the room.

"You look upset," says Nancy.

"Guess who's in the next room?"

Nancy shakes her head. "The Russian ballerina?"

"Dr. Bob and Carmensita—you remember them, don't you?—at the party?" At that very moment his beeper goes off.

"Sorry, it's the Coronary Care Unit. I've got to take this."

"Of course!"

He stands up and walks near the doorway to the entrance of the restaurant to take the call. The nurse relates that Anna was just admitted to the Coronary Care Unit after collapsing at Bloomingdale's, and that her relative wants to speak to him.

"Dr. Ali," says Mary. "Anna had a cardiac arrest while shopping at Bloomingdale's." He can hear the panic in Mary's voice. "She was lucky. There was a doctor close by who gave her cardio-pulmonary resuscitation. The paramedics had to use electric shock three times to get her out of it."

Ali fights to regain his composure.

"I didn't expect this to happen."

"Will you come, Ali?"

"It will take me sometime. I'm dining downtown."

After Ali hangs up, he returns to the table and apologizes to Nancy.

"I have to go to the hospital. The Russian ballerina had a cardiac arrest," he says, anxiety and remorse written on his facial expression.

"Please, don't worry—we'll catch up some other time," she says, barely in a whisper.

"Thanks Nancy, I appreciate that." As Ali waits for the check, Nancy stares at the tablecloth and fiddles with the demi-glass. A disquieting silence sits between them broken by the tickling of glass, the chatter of nearby customers and the sound of distant music, a sax and a guitar. Nancy is holding tight the glass of wine. She is flushed and hyperventilating. The crystal glass cracks. She is holding glass bits and blood in her hand. Ali opens her hand and scoops the glass and blood with the cloth napkin. The waiter brings a band aid, with which Ali bandages her hand. He can see she is visibly upset, but stiff. No tears. Luckily, it is a minor abrasion.

"I'm terribly sorry Nancy," he says.

They step out of the restaurant and Ali again apologizes for the abrupt exit.

"I understand," she says, abruptly, but calmly.

On his way to the hospital, it is Anna who is on his mind as he speeds on the West-Side Highway. A shroud of guilt descends over him; he was wrong to hold off on the defibrillator when Dr. Grimes all along felt that it was a reasonable decision to have one implanted. Now without it, Anna had almost died. She is damn lucky to have survived. But what about brain damage from the cardiac arrest? No, he didn't want to think about it.

And now it is Nancy he has to deal with. He wonders whether his relationship with Anna will leave Nancy bewildered and confused about his one-time patient, once his girl-friend, and now his patient again. At least he was entirely honest. He appreciates her understanding and selflessness, but her distress and anger had seeped through. And why not? He plans to call her as soon as he checks on Anna's condition.

CHAPTER 14

Anna's Cardiac Arrest

When Ali arrives in the Coronary Care Unit of the Medical Center, he finds Anna on a respirator and on intravenous sedatives. She lies there pale as a corpse, a mere shadow of herself, a few strands of hair are visible through the transparent surgical cap. Mary and Natalie stand by her bedside in tears. The machines drone on. Lines and shadows of dark green run across the flat TV screens. Ali listens to her heart and checks her reflexes on the soles of her feet.

"The next forty-eight hours are crucial," he says to Mary and Natalie. "We won't know until we take her off the respirator whether she suffered any brain damage."

Natalie begins crying and Mary embraces and consoles her.

Ali places his hand on Natalie's shoulder. "It's too early to tell. Let's hope for the best," he says.

It is past ten o'clock. He leaves the hospital and walks home, mentally and physically exhausted. His concern for Anna fills him with despair and at the same time anger at himself for not heeding Dr. Grimes's advice of implanting a defibrillator after Anna's fainting episode at the Met. What if Anna sustains brain damage now? What will happen to poor little Katya? How happy she looked when he had played with her at the party. He remembers the musical soiree and the walk in Central Park. Anna's life has unraveled and he feels somewhat responsible for it.

Suddenly there is a loud honk and a screech of the brakes.

"Hey, watch where you're going, man," the taxi driver yells. Ali stops in his tracks.

As soon as he enters his apartment still reeling from the events of the day, he immediately calls Nancy. "I'm terribly sorry for this evening," he says. He senses some hesitation in her voice.

After a long silence, she says: "I didn't except you to call."

"Well, my apologies again. It was unfair to you."

"Will she make it?"

"I hope so."

"You must be tired. I don't want to hold you up."

"I'm beat."

"Goodnight."

He takes out the prayer rug, prostrates in silence, and says a brief prayer for Anna. He pops an Ambien and lies on the bed in the semi-darkness thinking of the day just gone by: of Anna, of Nancy, but it is Anna's image that floats in his mind, like that of a wounded bird flapping its wings while falling down the sky. Soon, she takes the shape of a butterfly that appears and disappears from his peripheral vision, as cobwebs of sleep encroach, and the light goes out.

In a little less than forty-eight hours, Anna is taken off the respirator. She is confused and in a cloud for a couple of days, but gradually regains her faculties. Fortunately, she doesn't suffer any brain damage. She remains monitored in the Coronary Care Unit for another two days amidst the sterile surroundings, the hustle and bustle of the nurses and the resident doctors. Her celebrity status now somewhat dimmed having lost its novelty. The machines don't frighten her; the shades of green lines and curves of her electrocardiogram on the white screen are reassuring: that she is alive and her vagrant heart still continues to tick. This fearlessness doesn't last long. Gradually, her anxieties spew out into nightmares, sleeplessness, and the fear of not waking up. In one nightmare she sinks into a bottomless pit and wakes up short of breath. In another, KGB men in ski masks chase her down Fifth Avenue and hurl her into a black SUV. On anti-anxiety medications around the clock, she is transferred to the Cardiac Center where she goes along for the next few days with the ebb and flow of things. She has most of the tests all over again. Ali stops by every day but on the fifth day of her stay in the hospital, he comes with Dr. Tony Grimes. He sits by her bed and holds her hand. "Anna," he says, "you need the implantable defibrillator, without which you cannot go on. Dr. Grimes will do the surgery. He will explain the procedure."

"I don't want it. I'm a ballerina. This device—the defibrillator will deform my chest. Let me die if I must die," she says, tears forming in her big eyes.

"Dr. Grimes was right a year ago, if we had put it in then, this would never have happened," he says. "You are lucky to be alive, Anna. There will be no third chance."

Dr. Grimes, a bearded average built man, tucks her hand. "Anna, I promise to place it cosmetically under your breast where it will not show," he says. Ali takes her other hand. "Without it, you will be at a very high risk for another cardiac arrest."

Anna looks from Grimes to Ali and back, her eyes wide and bright with tears.

"I have total confidence in Dr. Grimes—he is the Head of the Arrhythmia Service.

"Look Anna, why don't you think about it. Give it some time. I'll return in the evening," says Grimes.

As they leave Anna's bedside, Ali taps on Grimes shoulder. "Thanks a million," he says. "You were very reassuring. And I'm sorry for not taking your advice in the first place. She should have had the defibrillator after the blackout spell at the Met."

"No problem," says Grimes as they part ways.

When Ali goes back to see Anna in the evening, she finally agrees to have the defibrillator. Apparently, Mary, her mother and the nurses convinced her.

The next morning, Dr. Grimes, gowned, masked, and hatted, walks into the operating theater. Anna is given local anesthesia and conscious sedation. Dr. Grimes cuts just below the collar bone, then quickly dissects the tissue under the skin, separates the pectoral muscle, and then threads the wires into her veins and finally into the heart. He does it with speed and diligence. He carries on a one-sided conversation with Anna about ballets and operas he has seen while all the time cutting and dissecting and cauterizing until the smell of barbecued meat wafts through the operating room.

"Don't worry Anna, I am only cauterizing a bit of your muscle. Your body is not on fire," he says, and holds a silvery can up where she can see it.

"Here, this is what the defibrillator looks like." A can hovers above her face with a picture of a heart and the brand name written in bold letters.

A few minutes later, he tells her that Dr. Ali has arrived.

The anesthesiologist moves her head to the side, as Ali looks at her, and for a brief moment, their eyes meet. "I'm here Anna." She blinks her eyes and smiles.

"We are now going to give you general anesthesia and induce cardiac arrest to make sure the defibrillator is working properly," Dr. Grimes says.

"I feel a lump in my throat," she whispers.

"You will feel as if you're floating away, and within a few seconds you'll switch off like a light bulb," says Ali.

Dr. Grimes sends a jolt of electrical current through her heart. The heart goes into *ventricular fibrillation.* The defibrillator instantaneously recognizes the abnormal rhythm, the rhythm of death.

"She's in VF...the device is sensing...no drop-outs... charging," Annette, the device tech. utters aloud. There is a dull bang and an electrical shock from the defibrillator jolts Anna.

Anna's heart is back in normal rhythm. The procedure is a success.

"Hey, that's great—I'm so happy for Anna," says Ali with a smile on his face.

Anna remains dopey for several hours. Back in the Cardiac Unit, the faces of Katya, Natalie, Mary, the nurses, the residents, Drs. Ali and Grimes are surreal images that come and disappear on a hazy screen. Katya calls out to her, but she cannot respond. Stretching her hand, she manages to wrap her fingers around hers. Natalie sits beside her stroking her head.

The anesthetic and the painkillers play havoc with Anna's mind. She hardly sleeps, tossing and turning like a boat about to capsize until an injection of morphine brings about a thickening shroud of cloudiness to her sensorium, and abruptly switches off her consciousness. The safety of sleep, of a deadened mind.

The following day when Ali appears at seven thirty in the morning, she awakens, startled by his very presence.

"I'm sorry to wake you," he says. "I wanted to see you before I left town to give a lecture. You seem a bit flushed. Do you feel feverish?"

He helps her sit up and places his stethoscope on her chest. "See, I told you the defibrillator would be a piece of cake," he says, after examining her. He waits for her reaction. She barely forces a smile.

"I'm afraid that your heart function has deteriorated further—it's around twenty-five percent. I'm going to place you on steroids."

"Maybe like before, my heart will improve at least *somewhat?*" she asks.

"It's possible—there is no conclusive proof that steroids work—but it's worth a try. Anyway, I will begin evaluation for a heart transplant as well."

"*A heart transplant?*" she says after a long silence as if the realization was late in coming.

"Jackie, our transplant coordinator will come and explain it all. I'll come back tomorrow, and we'll talk some more." Ali looks at his watch. "I'm sorry Anna for being so abrupt. I must leave to make my nine o'clock flight. I know you want to go home soon, and so I want to keep the ball rolling."

A couple of hours after Ali leaves, a nurse walks into Anna's room and pulls up a chair, and introduces herself.

"Honey, I'm Jackie, the heart transplant coordinator. We are going to get to know each other very well and for a long, long time."

She smiles at Anna, who suddenly sits up. "A heart transplant?" Anna asks. "How could Dr. Ali give me such bad news and then leave?"

"Dr. Ali had to catch a plane," responds Jackie. "It's not as if you are going to have a heart transplant tomorrow. You're only going to be evaluated for one."

"I don't want your evaluations and your heart transplants—I would rather die."

"Well, think it over." She leaves a card on Anna's desk. "Call me back when you're ready to talk."

"Go away. Just leave me alone." Anna lies back on the bed and closes her eyes.

"Look Anna, I know this is difficult for you. Just look at the bright side: with a brand-new heart, you can have a whole new life."

Anna rolls over and sobs into her pillow. The words: *heart transplant*, keep pounding in her head. They will take out my heart and give me someone else's? She feels like holding on to her heart, once a thing of grace and beauty that prolonged her life; in due time it will regenerate itself and give her back her life. But in the back of her mind she knows that her heart is badly damaged. It has lost its grace; it stumbles and falls, only to rise up again ever so slightly. Like the swagger of a drunk person. And yet, her heart is still able to barely maintain her life. But the very act of living: breathing, talking, eating has become an adventure, a barefoot adventure in the draught ridden Serengeti. No, her heart will not heal. Without a new heart she will ultimately die. But can she trust Ali's judgment? He is so young. Is he experienced enough? Don't most young people with a cardiomyopathy recover over time? And don't transplants last for only five years? What happens after that? So many questions and not a single answer that brings her any comfort.

In the meanwhile, Anna spends a restless night, and at last, after tossing and turning in bed thinking of her course of action, she finally comes to a decision, and requests the nurse for a sleeping pill. She wakes up at nine the next morning and gets out of the bed. A bit woozy, she has to lie down again. In another fifteen minutes or so she tries getting up slowly, sitting at the edge of the bed before she stands up. She washes up and dresses. Her left shoulder hurts as she tries to put her arm into the sleeve of her blouse. In the bathroom mirror she sees dark pouches under her eyes and a pale tinge to her face. After applying some blush, she tries to comb her hair. As she pulls up her jeans, her left shoulder and left chest hurt. She lifts her blouse and looks at herself again in the mirror. Black and blue marks surround her left breast and extend downwards towards her belly. She was told that the blood from the surgery would seep all over her breast and upper belly and would be absorbed over time. After packing her things in the carry-all, she calls the nurse. "I'm signing out."

"Why?" asks, the nurse. "You still have to be evaluated for a transplant."

"Call the doctor. I'm signing out."

The resident doctor arrives after an hour or so and goes about trying to convince Anna not to sign out. He tells her that it will be only a couple more days for the transplant evaluation, after which she'd be free to leave.

"I'll come later," she says. "But not now—I'm not ready for this."

The resident doctor asks her to sign the *Against Medical Advice form*.

The nurse provides a wheelchair and a hospital attendant drops her at the main entrance. She manages to walk out of the hospital in her weakened state, but feels strangely resolute and strong, her mind driving her weakened body. She arrives home in a cab and staggers into the lounge. The doorman rushes to her and escorts her to her apartment. She walks into the arms of her mother, who is busy vacuuming the floors. Her mother is shocked to see her home. Katya comes running and embraces her. Anna feels a sharp pain in her chest that makes her buckle and nearly faint. Her mother props her up and takes her to her room and helps her onto the bed. The pain in Anna's chest lingers on. Her mother brings her a cup of fresh Borsht and sits on the bed stroking her head and massaging her feet. After a few spoonfuls of the soup, Anna falls into a long capacious sleep that shuts out the world.

Later that morning, Mary visits. "How could you have signed out against medical advice?" Mary scolds.

"It's my decision. It's my life," says Anna.

"Ali is very upset," says Mary. "He called me late last night."

Anna goes to her room and comes to the kitchen with containers of heart medications and throws them in the wastebasket.

"All these pills are making me sick."

"Anna, you have to take the medications!" says Mary, raising her voice.

"It is none of your business. The last time I trusted somebody, he took away my husband. What do you want?"

Mary doesn't answer. She wishes Anna a speedy recovery and leaves.

When Ali finds out that Anna had checked out of the hospital against medical advice, he is viscerally upset. He tells Mary that she has to take responsibility for herself and bear the consequences of her actions.

Two days later, Anna, together with her mother, venture into Central Park on a hot summer morning, but Anna gets winded after walking one block, and they have to turn back. Because she has stopped all her heart medication, her legs swell up and she has to sleep propped up in bed. Without Anna's knowledge, Natalie calls Ali and relates what has transpired.

Ali goes over to Anna's apartment and is not entirely surprised to see her pale and all puffed up about the eyelids. She seems withdrawn as if nothing matters anymore, as if she has given up on life—the serotonins, the dopamines, the neural signaling are all crashing. He finds her congested and her heart is showing frequent extra beats, all signs of worsening heart failure.

"You have to get re-admitted to the hospital for treatment," he says.

"I don't want a heart transplant!" she says, repeatedly.

"It's only an evaluation," he says. "It may take months or even years for you to get one. Look, I'm sorry Anna—I was too abrupt the other day. I was afraid I would be late for the flight." There is no response from her.

She is re-admitted to the hospital the following day, and the process of getting the fluid out, the fine-tuning of her heart muscle, starts all over again. With intravenous medications within a couple of days, the fluid in her lungs, the swelling in her legs disappear and she is able to lie flat. However, Anna remains withdrawn and impenetrable. Ali tries to reason with her—even changing the subject to Katya, Natalie, ballet—but, Anna turns away from him. When the social worker asks Anna about her home situation, whether she has anybody to take care of Katya, Anna snaps. "It's none of your business. Leave me alone." She buries her head in the pillow and sobs. The social worker reports to Ali that she is angry and depressed.

Ali visits her in the evening and reinforces that evaluation for a transplant doesn't mean that she would automatically get a heart tomorrow or the day after.

"I understand your state of mind," he says. "You're in denial. You have the right to be depressed and angry... Illness like yours is difficult to absorb at your age. It is best you see a psychiatrist or at least a psychotherapist."

"There is nothing wrong with me. I don't want a heart, and I don't need a psychiatrist."

He is at a loss for words. He has dealt with difficult and demanding patients and their relatives. But with Anna it is different. He sits on her bed and stretches his hand and touches hers. He senses that she feels comforted.

"In our culture we don't trust psychiatrists," she says. "I will be labeled crazy—these things happened to political prisoners in Communist Russia. It happened to my mother. Do you really think I'm crazy?" she continues raising her voice.

He can sense fear and angst in her eyes, as she moves them from side to side.

"Nobody is going to label you crazy," he says. "It is natural for you to be anxious, to be depressed. You badly need help."

"I'm not depressed. Leave me alone," she snaps.

He looks down towards the floor. Defeated. He feels sorry and at the time responsible for her. He blames himself for not being more forceful in the past, for not preparing her for a possible relapse. When he entered into the relationship, his mind was consumed by optimism, by the prospect of her heart muscle weakness entirely regressing. Now, he doubts his own judgment but feels relieved that he is still caring for her, providing medical expertise she so badly needs.

And then, unexpectedly, Nancy comes to mind, and again his guilt surges like a rush. How easy it seems with Nancy. How understanding, how reasonable she is. And why not? Nancy is healthy, she has a good job, she is an American, this is her country; she's not an immigrant like Anna. The comparison is unfair and misplaced. He feels torn between his new fondness for Nancy and his love and concern for Anna. He looks at her again, absorbing the disappearing landscape of their past. He remembers when they nearly made love, her beautiful body, the face he had held in his hands and kissed with so much feeling. Turning towards her, he kisses her on the forehead. She doesn't react.

Anna is finally discharged from the hospital on heart failure medications and on steroid therapy. At home her anxiety spins out of control.

"It's all your fault," she says to her mother. You send me to America. You and the KGB."

"Why are you accusing me?" says Natalie.

"Da, you were in league with the KGB," she says. "The wild mushrooms. You knew they were poisonous."

"Anna, I didn't know they were poisonous," says Natalie.

"You and the KGB—your planned it all to keep me in Russia."

"If I'm upsetting you so much, it's best I return back to Russia and take Katya with me."

"Go ahead," says Anna.

Soon thereafter Anna calls Ali. "I'm going to audition for the American Ballet," she says.

"That's great, but I think you should wait until you get better," says Ali.

"Well, my Mum is going back to Russia. Maybe I should also go with her and audition for the Bolshoi," she says. There is no response from Ali.

"I don't want to live anymore. The KGB has poisoned me—it resulted in my heart problem. It's my mother's fault."

"Calm down Anna," says Ali.

"I want to die." She is sobbing now.

"No, Anna, no—you must not think that way," says Ali.

The rapid mind cycling, a sign of anxiety and depression, moves her life from grey to black interspersed with white spots, like the blackness of the night illuminated sporadically by the sparkle of fireflies.

"You have to see a psychiatrist," says Ali with a tone of authority. She hangs up.

He sees her in his office two weeks later, and nothing changes; her heart failure is under control, but his concern for her mental health heightens.

CHAPTER 15

A Romantic Interlude

Nancy and Ali waltz into each other's life confidently, like musicians at a performance. They glide into the relationship slowly in the beginning, then rapidly, like a raft down the river. However, in their euphoria, they don't deal with their cultural and religious differences, draping them over a chair somewhere.

They take in the city, each hurrying to show the other the glitter of Broadway, the museum row on Fifth Avenue, the jazz clubs and the restaurants in the East Village. Unlike for Anna, the Indo-Pakistani-Bangladeshi restaurants downtown are a novelty for Nancy, and she seems to enjoy the food: sort of. He makes time for her now, by leaving the hospital much earlier than before, and most of the time never after seven. They ride their bicycles in Central Park and the Riverside Park and order out. Any emergencies he asks Dr. Denzel to attend to, a good opportunity to build Denzel's practice. To Ali, the relationship with Nancy is easy, so different, from the complex emotionally charged Anna; and yet, they seem to wait for that moment, that inkling of time, when their togetherness will blossom into tapestry and art, with its intricate dance—the pas deux of love.

One chilly Saturday evening in late September, after a bike ride in Central Park, they walk back home to his apartment. They stop for fresh greens, olive oil, Greek olives, fresh oregano, basil, tomatoes, garlic, vinegar, pasta, a can of anchovies, goat cheese and French bread. At a neighboring wine store, they buy a bottle of Chilean merlot. She wants to cook her favorite pasta for him, the way her mother has taught her. As they enter his apartment, she heads into the kitchen, her suede jacket on, still numb from the cold. It smells of stale curry, a kitchen that hasn't seen a woman—or, for that matter any home cooked food—for some time. Soon, the smell of garlic, olive oil, balsamic vinegar and red wine, wafts through the room as he watches her cut the greens, crush garlic, her mouth caressing the glass of Merlot, a few droplets spangling her lips. He comes closer and guides his hand underneath her jacket, her bulky sweater. He fondles her breasts and she turns around and meets his lips. She stops the kissing to take a long sip of the merlot. Her breathing is rapid as she washes and wipes her hands. The odor of garlic mixed with that of Balsamic vinegar and Merlot and their pheromones, has an erotic quality to it. He whispers, "I love you," as he leads her to the bedroom.

The unmade bed is the only sign of life in this spotless, bare room. In the yellowish-semi-light emanating from a partially open window, her milky skin glows softly. He kisses her flat stomach, her navel, her neck, her back, and the inside of her thighs. His lips move down towards her shaven baldness, white and pink, and he so slightly keeps tasting her there. She pulls him towards her full, large breasts, moaning when he wraps his tongue on her pink taut nipple, his fingers stroking the other. She cuddles his face, kisses him hungrily. She whispers his name, professing her love for him. "I love you too, Nancy. I think of you all the time," he responds. She is about to unzip his pants when he does it himself. His tongue makes her nipples into erect buds; her sticky wet sex on fire. She pushes him on top of her and guides him between her parted legs.

He keeps on looking at her, fixated on her naked geography: her large ample breasts, the curve of her hips, her pink taut nipples like flower buds, the nakedness of her vagina. Why does the sight of beauty extol Eros into life? Does sex with a beautiful woman elevate us, apotheosize us somehow?

When they are finally finished, exhausted, she says: "Ali, we didn't use any protection."

"Don't worry, if you get pregnant, we'll get married and have the baby."

She smiles. "You want a child, don't you?" he says, and laughs.

"Are you proposing?" she says. "Let's eat. I'm hungry. I have to still cook the pasta."

When she serves him, he adds some crushed red chili to the pasta. After dinner, they sit on the couch in each other's arms and watch TV. He likes her practicality, her simplicity, and emotional stability.

She belongs in his apartment, in his bed, and in his life.

They continue seeing each other as often as they can, and once or twice a week she spends the night in his apartment. She always drinks a glass of red or white before her meals. She coaxes him to drink; mostly he refuses, at other times he takes a sip to please her, to be part of her. She can sense that he doesn't appreciate her drinking on a daily basis, although he doesn't mention it. Either his faith or his culture doesn't accept her indulgences, but she refrains from asking any questions, thinking that he will ultimately accept her habits; these, will slowly sink in through a slow process of osmosis.

They make love whenever they are together: in the living

room, the kitchen, in the bathtub, but Ali prefers the bed.

One day, after lovemaking, she walks naked in the apartment.

"Don't put your clothes on. I forbid it," she says.

"I don't like walking naked," he says.

"You're a bore,"

"So be it," he says, in a harsh tone of voice.

It upsets her. She feels he doesn't like the idea of seeing her walking around naked; she feels dirty and cheap. She showers and quickly clothes herself, and abruptly leaves the apartment without saying goodbye. It is the second time her anger seeps through. He calls her several times. She doesn't answer, nor does she return his calls. She calls him a week later.

"I will not walk around naked if you don't like it," she says.

"I'm sorry, Nancy for being such a prig," he says.

CHAPTER 16
Anna's Psychosis

One afternoon, three weeks later, Natalie calls Ali to tell him that Anna has locked herself up in her bedroom and won't come out.

"Did she answer when you knocked on the door?" he asks.

"I thought she was sleeping. She hasn't responded for the last hour. I just knocked on the door. Please help, Dr. Ali."

"I'll come immediately," he says. As he is changing from his surgical scrubs, he is paged stat to come to the Lab. Dr. Denzel has a heart perforation on his hands. Ali immediately calls Mary, who agrees to go to Anna's apartment.

Mary, together with the doorman knock on the door; there is no response. The doorman inserts a card in the lock and manages to open the door to the bedroom. They find Anna lying on the bed, eyes closed, her breathing shallow. A bottle of Ambien lies empty on the dresser. Mary catches hold of her shoulders and shakes her vigorously. There is no response. She calls 911.

The paramedics bag her. In the emergency room they pump her stomach.

She is placed on a suicide watch. A court order is issued to start her on psychotropic medications.

The social worker and the psychotherapist opine that her suicide attempt reveals a deep-seated mental instability not suited for the trials and tribulations of a heart transplant recipient. Ali is devastated with her suicide attempt; he quietly sits in his office and cries. He blames himself for all of this. He goes to see Anna.

"It's not hopeless Anna," he says. You are not alone. I'm here for you." She doesn't respond.

The following day, Ali pitches hard on her behalf to the transplant team, attributing her mood disorder and depression to her illness and the steroid therapy. It is mutually agreed upon to reevaluate her after anti-depressive therapy.

After fifteen days of drug therapy and intense psychotherapy, the psychiatrist deems her no longer a threat to herself, and Anna is discharged from the hospital.

CHAPTER 17

Ali and His Imam

Ali had mentioned to his mother without going into details that he was dating the Russian ballerina; his mother had seen Anna briefly perform and talked about her to her husband. Ali's father said it was a bad idea, and rather snobbishly stated: "These dancers revel in immorality and Godlessness." For several months now, they hadn't heard about the Russian ballerina.

When Ali visits his parents on the weekend, his mother raises the issue. "It's over between us," Ali says. She shows disappointment and distress as if suffering his bachelorhood in silence. "We remain good friends, she's my patient now," he adds. "I met someone, Mum. She's not Muslim and she's no doctor. But, you'll like her." It draws out a subtle smile from his mother. He knows what his mother is thinking: her son has a girlfriend and that is fine, but will it lead into marriage?

Ali mentions Nancy to his father at the dinner table and says that he wants to invite her for dinner.

"She's most welcome, but son is this relationship going to lead into something permanent?

"It's too early to tell," says Ali.

Ali's parents are both suspicious of his relationships with American women, both believing that cross-cultural relationships are fleeting and difficult, an enterprise prone to failure.

Before Ali has a chance to respond, his father continues: "Rolling stones gather no moss, my son! These women are not meant for you. You have to choose your own kind. I'm not asking you to go to Pakistan to find a bride. You can find one here only if you give me a chance."

"Well, that means you and your relatives in Washington are going to pick a mail-order bride for me? No thanks, Dad. See what happened to Safdar's arranged marriage—he ended up with a crazy woman who destroyed his life."

"I think you'd like Nancy—she's Irish-American, with Norwegian, German and Swedish genes on her mother's side. She has traveled widely in the East."

Turning toward his mother, he tells her that Nancy's best friend is a Bengali Indian doctor originally from Calcutta, a breast cancer specialist who works at Memorial-Sloan Kettering hospital. His mother smiles broadly, and this time around it is a smile of contentment. He doesn't mention religion but surmises that his mother suspects she is Christian.

"Ali, soon you are going to be forty. When are you going to start a family?" his father says.

"Khokon, please listen to your father," his mother pleads with folded hands. Ali keeps quiet, distressed by his mother's tears. This is his last chance to make her happy.

Ali's relationship with his father has been complex and confrontational since his father's refusal for him to pursue ballet, and since his bloodletting with his Imam. At the age of nine his father had enlisted him for one-on-one teachings of the Qur'an with Imam Rahman, whom he knew in his youth in Karachi,

Pakistan. The mosque, a modest one, perhaps the humblest in New York, was located in Queens in a two-story building situated on a row of small shops: a pizza joint, a Columbian bar and restaurant, an Indian restaurant, an Indian sari and jewelry store, a Korean Laundromat, and a grocery store specializing in Pakistani, Bangladeshi and Indian spices. The street reeked with the smells of paprika, asafetida, coriander, and curries—the exotic smells of spices transported thousands of miles from the streets of the recently arrived émigrés from India, Bangladesh, and Pakistan.

His father dropped him there in his black Mercedes; at times he came along to chat with the Imam in Urdu, about their childhood days. Narrow steps that creaked led to the place of prostration—al-masjid al-jami, and a door painted in blue with a Mogul motif opened into an empty space. In a room behind the large open area of prayer was the office of the Imam, with a desk on which were cluttered several Qur'ans, magazines and newspapers from foreign countries. "This is just a temporary place, Ali," the Imam would say. "One day soon, we'll have a big place, a mosque with a dome—*Allah-U-Akbar*. If not for your father's generous support, even this would be impossible." As he said these words, the whole place rocked with the rattling of the train passing up above.

The Imam was a tall, bearded, unsmiling, and lean figure for whom the young Ali never took a liking. It was his unkempt beard and the allergic rhinitis that gave him constant colds with sneezes and coughs that turned Ali off. But when he recited the Qua'ran in a shrill musical rhythmic voice, his arms wide open, looking towards the yellowish-green smudged ceiling, his teary eyes glowed, and his face elongated as he swayed his head wildly as if in a trance. "Listen to the music, the rhythm, the poetry—it is a miracle. Allah—*La illahah illalah* gifted our Prophet Muhammad—*Assalaamu Alaykum*."

Ali felt a sense of pity for the man, for his loneliness. Perhaps it was the shabbiness of the place the Imam called his mosque; perhaps it was his broken English, perhaps it was the sickly, disheveled Imam that Ali never synched with. Soon, Ali also began sneezing, coughing and tearing. His father gave him Benadryl, which made Ali sleepy. He never realized it then, but thinking about it, the place reeked with mold.

Ali liked the imposing modern Catholic Church with its Gothic arches, its statues of Christ, Mary the mother of God, whom he likened to his own mother. He liked the statues of saints, and the paintings of the Stations of the Cross that hung on the walls, and the large congregations, men and women together, happily holding hands, and the hymns they sang. Ali also liked the young smiling Irish priest who ruffled Ali's hair and hugged him tightly when he visited him in the sacristy after Mass. He was especially attracted to the priest's multicolored flowing robe, his baritone voice, and his mild Jesus-loves sermons he heard with his mother at the Church in Long Island, near their home. When eight, Ali secretly even contemplated priesthood.

The Imam wanted to make Ali a Hafiz, someone who could recite by memory the holy book in Arabic. "It will assure you and your dear father, *peace be upon him*, a place in Jannat—the Paradise."

"Have I to memorize the Qur'an in Arabic?" Ali asked. His mother kept mum. Shaking his head to and fro, his father said, "Behta, that would be nice."

"Are you a Hafiz, father?" Ali asked.

"I wish I was."

For almost three years Ali had come to this makeshift Mosque, but as he had difficulty memorizing the teachings of the Surahs in Arabic, he had pleaded with his father that he would try memorizing the Qur'an in English. "114 *surahs* in Arabic? I don't see the point!" he said, and his father had ultimately conceded, to the disappointment of the Imam. The visits to the Imam that began with "Assalamulaikum Imam," and lasted sometimes an hour, sometimes less when Ali arrived late, had gradually decreased in frequency. Sometimes Ali just strolled the length of Roosevelt Avenue to waste time before going to see the Imam, and then waiting for his father to pick him up; at other times they both engaged in some grocery shopping from a list that his mother provided before they returned to Long Island. But twice while waiting for his father at a corner store, once during a snowfall in the winter, he had seen a young white woman in jeans get out of his father's car. His father never mentioned the woman and Ali never asked who she was, but all along he wondered whether the woman was his father's lover, and whether the visits to the makeshift mosque was just a front for his father to pursue his extramarital forays. This angered Ali, and he felt deceived by his father. He began giving all sorts of excuses, even feigning headaches and colds not to go.

He liked many elements of the Qur'an, which he readily memorized, but as he grew older and into himself, he began questioning and doubting the concept of faith and dogmas he found in the teachings of both the Church and in Islam. Together with his classmate and friend Jerry Cohen, a Jew whose grandparents had perished in the Holocaust, he had been reading science and Darwin, and was taken up with Darwin's theory of Evolution. He didn't know it then, but Ali was a different cut of prime meat: of rational thinking and science. One day, when he and Jerry were playing Atari in the basement, Ali had asked: "Jerry, do you believe in God?"

"I don't know," he promptly answered. "We go to the temple, but my father tauntingly says to my mother and his in-laws who are deeply religious: '"But where was God during the Holocaust?"'"

"Nobody answered. There was silence," he said.

Then Jerry stopped playing and stood up, gesturing with his arms. "Even Albert Einstein expressed his skepticism regarding

God," he said. "According to my father, Einstein had said: "'I cannot imagine a God who rewards and punishes the objects of his creation, whose purposes are modeled after our own—a God, in short, who is but a reflection of human frailty.'" That night, Ali tossed and turned, until he woke up from a dream in which he saw himself burning in Hell.

He questioned the Imam about other faiths like Judaism, Hinduism, Buddhism, and reincarnation, which his mother had touched upon. He could see that the Imam was irritated.

"The answers are in the Qu'ran," he said.

The week after his father had forbidden the ballet lessons, when Ali went to his weekly meeting with the Imam, he said: "Assalamulaikum Imam—I have doubts about religions. I believe in Science, in Darwin, in Galileo, in Einstein."

The Imam, having sensed Ali's disinterest a long while ago, cast the stone quoting the second Surah: "But if you cannot—and of a surety you cannot—then fear the fire whose fuel is Men and Stones, which is prepared for those who reject faith." And, he continued: "After all these years of learning the truth, the absolute truth, if you still have doubts, and a lack of faith, The Prophet said that eventually all unbelievers will be destroyed." After a few coughs and grunts he continued:

"'The only guidance is the guidance of Allah'—according to the third Surah."

Ali stood in front of the Imam, stiff and defiant in killer silence. In the eyes of the Imam, Ali had wavered in his faith and rejected the one and only, the Absolute Faith. He became angry, an anger that made him pound his desk, tear at his beard, cough and grunt and sneeze, an anger that had made him puke, when Ali summarily ran away with no apologies, no regrets.

He had not waited for his father that day, but instead took the slow moving, old world Long Island Railroad, still plowing the rails in the New World. When he arrived home, he sustained his father's wrath. He was slapped on the face: once, twice then a third time.

"I saw you with a white woman. Who was she your girl-friend? Does Mum know about her?" said Ali, his face flushed with anger.

His father slapped him again. He took additional slaps calmly and stiffly without a single tear, with an air of defiance. It was then that his mother had intervened.

"Stop it," she said to her husband, banging her head on the wall.

"Why don't you tell Mum about the white woman? Great excuse to visit the Imam?" said Ali in the presence of his mother.

"Stop this nonsense," said his father at the top of his voice.

Ali's mother had continued banging her head on the wall silently, until his father, utterly defeated, had walked out of the house, shoulders drooping, and had not returned home that day. As in the eastern tradition this day was never talked about. The visits to Queens ended. But the distance between father and son established and solidified on that day would remain.

CHAPTER 18
Dinner in Long Island

When Nancy enters Ali's parent's house in Long Island, she is nervous perhaps as much as Ali, but determined to make a good impression. She has a black suit on and a dark blue-checkered scarf, which highlights her pale skin and her dark blue eyes.

Accustomed to the ambience at her friend Nalini's house, she gradually feels more at ease in Ali's father's posh modern home with inlaid wood furniture from India and Pakistan and exquisite Mogul ivory miniatures and oriental rugs. She is taken up with the photographs of his father and mother when they were young, before Ali was born, and those of Ali when he was a baby and a toddler.

In Ali's mother she notices the absence of the red and white bangles unique to Bengali married women, or the Tangali sari, or the thick stem of vermilion powder in the central parting of her hair. She has obviously cut her ties to Bengal and Bengali traditions. Thanks to her friend, Nalini, she is familiar with Bengali traditions and the smells of saffron, cinnamon, cardamom, chili and masala that lingers all around the house.

Ali's father seems stiff at first, very British in his manners.

At almost six feet, he is impressive in his blue suit, a white shirt, a blue Ascot, and the carved bone pipe from which he blows whorls of fragrant smoke, and authoritatively gestures with it. He is a senior partner in a large internal medicine practice in Long Island and now he is semi-retired, working two half-days a week. When Ali is helping his mother in the kitchen, his father mentions Ali's accomplishments in the world of academia to Nancy. "Ali could have any position he wants anywhere in the US in the heart transplant field," he says.

Nancy can sense that his father is proud of Ali. The way he talks, his mannerisms and his accent, reminds Nancy of an Indian aristocrat she has seen in movies from the British Raj. Ali's mother is dressed in a sari, and touching Nancy's face, she comments on the purity of her milky skin as she offers her a choice of Lassi, Pepsi, Coca-Cola, or Sprite. Nancy would prefer a tall martini or Sex on the Beach if she has the choice. Ali had warned her that alcoholic beverages are not served in their home.

Nancy asks for Coca-Cola to cool her stinging tongue after nibbling on tangy-spicy *churra* and a samosa. She notices that Ali has his mother's large, penetrating brown eyes; otherwise, his composure, the height, the hairline, is much like his father's. Ali's mother is all the time smiling and serving.

When Nancy mentions her father's Irish background, the senior Dr. Khan goes into the history of British dominance of Ireland and the IRA.

Waving his pipe, he says: "As much as I oppose violence, domination and subjugation can only be met at the barrel of a gun." Nancy doesn't know what to make of his aggressiveness and his bland humor.

"But what about Gandhi?" Ali's mother asks, in a low, subdued voice. "Didn't he rattle the British Empire single-handedly with his non-violent methods? I think the world would have been better off following his path." It is the only time she expresses an opinion. Ali's father concurs with the worthwhile bit of history; however, he says that Gandhi was one of a kind, and India is a large country with millions of people. "Look, after all is said and done, Gandhi was himself assassinated by a Hindu extremist."

"See how much Dr. King achieved applying his principals of non-violence and peaceful resistance," Ali interjects rather forcefully. His mother and Nancy nod their heads in agreement.

After a few morsels of the saffron smeared chicken biryani, Nancy changes the conversation to the subject of free markets and globalization, perhaps to establish her turf, to impress Ali's father, or both.

"Nancy, free markets and globalization are all too good for America and the Western economies, but not for the poor countries of the world," says Ali's father. "It's another method of Corporate exploitation; although, I confess it looks good on the surface."

As if to spice the remark, he offers her the gigot that his wife has just placed on the table. "You have to try this leg of lamb when steaming hot, spiced according to an ancient recipe of the Pashtuns," he says, hurriedly cutting into the flesh, as if he is tearing into some tribal enemy in Swat.

"It tastes terrific, the meat is so soft, and the ooze of spices tingles the tongue," says Nancy after taking a bite.

"How do you know so much about Indian cooking tastes?" Ali's mother asks in a singsong way.

"From my friend, Nalini." Nancy turns to Ali's father and smilingly states: "But Sir, coming back to globalization, in today's world, free-trade, and a capitalistic economy are here to stay." Ali's father shakes his head and seems unwilling to pursue further discussion.

After several morsels of the lamb, rather casually, Nancy inquires about the political climate in Pakistan, and General Musharaf's recent coup d'état.

Ali immediately goes on a lengthy explanation about the corruption in Pakistan: the plundering of the state coffers, the erosion of the economy and the social structure, and the constant coups. Addressing his father, he explains, that on the contrary, democracy has taken solid root in India. It is as if Ali and his father are waiting for the opening to discuss politics.

"Democracy in India!" his father raises his voice a notch higher, with a tang of sarcasm. "What about the destruction of the Babri Mosque, the police in cahoots with the Shiv Sena, the looting and the killing of the Muslims in Bombay, the suppression of the Muslim majority in Kashmir, and the ascendancy of Hindutva? There you have it—democracy in India." Ali's immediate silence suggests he is cornered and beaten. However, after a few bites of the spicy gigot and morsels of the saffron and almond chicken biryani, Ali is revved and promptly changes the subject.

"It is tragic that the Muslim world lives in the fifteenth century," says Ali. Nancy can feel the tension building between father and son, and wonders whether it is an old score that Ali is settling with his father, or vice-versa.

"You are expressing an entirely western viewpoint," says his father. "The rise of Islamic Fundamentalism is related to frustration, injustice, and the lack of hope."

"That's exactly what I am trying to say," says Ali. "Wasn't it Karl Marx who said that religion is the opium of the people?"

The very mention of Karl Marx is blasphemous. The furrows on Ali's father's forehead; the flush on his cheeks, and the droop on his face reveals anguish, anger, and disappointment. Perhaps Ali has gone too far into forbidden territory.

"It has nothing to do with religion. As I said before, it is related to frustration, injustice, and the lack of hope." Ali's father says with a certain vigor and determination.

"Nancy, I hope our political arguments are not bothering you," says Ali, apologetically. "It's a family tradition to argue the politics," says his father addressing Nancy. My father and my uncles were involved in politics during the British Raj and were imprisoned for their outspokenness and their alignment with Mohammad Ali Jinnah, the founder of Pakistan."

Ali's mother, the peacemaker, interjects that it's time for dessert and asks who would like coffee and who would like tea. "Masala tea for you Nancy, like for Ali?"

Later that evening, when Ali and Nancy are by themselves, Ali expresses the view that the rise of Islamic Fundamentalism is at least partly related to the marginalization of Muslims in the Middle East without hope or a promise for the future, notwithstanding, and the constant Western interference. He sees a parallel to the rise of Communist ideology and radical guerrilla movements in South America and Africa among the poor and dispossessed before the fall of the Soviet Union.

When the conversation changes to religion, Ali reveals that for him, faith is shrouded in complexities. Perhaps there was a mutual understanding between his father and mother that he be exposed to both faiths: Muslim and Christian. And so, he had gone on and off for Sunday Mass with his mother during his childhood years, and they still have a Christmas wreath and a Christmas tree every year. Then one day, he had found a small shrine hidden in the basement with a statue of the Hindu God Shiva depicted as a multi-armed divinity deftly balanced on one leg. Pointing to Shiva, he had asked his mother why this God stood on one leg unlike the crucified Christ that hung in the Church. His mother had told him that the God was Nataraja, a Hindu deity, the Lord of the Dance. She danced a few steps of the Bharatnatyan.

"Look, I can do it, too!" he said. And he had attempted the pose quite successfully. His mother had found in him a talent for imitating a most intricate dance sequence after being shown it just once. A week later she signed him for ballet. Almost three years later his father had strongly opposed the ballet.

"'I want my son to be a doctor—a heart surgeon, not a dancer,'" my father said. "He had his wish."

"You resemble him physically. And he is so proud of you," says Nancy.

"It was on the day that we danced the Bharatnatyan that my mother mentioned to me her past Hindu background. But she never went into any details, and her Hindu past still remains an enigma in my mind."

"Muslim, Christian, Hindu—I see it. So, what do you see yourself as of now?"

"I don't know," he says softly, as if in deep contemplation. She kisses him tenderly, thankful for sharing these slices of his past.

On her way out, Ali's father tells Nancy that he hopes to see her again. Ali's mother tenderly strokes her face. As they drive away, Ali tells Nancy that his parents liked her, and asked her in turn what she thought of them.

"I think your mother really does," Nancy smiles. "And I like her too. But your father..."

"He told me he was very impressed with you—your smarts and looks—coming from him that means a lot."

"In my family we hardly ever discuss politics," she says as the car idles on the clogged Long Island Expressway. Ali dials the radio to NPR News when Nancy unexpectedly asks him whether his parents minded that she is Catholic.

"They might be concerned about the cultural differences but not religion per se," he says. "The Qur'an states: "Lawful for you in marriage are...women from among those who received revelation before your time." The latter are usually seen as Jews and Christians."

"You are so much like your mother," she says.

"Yes, indeed," he says. "I inherited from her my love for dance and poetry. She has an exquisite sensitivity for the arts; she read me Tagore's poetry in my youth. I regret not knowing much about her Hindu background, and her conversion to Catholicism. Sometimes I wonder whether it was entirely reactionary."

After a long pause, he says: "Have you read Tagore?"

"I heard of him, but no, I never read Tagore. I'd be happy to read his poetry," she says.

"The next time I go home to Long Island, I'll get his poetry book."

"Was it difficult for your mother to give up her family and her Hindu Bengali traditions," she asks.

"I don't know," he says.

"Why don't you ask her about it?"

He doesn't answer. It is amply clear to her that Ali has great respect for his mother, and it bodes well for her. She remembers Nalini telling her that in the Eastern tradition some things are just left alone. Bottled up. Pickled forever. Perhaps, it is better that way.

CHAPTER 19

Anna's Recovery

Anna reconciles with Mary, and after her discharge from the
hospital and her mother and Katya leave for Russia, she stays
with Mary in their apartment on the West Side. She has a room
for herself and a baby grand to play on. To Anna, Mary and
Brad are an odd couple. Mary, with her fine New England upbringing, her generosity, and humanity; and Brad with his ponytail, jeans, his sax and the scar, and yet they seem to communicate, perhaps through music or some other chemistry that is
beyond her reach. There is something wild and brutish about
Brad and yet, in Mary's presence, he seems subdued, tamed like
a domesticated animal.

During Anna's stay at Mary's, Brad happens to be in town,
playing at New York City jazz clubs. He often practices playing jazz mixed with Native American tones he composes. Anna
attentively listens to his music and observes every movement:
the arching of his body as he raises his sax to his thick lips, the
puckering of the mark on his face as his eyes close, and the tones
from the sax as if spelling out words:

"Once upon a time

"Buffalo roamed the land

"And the Navajo were free…"

The image of Brad playing his tones in the Paria Canyon during sunset, that echoed through its sinuous sheer-walls, emanating deep sounds, like echoes of a distant time—that music she had heard during her trip to Vegas now repeats itself; music that soothes and heals, helping her get over the depression that brought about the panic that kept her awake at night. Brad's music and the drugs gradually work their marvels, not only on her depression, but also her whole attitude towards life.

When Anna plays the piano, Brad often joins in. But it is his lips, those thick lips that drool when he blows his sax, those lips she wants to press to her own. These thoughts arouse her as she regains her strength, but she shows restraint. Brad hardly talks, words are sparse, but his music communicates a story more than words can tell.

One day when Brad plays, Anna begins dancing a slow voluptuous sway, a movement without jumps, with eyes closed, her mouth wide open, as if she is floating in thin air. Brad stops playing. He comes from behind and places his arms around her waist, and they sway without music, the rhythm dancing in their bodies. He turns her around and they dance clinging to each other, his body pressed on hers, and then she sees the image in front of her, the image of the great betrayal—Aloysha and Jack making out. She immediately disengages. Perhaps Brad sees fear in Anna's eyes, the fear Anna feels in her heart, the fear of betrayal, of how much Mary means for both of them—Mary the fulcrum, the giver of life—and Brad walks away. At that moment, and at subsequent moments when Anna thinks about the episode, it seems to her as if fate, an instinct, had pulled her away from Brad. They never talk of the episode.

Anna's initial euphoria and burst of energy stabilizes after the dose of Zoloft is cut down, and she begins seeing things with a new clarity. She feels confident to return to her apartment and live there. When she sees Ali for a checkup, she tells him that she wants to have the transplant. "I am ready for the evaluation."

"Why don't you call Jackie, the transplant coordinator and make an appointment?" he says.

Jackie explains to Anna all there is to explain and sends Anna's blood for a variety of tests. But it is the evaluation by the transplant psychotherapist that is the clincher, since Anna had attempted suicide.

Anna is somewhat nervous on the day of her meeting with the therapist. To her pleasant surprise, the therapist reads Ali's letter, and after asking her a few questions, like where she lives, whether she has family and friends, he smiles and dismisses her. Ali's lengthy letter regarding her illness, the loss of her profession that meant so much to her, her immigrant status, her single motherhood, a strong support system in Mary and her mother, and that her depression was entirely related to her illness, does the trick.

Anna passes the test. She is accepted for a heart transplant.

CHAPTER 20
Thanksgiving Dinner

Summer rapidly advances upon Nancy and Ali, and in the month of August, they fly to Lima, Peru, then into Cuzco, and trek on the Inca trail to Machu-Picchu. It is there, amid the ruins of the Inca civilization, in the heights of the rain forest and snow-capped mountains that they connect in a spiritual way. They look at each other, expressing how much they love each other, and lock themselves in a long embrace. Within this physical union, they both feel a desire, a longing, to spend the rest of their lives together. At this moment, love is solid, firm; they can hold it in their hands like a book of scripture.

In Aguas Callientes, at the foothills of Machu-Picchu, that evening, after a filling meal of *Olloquito com Charqui*, Ali takes Nancy's hand and asks her if she would like to spend the rest of her life with him. With her lips stained with dark sweet Andean chocolate, she says: "Do you have any doubts?"

Within this newly discovered ancient world of clarified emptiness, that evening, they see a future of promises, and when they arrive back to New York, the summer fades, tumbling into the fall, and a new season, a new life begins.

When in Machu Picchu, the excitement of the ethereal, and the vast distance has kept the image of Anna out of Ali's mind. He had dismissed previous girlfriends without much ado, saying very little, and they had faded away, no fuss, no drama. But not Anna; she isn't easily forgotten. He calls her the day he returns to find out how she is doing and leaves a message on her phone to call him back.

When Ali returns to work, he finds an urgent message from Dr. Bob requesting a meeting at seven o'clock in the evening.

As Ali is about to knock on Dr. Bob's office, all of Bob's secretaries having left, he hears voices coming from inside the office. He sits in the waiting room, expecting someone to exit anytime soon. After almost ten minutes, the noises stop. Ali is about to knock again when Dr. Bob abruptly opens the door and passes by him. Ali is taken by surprise that there is no one else in Dr. Bob's office, and Dr. Bob seems distant as if he doesn't know why Ali is there. He is startled at the blank stare, the sweat on his brow, and Dr. Bob's silence.

"Dr. Bob, you asked to see me."

"Go in. I need to take a leak. I'll be with you shortly." Ali anxiously waits for him seated in his office. After almost fifteen minutes, Dr. Bob bursts in.

"Oh yes, the Cardiospeed study," he says, after a long silence broken by his footsteps as he rapidly and purposefully paces the floor as if to get his memory going. The smell of a foul fart fills the room.

"You are behind in the recruitment of patients," he says. "In fact, you haven't recruited a single patient. Mr. Fusco is threatening to terminate the study and recruit the Downtown Medical Center, our competitor. And let me remind you: we are going to lose the funding."

"I just returned from a holiday," says Ali apologetically. "It's a difficult study and the recruitment is not easy. Besides, I'm not the Principal Investigator on the study."

Dr. Bob's face starts twitching. "Look Ali, I'm giving you a month to recruit at least two patients, so that I can hold off Mr. Fusco," says Dr. Bob. "If not, I'll have to take you off the study and offer it to Dr. Cain, the new head of the Heart Failure Program."

"Currently, I have my hands full. Please, by all means go ahead and hand it over to Dr. Cain," says Ali.

At that moment the phone rings. "One moment Ali, it is Dr. Claudette Pèpin—my new research assistant from Paris," says Dr. Bob.

"Sure."

"Hold on Claudette," he says on the phone. "Well, I'll call you in four weeks; I expect some progress," Bob says to Ali, as he gets off his chair.

Ali is angry as he leaves Dr. Bob's office. Claudette's call poured cold water on the tension brewing in the room. Anyway, the study was his idea and he isn't the Principal Investigator— Dr. Bob is. So, let him recruit the patients. He is not playing the *political correctness game* and he could pay a costly price for it. But his research is going well, he has tremendous success of late in getting his work published, and he is on a meteoric rise nationally and internationally. So, the hell with Dr. Bob.

There, he is again challenging authority just as he challenged his father and his Imam. It is deeply rooted in his genes.

Nancy had mentioned to her mother, Pat, that she was dating a doctor; she had shown his picture. Pat had asked her to invite him over, but Nancy had procrastinated, saying that he was on call or out of town lecturing. To some extent, these were excuses. At first, Nancy wasn't confident of the relationship; now, she isn't sure how to broach the subject of his Muslim faith. She is certain her father would object, and she isn't sure of her mother either.

Finally, after her return from Peru, Nancy decides it's time for Ali to meet her parents, and Thanksgiving dinner seems a great opportunity.

It is on the day before Thanksgiving when Nancy and Pat are baking cookies and pies that Nancy whispers to her that Ali is not of the Christian faith. Pat asks her whether he is a Hindu, knowing that her friend, Nalini, is of similar faith. When Nancy, after some hesitation, relates that he is sort of half-Muslim and half-Christian, Pat nearly faints. "You must be kidding Nancy," she says, after recovering her composure.

"Wait till you meet him. His looks, the accent, and his smarts—you'll love him, Mom. Besides, he was born in England and educated in the US, and he is after all half-Christian."

"Is it serious?"

Nancy nods.

"It's going to break your father—you know that, don't you?"

Nancy doesn't reply. She keeps her head down, slicing the apples for the pie, faster and faster. She knows her mother will tell her father, pick the right moment, and choose the right words as only her mother can do.

Thanksgiving Day, Nancy is nervous, and looks slantingly at her father to detect any concern or disenchantment. She remembers her girlhood days when her father took her on fishing trips to Coney Island or Arthur Kill—their love was like sunshine on oily water. In the beginning these were enticing trips, quality time with her father but as she grew into her teens, she hated them, but went anyway, not to offend him. There was one memorable trip on a small lake in Upstate New York when her mother was visiting her sister in California. They had barbecued lake trout on logs of cedar, and with the fragrant smoke en-shrouding them, she had snuggled close to him by the lakeside in the moonlight. He had told her of how the Verrazano Bridge was built, how dangerous it was, and about the men who had fallen to their deaths, and how he had been one of the top en-gineers. She always marveled as she crossed the Verrazano and told all her friends that her father had built it. He had bought a house on Grymes Hill with a view of the bridge, and she often found him looking over the narrows during sunrise, as if it was a marvel, a feat of engineering he was part of. She wondered what he was thinking, and much wanted to ask him, but some-how felt it was his own personal secret.

When she was a teenager, her mother had told her that a close friend of his, a classmate, an engineer, had met his death, and ever since, her father had never been himself. "When you were born," she said. "It was the happiest moment of our lives. It was as if you father was reborn."

Nancy runs upstairs to her mother's room and asks her whether she has mentioned Ali's religion to her father. "I talked it over with him. I stressed he was half-Christian. He was a bit upset. I took care of it."

"Thanks, Mum," says Nancy and hugs her.

Out to impress, Ali wears a brand-new-from-Barney's dap-per double-breasted blue Pierre Cardin suit for the Thanksgiving dinner. He immediately takes to Nancy's spacious two-storied Victorian with its spectacular view of the Narrows. Her father's brothers, both retired firefighters, their wives, and his half-sister are there. They are all respectful towards Ali, perhaps because he is a doctor, but conversation is awkward. They keep staring at him. Is it because he is overdressed? He wonders. Finally, Ali points to the view of the bridge and asks Sean, Nancy's father, what it was like building the Verrazano. "Awesome," he says, as his face lights up, and he relates in some detail the history of the Verrazano Bridge.

The men drink beer or Sean's special martinis and watch a football game in the living room. Ali can hear the women chatting aloud in the kitchen. Ali, Nalini and Nancy are seated on the living room couch. Ali and Nalini talk about chemotherapy in terminal cancer. They discuss what constitutes an honorable death while Nancy listens.

During commercials, the men make simple talk of the Indian summer they are having, and comment on the downs and yardage and the tackles.

Ali can see that the family views Sean with respect and deference. He is the educated one among them, the engineer who has done well. He takes pride in his home on the hill, and they comment on the location of the house and the views, which they must have done to no end.

Nancy's aunt, Rose, bursts out of the kitchen a couple of times, wanting it seems, to strike a conversation with Ali, but Nancy pulls him away to show the house, and the garden. He gets the impression that Nancy is protecting him from her aunt. Finally, when Nancy goes to the bar in the basement to fetch a beer for one of her uncles, Rose approaches clad in fiery red slacks and a loose white blouse.

"Heart Doc? Right? I didn't get your name, dear."

"Ali."

"Dr. Ali?"

"Ma'am, you can drop the doctor bit."

Nancy comes rushing with the beer and addresses her aunt: "Aunt Rose, did I tell you that Ali is one of the most prominent heart transplant doctors in New York?

"Yes, Pat told me. Hmmm—what name is that? Ali! You are not Catholic now, are you?"

"No ma'am, I'm Muslim."

"He is half-Christian, half-Muslim," says Nancy

Rose's face tenses, her light eyes squint, and her mouth opens wide. "I'd better go to the kitchen and help your Mum," she says to Nancy, and leaves. Nancy shows Ali her room, going over the photographs, the class of 1984 at Notre Dame Academy, and her basketball trophies. And then, dramatically she opens the window curtain in her room to the spectacular view of the Verrazano Bridge over the Narrows. She points to the autumn leaves of yellow, magenta, and green bouncing in the wind. Soon thereafter, the bridge lights up like a glittering emerald necklace connecting Staten Island to Brooklyn. He can see why Nancy is attached to the place.

They venture into the garden and sit by the fishpond, until the autumn wind, fast and crisp, and a sudden chill, send them in.

At the dinner table, talk centers around the food: the virtues of white versus dark turkey meat, stuffing, cranberry sauce, beans, turnips, sweet potatoes, pecan and apple pies. Ali considers interjecting politics but desists; in his home politics is always on the menu no matter what the occasion.

When Aunt Rose is about to pour some champagne, Ali cups the flute with his hand and instead asks for some water. He had decided that he would abstain from alcohol, fearing worsening of the reflux.

"Muslum's don't drink, right?" Rose asks, trying to lift her short neck, her head sitting directly on her shoulders. The dinner table is suddenly overtaken with a strange silence, as if his response is a matter of the utmost importance, as if, somehow, he would dignify it with a flourish of an answer or slaughter it with a resounding no. Ali sees Sean's hands shake, and the next moment inadvertently, or perhaps purposefully, Nancy smacks her champagne flute, spilling its contents on the table. Ali can see a fiery flush on Nancy's face.

Pat's hand moves to her lap, holding her at the table.

Rose's light eyes dash around the table from Ali to Nancy to Sean, to Pat, and back to the food on the table like those of a hungry mouse.

"Dad, what's this about the tremor? Maybe you should talk it out with Ali." Says Nancy, loudly to change the subject?

"You're right. Observing Muslims don't drink," Ali responds with a smirk. Sean and Pat keep a dignified silence as if waiting for the storm to blow away.

"So, you are an observing Muslum, Dr. Ali?" mouths Rose, in a shrill voice.

"Aunt Rose, Ali is half-Christian," says Nancy.

"Today, I don't quite feel like a drink," says Ali.

"Aunt Rose, will you cut it out!" says Nancy.

"That's enough," says Sean, looking at Rose and Nancy.

"Let's raise a toast: to health and happiness," interjects Sean.

"And bon appetite," adds Nalini.

Pat promptly gets up and thanks the Lord, and they all say: "Amen".

After dinner, Nancy takes Ali to her room. "I'm sorry Ali," she says. "My aunt is opinionated, and a bit cucu."

"I thought Aunt Rose's eyes were going to fly out of her head when she came to know I was Muslim," he says. "By the way, do your parents mind I'm Muslim?" In his own mind, his religion didn't even arise when he had dinner with Anna and her mother and her friends.

"My mother is very liberal in her views," says Nancy. "I'm not sure about my father. Perhaps he will have a chat with me tonight. He is a man of few words. By the way, it would be nice if you speak to my dad about the tremor."

"I think he has the beginnings of Parkinson's. I can refer him to a Neurologist at the Medical Center."

That evening, after the guests leave, Sean comes into Nancy's room and sits on the bed.

"Honey, I was very impressed with Ali, but I'm concerned by the religious and cultural differences," he says.

"I love him, Dad," she says. "He has asked me to marry him. Besides, he is half-Christian after all. His mother is Catholic, and Ali went to Church in his youth." She plants a quick kiss on his cheek as if to reward him for his understanding, or better still, to silence him, for she is uncertain of what is actually going on in his mind.

"He thinks I have the beginnings of Parkinson's," he says. "He gave me the name of a neurologist at the Medical Center."

As he turns to leave, she notices a concerned look on his face: the eyes are glazed, his back is hunched, his walk a shuffle. Suddenly she sees a bent, wasting old man. She runs to him and hugs him.

"I'll be okay, Dad," she whispers.

CHAPTER 21
The Omen

In the hospital, Anna, with Helen, Tom, Rick and Jay R, heart-mates, walk ritually up and down the Cardiac Center and into the lounge with their tall IV poles from which dangles a bag with the drug Primacor. It keeps their hearts running like some high-grade gasoline. Because of the deteriorating condition of their hearts, they are admitted to the Heart Center to receive intravenous medications continuously and upgraded to Category I for heart transplantation. Like Anna, they are young and they are bonded by their disease if nothing else. Like prisoners in a cell.

One day, a ten-year-old boy, visiting his father recovering from a heart attack, points to them and says aloud: "Dad, look at the pole people." And the name "pole people" sticks like that of some dwindling Peruvian-Amazon tribe. Anna often stays by herself, but on some nights, they group together for a hand of Rummy or Blackjack.

That night, Anna shuffles the two packs of cards and deals to Helen, Tom, Rick. and Jay R. The tall poles with hanging fluid bags stand around them, to the right, to the left, like sentries on guard. The Blackjack table is Helen's bed. She is seated at the head end of the bed, Anna at the foot, and Jay R and Tom on chairs.

"I'm out," says Helen.

"Me too," says Tom.

"I'm in," says Anna.

"Deal," says Rick.

"Blackjack," says Jay R, and scoops up the wins. "I was a rappin' Man, and a damn good one—the coke, crystal, Mexican X—kept me going. Ten grams of my heart muscle just died. I'm born again, man...Jesus, man...I knows it man...I have Jesus, right here, in my heart. It's been two whole years I'm off the stuff! I is going to school, Man, law school someday." He gets off the chair.

"Hey you child," he sings pointing to Anna. *'You look so good.*

Yeah, you look all right. Hey girl, hear me
Callin' your name. Baby, the way you look
Say you drive me insane. Oh you're lookin' so good..."
They all clap. "Thanks," says Anna. "You sing great!"

"Sister, when you get a new heart, you go back dancin.'"

"You go back rappin' friend!" says Tom. They high-five.

"Let me tell you, man...we spend a cool five grand at one party doing Blow...and the chicks...I was flying high those days," says Tom. "Five hundred grand—that was my bonus... bought me a Porsche and pied-a-terre in the Hampton's—all gone down the drain, man...this damn heart...just gave way—it came out of the blue. Wham! I was running in Central Park. I just couldn't catch my breath. Dr. Ali tells me its cardiomyopathy—the viral type."

"Like me," says Anna.

"You'll get a new one," says Helen. "They'll take you back on Wall Street, and you'll make your millions. Look at me—I'm a straight girl, a mother. No alcohol, no cigarettes, no drugs, good family, high school grad. "*Postpartum cardiomyopathy,*" they said, after the first baby. I recovered completely. My doctor in Long Island said I could have another, and here I am. If only I had aborted. How could I? I'm a devout catholic."

"We'll all get a new one," says Tom.

"Let's hope so," says Anna.

They anxiously await a heart in their own single bedded rooms that each convert into a homeroom with TVs, VCRs, sound system, postcards and personal photographs. On Sundays, they attend services in the hospital Chapel. In the beginning, Anna accompanies them and tries to pray, but never fully engaged; later on, she intently observes the services, reciting the words, looking for something to hang on to, to be struck by a revelation, to be born again so to speak, but it never happens. When she grew up in Communist Russia, God was no part of her world—the Communist State had been her God, had provided all, and now that world crumbled into the rubble. The faith, the belief and trust of her fellow patients in God, particularly Jay R, takes her by surprise. And her own lack of faith leaves her confused, empty, and longing for a God. She asks of herself: what has she done to deserve this? If there is a God, where is he?

In her room, she listens to Tchaikovsky and Chopin, reads poetry and books she never had time for in the ballet Academy in Leningrad. Akhmatova, Pushkin, and Dostoyevsky are her favorites. She is deep into *The Brothers Karamazov*, after which she contemplates reading the *Gulag Archipelago*, thinking that perhaps Solzhenitsyn will help her understand her mother's bitterness towards the ex-Soviet Union.

Time passes, and nothing seems to change. The days, the months, slip away—three tedious months with Christmas, New

Year, her birthday, her daughter's birthday, come and go—the interminable tedium of one uneventful pointless day superimposes on another, and still Anna waits for a heart. To make the priority list the transplant candidates remain hospitalized to receive their drugs.

Then with no warning, Dr. Ali appears one day, and tells them they can all go home. The policy is abruptly changed, as often happens in the health care industry; new guidelines are drawn because of soaring hospital costs, and they are all allowed to go home. They cry and hug each other and they all hug Dr. Ali. Anna calls her mother in Russia to tell her that she is going home. She says goodbye to the other patients.

As Anna is packing her bag, all excited to go home, she suddenly feels dizzy. She immediately lies down on the bed when a blast rips through her chest. She screams. A nurse comes running to her.

"Page Dr. Grimes and Dr. Ali," she yells. "Anna's defibrillator has gone off."

"I am feeling dizzy again," says Anna, as her eyes roll in their sockets, and she begins gasping for breath, as if the little she can inhale is nowhere enough. She barely sees the nurse looking at the monitor—her heart is erratic; and then comes another searing shock and another, and at each shock her slender body bounces up from the bed.

Anna loses consciousness. Anna stops breathing.

The nurse calls Code 7000. A cardiac arrest is in progress. Rick paces the floor. "Jesus, Jesus, don't let her go!"

Anna sees herself detaching, pulling away, deserting her body, staring at her lifeless carcass from a distance as she watches the doctors and nurses surrounding her, ceaselessly working, pumping her fragile chest, and shocking her repeatedly. She hears a doctor order the nurse: "Go on, shock her again, up the current to 360 Joules."

The internal defibrillator worked initially, but now she needs external electric shocks to bring her out of the rhythm of death that chases her incessantly. She feels no pain, welcoming the departure, the exit, as she floats away into a tunnel losing sight of her body, the Code that is in progress, until all of a sudden, she is at the entrance of a realm of scintillating lights faceted like emeralds, rubies, and diamonds, like in the ballet *Jewels*, in which she had once danced. She turns to look back one last time, when she sees a hand of a child, stretching for hers, pulling her back forcefully into the tunnel. She hears a soft voice, Katya's, in the distance, calling, "Mama, Mama," and Anna flies to her. It is then that she hears faint voices from afar, Dr. Ali saying: "There is an ECG complex; I feel a pulse—she is coming back." Slowly her heart starts beating again—she is sucked back into her body—to life.

She is immediately transferred to the Coronary Care Unit and placed on a host of intravenous medications. When the storm subsides, and she realizes that she had had several cardiac arrests and survived, she relates to Dr. Ali, Jay R, and the nurses what she has seen and felt.

They tell her it was a "near-death-experience."

"Jesus, Lord Jesus, Alleluia!" says Jay R, repeatedly.

"Yes, Anna, some say they see tunnels, bright lights, angels, heavens and the like," says Ali. "I don't know what it all means. Perhaps it is all a dream. Perhaps it's your will to live for your daughter."

"It was so real," says Anna. "Katya is my angel. She brought me back to life."

"Jesus, Lord Jesus, Alleluia!" says Jay R, repeatedly. "This is it, Anna—the omen, the call to Jesus." You were at Heaven's gate. You've got to embrace him child."

The cardiac arrest further delays Anna's discharge from the hospital. She is alone now. The others have left. Her implantable defibrillator is upgraded to a high-energy shock device and she has to undergo surgery. Her *near-death-experience* raises many questions in her mind she has never contemplated upon. She wonders whether life has a bigger meaning: a purposefulness, a destiny yet to be fulfilled, and whether there is another life beyond the world she lives in. Rick's words: "The omen, the call to Jesus," keeps repeating in her mind.

Dr. Grimes and Ali's words that the defibrillator would protect her until she gets a new heart were so true. She had gone into the rapid, irregular rhythm the doctors called ventricular fibrillation as if she had been sucked into a death twister. The defibrillator had recognized the deadly rhythm and shocked her instantaneously not once but five times. And yet, she isn't convinced that that is all there is to it. It was as if she were forever dying and forever kept reviving. Did it all confirm a purpose for her to go on living? Was she challenging fate, or reclaiming it? Or was it modern medical technology at work? Was she simply lucky to be there at the right time, the right moment? These questions keep repeating in her mind. The dedication and commitment of the doctors, particularly Ali and Grimes, overwhelm her. Ali comes by, sits by her side, holds her hand, expresses his concerns and prods her on. It is during these moments that she feels a special love for him, as if he were some savior, her guardian angel sent to protect her, to pump her arteries with life. He was there during the Code, and perhaps without his presence, his command of the Code, ordering medications, telling the residents what to do, how to proceed, she wouldn't have made it. She remembers the dinner at the Café des Artistes, when he told her that she had to believe in God, and that we all need something greater than ourselves to lean on. The memory of the first time they nearly made love in her apartment flashes back like a dove flying by—she held onto it in her failing heart like a sacrament. She wishes she had made love to him. Perhaps the opportunity will surface again. Who knows?

"What are you thinking?" he asks. She shakes her head and looks away from him. She feels relieved to be physically detached, and even more relieved that they have stayed emotionally close to each other, loving each other in many different ways—her love for him has kept growing.

"Hold me tight," she says.

He hesitates for a moment, and then pulls the curtain to enclose them in a cocoon and embraces her. She offers her lips, and he kisses them.

The recurrent near-death experience changes Anna profoundly. It fills her with inner peace she had never known before. She begins reading the scriptures and through them, she begins searching for explanations. She makes an effort to kneel and prostrate herself in prayer. When she prays, she feels relieved, knowing that there is a Being watching over her, that there is another life waiting for her. The image of Christ, slowly, but surely, like a beacon, begins taking shape in her mind.

She is thankful for the attention and care she received, and promises that, if she were ever to dance again, she would perform for the doctors and nursing staff.

After her discharge, Anna begins attending the Russian Orthodox Church, where she is taught the Nicene Creed, the liturgy, and sacraments. Dostoyevsky', *The Brothers Karamazov*, and her out-of-body experience has a profound effect on her, as she turns towards Christ. She is taken up with the long discourse of the Elder Zosima, in the book: that we all share the common responsibility for the ills of the world and must share in the common suffering. Like Dmitry Karamazov, an army officer in Dostoyevsky's novel who came to repent for the guilt of social privilege, Anna repents for the guilt of her own ego, the vanity at the greatness of her dancing talents, and her beauty. Like in Dmitry's dream, when he finds himself in a poor peasant's hut, the helpless mother beside her starving baby, and he wakes up, "his face radiant with joy." Similarly, Anna wakes up from a dream where her suffering brings release in the kingdom of Christ—the kingdom of scintillating lights. She begins living with a new determination, a newfound strength to survive. She feels that she has a destiny, one preordained by God. She doesn't know what that destiny is all about, knowing only that when the time comes, she will face it with God given courage and joy. Her affair with Ali, the physical break up, the emotional attachment—she believes, is also predestined.

She invites Ali for the ceremony of baptism, but he cannot attend. He is lecturing out-of-town. On the day of her Baptism, Anna and her daughter dress in white gowns and stand in the Church, just inside, in the corridor. The Rector, a tall bearded priest in his canonicals, comes out and asks: "Who art thou?" And Anna, and then Katya, reply in turns: "I am one who desires to know the true God, and seek salvation."

They are led and immersed in a large circular wooden font draped in white, as the worshippers sing Baptismal hymns. Anna is ecstatic after the ceremony, and a radiant glow reflects on her face from the candlelight as if she is deified. For her, a new life is about to begin. It is as if she has come into a new orbit, the sphere of a good and merciful God.

CHAPTER 22

The Saudi Arabian Princess

At eleven in the morning when Ali is in the catheterization laboratory performing heart biopsies, he is paged. "Dr. Ali, its Dr. Bob's office—he wants to see you immediately," says Noreen, the Cath Lab nurse.

"I'll be there as soon as I finish here." Ali sighs. He is sure Dr. Bob wants to address the Cardiospeed study; he hadn't recruited any patient since they last spoke. Ali expects fireworks.

An hour later, Ali takes a seat in Dr. Bob office. Dr. Bob relates that he has a Saudi Arabian Princess who needs a fast-track transplant evaluation and a fast-track heart transplant. He says it at a rapid pace, giving Ali little time to digest his words.

"I'll move quickly with the evaluation," Ali says. "But she'll have to be listed, categorized, and wait her turn."

"How long will that take?" Dr. Bob shakes his head.

"Months, possibly a year, depending on severity of heart failure, her blood type, and obviously, the availability of donor hearts. I will see her this week or the next, however."

Dr. Bob wheels around in his pacing and faces Ali head-on. "She is a Princess from Saudi Arabia!"

"She can always stay at the Waldorf Astoria and wait, can't she?" says Ali, calmly.

"Well, I want you to do the evaluation immediately, and then we'll talk." Dr. Bob's face is red, his eyes hard.

As he leaves the office, Ali notices a tall, young, shorthaired brunette in a white starched coat reading a journal in the waiting room.

"Dr. Ali," says Linda. "This is Dr. Claudette Pèpin from Paris. She has just joined Dr. Bob's research staff. Meet Dr. Ali, our Head of the Transplant Program."

"Welcome to New York. It's a great city. Not exactly Paris, but I'm sure you'll enjoy it."

"Thank you, merci, merci," says Dr. Pèpin. "I'm sure our paths will cross again."

In the elevator, Ali receives a page from Dr. Blair—Dr. Bob's mouthpiece who thanks him for seeing Mr. Lieberman, and that his opinion was very useful. "We're lucky to have someone with your expertise on hand." Ali hears him draw a deep breath. Then he goes about repeating what Dr. Bob has just told him about the Saudi Arabian Princess, Fatima.

"Her father is a big donor and the department could go a long way with the funds, what with the budget cuts, etcetera," he says.

"Dr. Bob already spoke to me about it. I'll see what I can do," says Ali.

One week later, Ali sees the Saudi Arabian Princess. As he enters the examining room, he finds her surrounded by middle-aged women in black *burqas*.

"Please, just one companion. The others must wait outside."

Ali is firm. After much discussion, three of the women leave like a flock of crows.

The Princess is of medium height and draped in black except for a pink scarf with sparkles of metal thread work. He notices the light brown complexion of the skin on her cheeks;. Her black cloudy eyes have a sad gaze, a-dog-in-the knell-gaze of submission and fear. When Ali's female assistant asks her to undress, she and her chaperone just stare at the assistant and shake their heads. She speaks in whispers and is shy when he asks details of her medical history. He examines her with her clothes on in the presence of the bulky female chaperone who keeps on shifting her position as Ali shifts his, to see what he is up to with his hands and his stethoscope. He finds the Princes to be stable on her current medications.

After the examination, her father, dressed in a suit with an Arab headdress, tells Ali that he wants his daughter to get a heart as soon as possible. Ali tells him that he needs to admit her for evaluation and a heart catheterization.

"Your daughter is in *well compensated heart failure,*" says Ali. "There is a waiting list of sicker patients. She might have to wait a year or more before she gets a heart."

"A year?" says the Prince. "Dr. Bob said she would get priority. Besides, I'm ready to pay for the heart."

"It doesn't work that way, but, I'll do my best," says Ali, not to further belabor the discussion.

Princes Fatima is finally worked up and listed in the Heart Transplant Program; however, her O blood type could make the wait longer, and there are many others like Anna waiting before her. Not for the first time, Ali wishes that there were more hearts and fewer patients needing them. But even more, he wishes that Dr. Bob would stop playing favorites for the sake of donations and give all patients the same chance to survive.

When Ali calls Dr. Bob, he is informed that he has left on a short holiday. Ali emails him his findings on Princess Fatima, and the future course of action, well aware that he's not going to take it well. Ali promises to discuss her case personally after he returns from his holiday.

PART

III

2001

People change and forget to tell each other.
—Lillian Hellman

CHAPTER 23

Nancy's Surprise

On a Friday, a month or so later, when Ali is on his way home from a five day meeting in Dallas, his cell phone rings as he waits for a cab at La Guardia airport.

"Hi honey, I have something important to discuss," says Nancy. "If you don't mind, can I come over? It's very important."

"Well sure," he says, sensing urgency in her voice. "Should I pick up some food on the way home?"

"Can we go for Italian?"

An hour later, she bursts into the apartment and rushes into his arms. There is a bottle of Moet in her hand that almost falls to the floor. She happily bounces around and seems to want to prolong the telling. He waits expectantly. She goes to the kitchen and uncorks the champagne.

"Nancy, I cannot take the suspense any longer," he says, as she comes back to the living room with two glasses of the bubbly.

"You made a killing on a stock? A promotion?" he asks, as he takes a sip of the champagne.

"I'm pregnant!" she blurts out.

Stunned, he freezes as if hit on the head with a bat. After he quickly regains his composure, he embraces and kisses her. He finds himself thrilled, perhaps not as much as she—a huge relief given Nancy's age.

"Aren't you happy?" she asks.

"Oh yes, oh yes," he says, his expression rather subdued and thoughtful.

"We have to marry soon," she says and gulps down the champagne. And, to crowd up the silent space, she laughs, a luminous hearty laugh. Typical Nancy, he thinks, always happy, no matter how difficult the terrain.

"No more champagne, Nancy. You're pregnant, no alcohol" he says.

"Just this one time. No more," she says.

"But how will your parents react?" he asks, with a concerned look.

"My mother had her difficulties with pregnancy, and she's been worried for me. I'm sure she'll be happy. And one more thing; promise you won't get upset."

"I promise."

"I've been on a small dose of Paxil on and off. It has given me an even keel. Should I stop the drug? Could it have effects on the baby?"

"I don't know Nancy. I think I saw you pop in a pill a couple of times. Why didn't you tell me about the Paxil?

"Sorry Ali. I should have told you. I didn't think it was a big deal since I'm on a small dose, and that too, on and off—when I feel stressed out."

"Why are you on Paxil?"

"A mild case of bipolar disorder: the highs and lows. I like the high's but not the lows."

"I think you should talk to your Ob/Gyn doctor,"

"I'll give him a call."

After Nancy leaves for Staten Island to inform her mother, Ali lies on his bed contemplating on Nancy's pregnancy. He didn't want it to happen this way. He wanted a child, but after marriage. He wanted to marry Nancy but preferred to wait another year. His situation in the hospital, particularly his relationship with Dr. Bob is deteriorating. They have to jump into marriage without discussing important issues like cultural and religious differences that could come in the way of their married life, and now the mild bipolar disorder to top it all.

Since his complicated personal and professional relationships, he began attending the mosque once in a while on Fridays; and now, he will soon have to face the responsibility of bringing up a child. What will the child be brought up as: A Christian or a Muslim? There are other important issues to resolve urgently: the religious marriage ceremony and the reception. Will his father demand Nancy's conversion to the Islam? He pops a sleeping pill and turns off the light.

On her way to Staten Island, Nancy realizes that there is no time to look for a wedding hall; they have to hurry up with the wedding. She doesn't want to look pregnant on her wedding day.

To her pleasant surprise, her mother accepts her pregnancy without much ado, and promises as usual to speak with her father. They spent half the night talking, and frantically making preparations.

Ultimately, Ali's father insists that the wedding ceremony be held in his home in Long Island; however, Nancy wants it in her home in Staten Island, what with the beautiful lawn on the hill, the azaleas, the rhododendrons and roses soon to be in full bloom, and the spectacular view of the Narrows. Finally, over the next few days, after much back and forth discussion between Ali and Nancy and their respective parents, Pat seeks the bishop's dispensation and her friend Father DiPietro agrees to marry them, following which there will be a Muslim wedding ceremony, the Nikah. Ali's father arranges for the young Imam Zaman of the new spacious mosque for which he has contributed generously to perform the ceremony. Nancy's parents welcome the idea, overtaken by the exotic nature of Islamic wedding rituals. Besides, this marriage is no mésalliance. The invitations are sent out.

When Anna reads the invitation, she feels a sudden chill, a heavy feeling in her stomach. She keeps reading it again and again, and it finally sinks into her. She slumps onto the couch, consumed by a kind of a loss, of un-possessiveness. Her eyes well up in tears as she stares into oblivion. There is no anger, no tantrum, no beraking of china. She takes a Xanax and falls asleep.

When she wakes up, she wonders why Ali never mentioned that he was dating. Was it guilt? Or was this an arrangement by his parents. She remembers him mentioning that it is quite common for arranged marriages in the Islamic culture. But an arranged marriage would be to a Muslim girl not an American Catholic. Anyway, she is his patient—she has no future with him. He had to move on with his life.

She brings him a gift: a tall, elegant Lladro porcelain ballerina that she takes to his academic office. She wants to tell him that it is something for him to remember her, and that, no matter what, she still loves him, but her precarious emotional state dumbfounds her.

"You didn't have to do this," he says, as he un-wraps the gift. He kisses her. She begins to cry.

"I will not abandon you," he says, stroking her back. When the sobs stop, he wipes her eyes with his handkerchief.

"Are you coming for the wedding?" he asks. "I can ask Dr. Denzel to pick you up, or I can send you a car."

"I'm not sure. I'll let you know," she says, in a whisper.

On her way out, she sees Nancy's picture on his desk. She feels a sudden crushing pang in her chest. There she is—beautiful yes, but nowhere compared to her before her illness. When she gets home, she keeps herself busy preparing for Katya's departure to Russia for the coming summer.

CHAPTER 24
The Khutbah-tun-Nikah

Ali, dressed in a white, gold threaded silk sherwani with princely headgear gallops down Grymes Hill on a white horse, escorted by Dr. Grimes, the best man, also dressed in sherwani. They are accompanied by a coterie of musicians and the beating of drums. The guests are captivated by Ali's handsomeness and princely appearance as they line up the downhill road and shower him with rose petals, and loud bursts of firecrackers, as he smilingly glides down from the horse. Pat welcomes Ali to the family and Ali's mother, Lila, ushers him into the wedding canopy laid out on the front yard of Nancy's home overlooking the Verrazano Narrows. He sits on silk cushions and Kashmiri rugs spread out on the ground under a tent.

Nancy arrives in a gold embroidered palanquin carried by Ali's cousins from England and Washington, dressed in multicolored kurtas and elegant headgear. She wears a beige-turquoise georgette choli dress with a gold-embroidered dupatta, a long headscarf, and jewelry set consisting of a necklace of gold with rubies and diamonds, a pair of bell earrings, and a head ornament that rolls down her forehead. She is ushered by the bridesmaids, among them her friend Nalini, and takes her seat by Ali's side. They look like an Oriental Prince and Princesses, a royal blend of East and West. A large mirror is placed skirting their lap. They are surrounded by the glow of candlelight.

Nancy's family and the seated guests observe all this with utter fascination, except for Nancy's aunt Rose, who grunts and questions the other family members what they think of the "pagan rituals" soon to be under way. Several doctors and nurses from the medical center, including Dr. Denzel and his wife Cindy, as well as Carmensita with her husband Ramon, and Linda Rivera are there. Dr. Bob, who had insisted in making a speech, calls in sick at the last moment.

The Khutbah-tun-Nikah begins with the praise of Allah: "There is none worthy of worship except Allah and Muhammad is His servant and messenger," the *Maulvi* declares. He continues reciting Qur'anic verses, and the Arabic text that comprises the traditional sermon during the *Nikah*. In the middle of the sermon, Nancy feels as if everything is closing in on her—she begins breathing rapidly overtaken by a sudden panic. She feels as if she is in a strange land, among strange people, the Maulvi and Ali's many cousins she had not met before. She uncovers her face, although she is not supposed to do so before the ceremony is over, and lifts her bowed head, controlling her breathing, and the anxiety slowly dissipates.

She had had doubts about marrying Ali from the start: the cultural differences between them had held her back; besides, he seemed elusive and distant at times, someone she couldn't fathom, and yet she was physically attracted to him and she loved him. Physical attraction, love, and smarts—these attributes are important to her, and drown all; the others like culture and religion don't seem to matter—they are evanescent like the fog the sun will burn out. When she became pregnant, whatever doubts she had, had dissipated, as often they must in pre-marital pregnancies. She had continued half-a-dose of the Paxil, and so far so good. Although, the wedding is a prolonged insurmountable high, she didn't want to risk it.

She looks into the mirror in her lap, and there in the mirror, she sees Ali's handsome face, the face of her husband, and it reassures her. She looks at her mother and father. Her family is with her—they will always be there for her. Things will work out. She notices Ali looking and smiling when he sees her face in the mirror on her lap. She is his Queen—his wife-to-be.

They sign the revocable marriage contract, witnessed by Dr. Grimes and Dr. Nalini, after which Ali hands Nancy a gilded purse containing money and jewelry. The Mahr—the marriage-gift.

A new planet has swung into her sphere. She smiles—a smile of reassurance.

Pat and Lila shed tears of joy; Nancy's father has glazed teary eyes, while Aunt Rose stomps away brashly into the house.

"I don't know why my brother went along with this Muslum ceremony," she utters to her eldest brother, the firefighter, who motions her to keep quiet.

After the ceremony is over, Nancy rushes into the house to her room and changes into a champagne colored gown that is flattering to her complexion; the open neckline accentuates her cleavage and showcases the sapphire necklace gifted to her by her mother-in-law that heightens her dark blue eyes. She carries a cascading bouquet of rubrum lilies, open roses, tea roses, irises, and ivory colored ribbons. She is a full-bodied, sparkling, gorgeous bride. Soon, the embracing, the kissing, the speeches, the dancing, and the eating begin, and a new joyous reality takes over.

CHAPTER 25
Marriage Blues

Nancy and Ali move into a spacious two-and-a-half bedroom condominium on Seventy-six and Second Avenue. Ali wants something more modest, but he ends up giving in to Nancy. They pay over a million for the space, the sunlight, and a slit-view of the East River.

Nancy is busy nesting: hanging her photography on the pastel colored walls in the corridors, an abstract blue and white painting over the new Ethan Allen beige leather sofa, and, on the bedroom walls three black and white nudes she finds in a Village antique store.

The preparation for the arrival of the baby begins in earnest. But Nancy's happiness is smudged with anxiety.

"Trust me, you should have faith in God," Ali proclaims. The amniocentesis finally allays her fears.

They spent whatever is left of their evenings together, making small talk, and taking walks, jogs, and bike rides in Central Park when he gets home early, which is not often. On some weekends they go to her home on the hill on Staten Island. That's what she calls it: "my home on the hill," as if it belongs to her, as if it were there, they should be living rather than in Manhattan.

Bush's election as President by the State of Florida unsettles Ali who sees dark clouds encroaching on the horizon. But they hope that the stock market will continue to soar; Greenspan—the Maestro—is still around, and will easily swing his baton and the economy will follow despite the "irrational exuberance" of the market. But the bubble bursts, and Wall Street doesn't re-bound—the stocks, the highflyers, and the Internet start-ups continue to tank. Nancy gets out of some of the biotechnology stocks at the right moment, and manages to save some, but not all of her investments. Most of her clients are still aboard the Titanic.

"The Supreme Court shouldn't have interfered," says Ali, on a Sunday morning at breakfast, after reading *The New York Times*. "Read this article, Nancy. There should have been a recount." And he continues tauntingly, "America shouldn't preach about the electoral process to other countries. They do a better job in India with hand counting. Talk about Pakistan, this was a certified coup d'etat."

"If you don't like it in America, then leave," says Nancy, curtly. "You'll have to go by yourself, and maybe you take with you that Russian tart who keeps on calling you all the time."

"There you go again..." He gets off the sofa and hugs her. "I'm only critical of the process, not the country. I'm surprised Wall Street hasn't reacted positively to Bush's election. Where's the silver lining? And what's this about the Russian tart. She's a ballerina; not a Russian tart. Besides, she's my patient, a very sick patient, awaiting a heart transplant. That's all."

They discuss the election: Bush, Al Gore, the Clinton's, and Middle-East peace talks, but they don't resolve their differences.

Ali is sensitive to Nancy's patriotism, and her resistance to criticism of the country, but they end their discussions amicably and without hard feelings. But her attitude towards Anna remains. Locked in!

Within three months of their marriage, their financial expectations collapse. Now Nancy cannot count on her handsome bonuses, and Ali has to give up on a raise; if anything, he and many of his colleagues see their salaries cut again by another fifteen percent.

Several months before, the arriviste Dr. Bob had advised them to apply for grants to study alternate medicine and the effects of herbals on heart function. "It could be an additional source to supplement your income," he had advised. Ali was taken aback at Dr. Bob's pronouncements. After all, he was no ayurvedic doctor. All this interest was initiated by Carmensita's involvement in herbal medicine, which had aroused Dr. Bob's curiosity and a certain degree of excitement. It was as if he were searching for something new, a new scientific adventure to embark on. He had given ayurvedic medicine in India, and acupuncture for general anesthesia in China, as prime examples. "There's got to be some hidden potential there," Dr. Bob had maintained. He obviously smelled millions in grants. But more recently, Dr. Bob's enthusiasm for the project seemed to be waning. He had not even raised the issue on the monthly departmental newsletter.

"I can understand his interest in Carmensita, but why all the interest in herbals?" asks Nancy.

"He no longer talks about it," ponders Ali, "and that means something's amiss."

After her first trimester, their life changes radically. Nancy loses interest in restaurants, the theatre, and friends. She attributes this to her pregnancy. She is slowly sinking into depression, and now she cannot get out of it. She sometimes cooks, but she isn't into cooking, and soon she senses that Ali doesn't like her bland food. He is entirely into Indo-Pakistani curries, which she cannot now tolerate, and often they end up ordering out; she, sushi or pasta; he, biryani and an assortment of beef curry, mutton curry, lamb curry and kabobs. She loves a glass of wine and sometimes a beer for dinner, and regrets that her pregnancy forbids it. She is somewhat incapacitated with morning sickness that has continued well beyond the first three months. She cannot tolerate even the smell of the foods Ali relishes. Often they end up eating separately. The morning sickness further sours her mood, and recently her obstetrician notices a slight rise in blood pressure. Ali often finds her testy when he comes late in the evenings from work.

When Anna calls Ali with her usual complains of shortness of breath or the extra beats, she and Ali often go on talking animatedly about how she found God, and how Ali was partly instrumental in it. Nancy is flustered not knowing what to make of these intimate conversations.

Ali wonders whether Nancy's depression has anything to do with the discontinuation of the Paxil. He doesn't want her to be medicated, and at the same time he is fearful of the outcome of Nancy's depression on her and the baby. He takes to prayer, and often reads the Qu'ran out loud. After the wedding, he had connected with the younger, more seasoned Imam who runs a large brand new mosque in the city. He makes it a point whenever possible which is not often however, to attend the mosque on Friday afternoons. In their conversation, he expresses the plight of Muslims around the world, and in particular the Middle-East. His pace of religious transformation almost unnoticeable in the beginning accelerates like Voyager heading into outer space. He grows a beard, and talks of not trimming; even his mother affirms that he looks wild and unkempt. It doesn't end there. On weekends he walks around in Punjabi pajamas, a shirt and a vest. There are also the *salaat* alerts on his mobile. He begins praying at odd places: in the early morning hours in the corridor, and when Nancy asks him why the corridor, he counters by saying he has to pray five times a day facing Mecca, and the corridor for sure faces east.

"Bullshit," she says aloud, "you just didn't want me to see you pray so many times."

"Five times a day—that's all. It looks a lot to you because you hardly ever pray. All that I have seen you do is the sign of the cross when you go to sleep. The *salaat* alert is great. One of my brothers informed me about it."

"I didn't know you had a brother?"

"I mean a Muslim brother."

"Jesus, Ali! What's gotten into you?"

"And what's gotten into you?'

"I'm depressed and anxious. Don't you see it?"

She remembers the first time while they were dating when she saw Ali pray in his apartment in the morning before breakfast. He had knelt on a Pakistani prayer rug, placed his hands one on top of the other on his chest, and assertively uttered strange sounding words with eyes closed.

She had felt a strange power emanate from him, perhaps because she loved him or it was a novelty to see him prostate on the prayer rug uttering indiscernible incantations. It made her blood pound and her heart race as he knelt on the prayer rug, his hands on his knees, his head bowed, and when he had gently stood up, and rolled up the rug and safely placed it in the closet she had embraced him and cried. She regrets the derogatory word—*bullshit*—she just uttered. At the same time, she wonders whether he was entirely honest about his religious beliefs before their marriage.

"I'm sorry Ali, I'm terribly sorry," she says. He doesn't respond and walks away.

Soon thereafter, the alcoholic beverages: the wine, the whisky and the beer disappear. She notices it when her parents come on a visit, and her father asks for a whisky. When she asks him what he has done and why with the alcohol, he tells her he poured it down the drain, and that it is not a good idea to have alcohol in a Muslim household.

"But ours is not a Muslim household," she curtly counters. She has an urge to do something dramatic: to break the china, to kick the door, to trash the furniture, to hit him, to kill herself, but she bites her lip, kicks the door and holds on tight to the chair.

Ali has also questioned the figures of St. Patrick, St. Anthony, Saint Jude, and the Virgin Mary that her mother piled up on their dresser, and calls it "paganism."

The Qur'an remains in its place in its cloth case on the mantle in the living room.

One evening when she gets home after a tiring day, she finds that all her nudes have vanished from the bedroom walls and are closeted in a box.

That night, Nancy finally garners the strength to talk to him. She is willing to live to some extent with his newfound idiosyncrasies, but she hadn't bargained for all this. They are turning into a dysfunctional couple: she with her depression resurfacing, and he with his religiousness. She asks him what on earth has brought about the change. He tells her that perhaps it

is middle age creeping up; perhaps it is the coming child, at last
a family, or perhaps her mood swings.

"Are you blaming me for your religious craziness?" she says.

"I never said that!"

"But you did!" He keeps quiet as if in contemplation.

She understands that he never had a clear religious foundation; while his mother pulled him towards Christianity, his
father and the Imam overwhelmed him with the Muslim faith.
His father had told him that they were *Sayeds*—descendants of
Mohammed through his son-in-law Ali.

He gives her the same reasons he had given before: that he
simply didn't know where he belonged; and now that he has
a family, *a son on the way*, he feels the need to belong. He is
consumed with guilt, which is ingrained in him like it was in the
Christians of the Middle Ages—the guilt of martyrdom. He rec-
ollects the story he had told her about his experience during the
Ashura celebration: that bloody day, the dying young man in
his arms, those events deeply hidden in the crevices of his mind.
That dream has re-surfaced, and it is the source of his guilt for
not living his faith.

As he is deep in thought, something comes over her, a desire
to fight back.

"What about you mother's religion?" she shouts. "There is
enough equality and love in Christ."

"Christianity was not my mother's true religion," he says.
"She was a Hindu and her conversion was reactionary. Perhaps
she converted to be one of the 'people of the Book.'"

"I know. You told me that before."

"I went to Church with my mother on Sundays, but when
I became fourteen, I began questioning everything. It was then
that Christianity ended for me and I stopped going to Church. I
gave excuses. My mother never asked me why; she never insisted. Perhaps her faith was not as strong."

"I've heard all that before."

"Doesn't the crucifixion of Christ, his death on the Cross fill you with guilt?" he asks as if to drive the point.

"Cut the bullshit," she says. "We have discussed all this before. Suddenly you have embraced a degree of fanaticism and orthodoxy—dumping the alcohol down the drain, the unkempt overgrown beard, the excessive praying." They are facing each other now, as if about to pounce on each other.

"Honestly," she says, and I'm not sorry to say this, I think that this religion business is all childish."

"You have no right to call me childish. You don't understand."

"Well. I'm sorry. I may not entirely understand what you are saying. I stand by my characterization."

"One is a Muslim or one is not. It is the all or none phenomenon. You Catholics are token Catholics—Catholics in name! I have been a token Muslim myself and it's time to make a change."

"Now you are making me very angry," she says. "You don't have to challenge my Catholicism. I like it that way. We do what we believe in—what's okay with our conscience. Well, honestly, Muslims believe in one thing and do another—they drink, smoke, visit prostitutes, some even eat pork, and at the end of the day deny it all. We are a mixed couple, and we can only survive if we take the middle course.

He listens without a word.

"You can practice your religion as long as it doesn't infringe on my beliefs and our lifestyle. We agreed on that didn't we? It is those new Middle Eastern friends of yours—isn't it? Don't you see that all this craziness is making me sick, more depressed?"

"I pray for you, Nancy. I pray for our son."

"I don't need your damn' prayers!" She shouts at the top of her voice. And she begins sobbing.

"I'm terribly sorry," he says, and embraces her. She pushes him away.

"Life cannot be defined as all or none—as black and white," she says. "After all what does it matter this religion or that? They are only different clothes on the same Emperor; different symbols, different rituals for the same message." She scores a big point, and she feels it.

He walks out and slams the door. She goes to the bedroom and cries some more. She wants to start back on the Paxil. *Why is Ali doing this? He wants to drive me away? Is it that Russian tart? He loves her more than he loves me! The way he speaks with her, so calmly, so reassuringly. Perhaps she had come on too strong and spewed out anxieties in both of them?*

She remembers Ali telling her about the events at the Ashura celebration on Thanksgiving day, and these tragic happenings have resurfaced in his mind. She was at a loss, and couldn't understand the flagellation bit, and the difference between the Shia and the Sunni sects. She was utterly disturbed at his beating his breast, and wishing he had iron shards. Utterly shaken, she could not fall asleep that night sitting by her bay window for hours, looking at the lit Verrazano Narrows Bridge. That night, her sleep was constantly interrupted by dreams she couldn't remember. The next morning, she had woken up wondering about Ali's culture, his faith, and his inner self. At the same time, she longed for him, to make love to him, and it frightened her. A cloud of depression had descended over her. She called her shrink, who told her to start back on the Paxil. She should have discussed her fears and uncertainties with Ali. It seems too late now.

She lies on the bed exhausted and dozes off to sleep after taking a Xanax. Three hours later, he returns and finds the lights off and Nancy asleep. He nudges close to her, putting his arms around her.

"You are right, Nancy," he says. "Perhaps it's the pressure—perhaps it's guilt. Our son needs a foundation."

They both get out of bed and enter the kitchen for some

chamomile tea with honey. The hours of sleep she had managed has calmed her raw nerves.

"Ali, I must find a new investment focus. Nobody buys stocks these days. My commission is dead in the water. I'm afraid I'll be laid off," she says.

"Come on, don't say that," he says. "Is that the source of your anxiety?'

"Partly. You don't know what it's like in the corporate world. They send you packing like ground meat. Maybe I should focus on device and drug companies. What do you think?"

"I can help you there," says Ali. "With advice I mean."

"I don't have much energy left. I don't even feel like going to work."

A week or so thereafter, Ali is scheduled to lecture at the Mayo Clinic in Rochester, Minnesota. The night before, he shaves his beard. Nancy is lying on the bed half-asleep glancing at the *New Yorker*. He comes to her and juts his face in-between hers and the magazine.

"Now you look like the brilliant Dr. Ali, my husband," she says. He hugs and kisses her.

"You seem in a better mood," he says.

"Yes," she says, without mentioning that she has gone back on the Paxil.

That morning, waiting for a cab, Ali revels in the sounds and colors of a New York awakening: the smell of coffee, do-nuts and pretzels intermingling with exhaust from zooming tax-is, buses and cars; a sanitation truck, its large circular brush-es washing the street; another huge truck revving its motors. Steam from the street circles in the wind, as a taxi with a Punja-bi driver stops in front of him. Invigorated after a cup of coffee and a glazed donut, in the taxicab on his way to La Guardia,

Ali contemplates on the argument with Nancy, and how in spite of it, they ended making love that night. He feels overpowered by a need to hold her in his arms, to make love to her all over again. And then as suddenly, all desire leaves him, when he is reminded what lies in front of him that day: his long awaited lecture at the Mayo Clinic, his alma mater. But somehow he lacks concentration that morning. His attention shifts back to their conversation, to his religious fervor—his newfound orthodoxy—as she had put it. He examines his own life of material achievements and accomplishments, where religion and faith played no role, and contrasts his ways with the way of life of his fellow Muslims and their universal suffering, and it makes him all the more guilty. He owes to his coming son what he himself was not privy to—a true belief in the faith. But what effect will her depression have on her pregnancy and the baby? And will she have post-partum depression of the severe kind? These issues linger on his mind, so much so that he cannot quite concentrate on his lecture. Luckily, he is to speak on the role of devices in heart failure, a subject he has lectured on many times before. But he needs to re-focus, however.

"We are here sir. Northwest Airline."

As the plane takes off, the sky shimmers in the early morning sunrise, light blue and transparent like ice.

His day at the Mayo Clinic surpasses his wildest expectations. It is the highest point in his short career to lecture at the Mayo House, that cathedral of medical education where he had intently listened, mesmerized by the Visiting Professors. He is unnerved as he stands in that hall on the podium, amid his old teachers and a sea of respectful students. He introduces the lecture he is about to deliver, which he executes with perfect diction despite his initial nervousness, and when he finishes ten minutes before the hour, he is filled with exhilaration.

On his way back to New York, he begins thinking again of what Nancy said about letting his religion come in the way of their relationship. As Nancy so eloquently reasoned, the only worthwhile expression of religion is love. Everything else is symbolism and different sets of clothes on the same Emperor.

This idea of a religion, of an abstract God, or an anthropomorphic God of flesh and blood, that Man has usurped to keep on further separating mankind, labeling man into different paradigms beyond and above his genetic traits—these Man-made Gods vying for supremacy, for power, for righteousness. And where does it all end? He had made the choice when he asked Nancy to marry him; besides, he had not sought her conversion to the Muslim faith; he cannot change the script now. He has to place this religion thing on the back burner. It is causing anxiety in Nancy and it could affect her pregnancy.

Ali looks out of the window as the plane makes its way Southwest, up the Hudson, crossing the city line to land at LaGuardia Airport. The Statue of Liberty holds its everlasting flame of freedom. The downtown skyscrapers glisten in the sunset like towers of gold, while fiery pillars shimmer in the waters of the Hudson below; necklaces of diamond and emerald glitter on the Verrazano Narrows and the George Washington Bridge. He remembers how impressed he was with the Manhattan skyline when he, as a young boy, had migrated to America together with his parents. He never stops taking in the New York City skyline when he returns from his lecture trips. The sight of the city at night, this island of Manhattan, disintegrates Ali's tribulations into speckles of dust and fills him with slivers of renewed hope for the future. He feels a rush of optimism, and his lecture at the Mayo House reconfirms his aplomb. He has made it in New York, and the doubts that he had when he moved from the Mayo Clinic, to take the position as Head of the Transplant program, has all but vanished. Life is good and he has to keep it that way. Then he remembers Nancy's depression, but he sup-presses the thought, pushes it away from his mind.

CHAPTER 26
Death and Insanity

When Anna goes to see Ali in the clinic, after examining her he says: "I hear a few crackles in your lungs and you've gained a few pounds. Five to be exact. I think it's time to upgrade you."

She immediately wants to ask him what he means by that, but finds him constantly looking at his watch. Did it have something to do with the sudden death of Helen and Tom? Of the six of them who were with her in the hospital, only Jay R received a heart. The news of Helen and Tom's sudden deaths devastated those remaining on the transplant list. They needed a great deal of support from the social worker and the psychotherapist.

This idea of a life, a life shadowed by death, a death randomly ordered, a death that comes suddenly and unexpectedly to those suffering a common ailment, well knowing that they could be the next in line while waiting for the heart that is difficult to come by, and yet, above all odds, hang on with hope, of living yet another day, another month, possibly another year...

Anna takes the news of the sudden demise of her companions philosophically, rationalizing that she will await her fate, determined by God alone. And yet, the wait has been too long.

When will her turn come to die? The very thought, the idea of waiting for one's death, this idée fixe—a realistic afterthought impossible for a young single mother to hold, to ponder with, renders her world, the world of patients waiting for a heart into a fractured, Koyaanisquatsi-esque world.

"Anna, are you okay? You seem distant," he says.

"Just thinking," she says. "Are you in a hurry?"

"I have a meeting with Dr. Bob at one, and it's past twelve."

"How long do you think I'll have to wait for a heart?"

"It may be soon, Anna. Keep up your spirits."

"It's easy for you to say that. It maybe another six months, one year, or more years, right?"

"Let's hope it's not that long. I'm going to upstage you to Category I. This means that you'll have to be on continuous intravenous medications at home."

"Humm..... Okay, if you say so."

"I'll call Jackie and instruct her about this. Please go and see her on the way out. She will set you up."

"I'm considering starting a ballet school after I get a new heart. I have a lunch meeting with Mary and her father. Can I go?"

"Your own school?" Ali smiles. "That's a great idea! Yes, you can come off the intravenous medications but not for more than six hours, and take an extra water pill the night before. When is your meeting?"

"On the eleventh."

He takes out his PALM, and looks at his schedule. "I'll be in Boston that day. Call Dr. Denzel if you have a problem. I'll alert him."

"God will keep an eye on me."

"I'm sure of that."

"By the way, you seem stressed out," she says.

"It's the job. I don't know how long I'm going to be here."

"If you leave what will happen to me?"

"Don't agonize over it. I don't even have a job offer."

"Promise you'll be my doctor, wherever you go."

"Cross my heart—I'll be your doctor even if I move to another continent. I have to leave now, Anna." He gets off his desk and hugs her. She doesn't want to let go.

As Ali makes his way to Dr. Bob's office, he wonders about his deteriorating relationship with his boss. He has taken solace in the fact that he is locally and nationally credited for building the heart transplant program at the Medical Center. He has excelled not only clinically, but his research is going better than he expected. He had hired a Ph.D. with monies donated by a wealthy patient of his and recently was awarded a research grant from the National Institutes of Health. However, Ali hadn't met the required recruitment quota for the Cardiospeed study, and consequently the study was terminated at the Medical Center. Ali was surprised that Dr. Bob hadn't raised the issue with him; perhaps he had too many things on his plate. On top of all this, the recent row regarding Princess Fatima had not yet been settled, and Dr. Bob had requested the meeting to discuss the Princess. Ali's intention was also to bring up the raise and promotion issue that had been placed on the back burner for too long a time.

Linda waves Ali into Dr. Bob's spacious office, and the door opens on Dr. Bob pacing compulsively around the desk. His gaunt face, the blood shot eyes, and rapid facial tic alarms Ali. Dr. Bob looks ill, as if he had not slept for days. He is rather surprised that he did not mention his wedding. Ali's clinical acumen tells him that there is more than meets the eye—an insanity brewing in the deep recesses of the mind?

Dr. Bob slumps in his maroon leather chair, whirls it around, ignoring Ali, and stares into space through his tenth-floor window. Ali doesn't know whether he should sit down or walk away. He takes it upon himself to take a seat and speak up.

"I've listed Princess Fatima in the Transplant Program, but she has to wait her turn. I told her father not to be optimistic, that the wait could be long and trying since her blood type was O, and she is in well-compensated heart-failure." He waits for Dr. Bob's reaction.

After a long silence, broken by the siren of a passing ambulance, Dr. Bob suddenly whirls his chair back to face Ali: "Did you say she'll have to wait her turn?"

Now why did he say that? Where is political correctness? Why did he have to challenge authority? Didn't he challenge his father and the Imam in his youth, and now Dr. Bob? And he always does it with a tinge of sarcasm as if subconsciously he wants to slight the guy who has all the power over him.

"What did you say?" Dr. Bob asks again. The boom in his voice has faded to a shrill cry, like that of an alley cat crying for milk.

Dr. Bob bangs his fist on the table. "She will have to wait her turn?"

"Well, there are people ahead of her who have waited for over a year." He has him there. He has taken the moral high ground. He is in the mood to fight: right versus wrong, good versus evil. Another part of him, the cautious part tells him: cut it out, ease it off now, just shut up, let him do the talking, let him blow steam. You have ruined your chances of promotion. Forget about the raise. Start looking for a new job. Don't forget you have a son coming. You have to meet the mortgage payments.

"I'm sorry if I upset you," says Ali. Dr. Bob abruptly calms down. Has Ali slaughtered the devil?

"Wasn't there a politician, some Senator or Governor—I don't exactly remember, who received a heart and a liver—or a lung—a pancreas—a kidney—or something like that—in one month, ahead of the others on the list?" Dr. Bob asks in a quick, shrill voice, drumming his fingers on the desk.

"I cannot speak for the other programs," Ali says. "Anyway, there is a strict national organ procurement list now, and they are the ones that do the matching. We have nothing to do with it." Ali sounds firm.

Dr. Bob's face reddens and begins twitching again, and the hemi-facial spasms begin spreading all over his upper torso. It is as if he is playing a Hungarian rhapsody on the piano. He wonders whether Dr. Bob has gone bonkers. *It's best to back off now,* he thinks. He can see hatred and madness staring back at him.

"If there is anything else I can do for her, I will be more than happy to accommodate," Ali adds.

Dr. Bob expression changes—he stares at Ali with a dazed look. "You may go now," he says, subdued. "I'm off to California tomorrow. After I return, we'll talk again."

The rapid mood swings, the flight of ideas, the fast recycling in Dr. Bob alerts Ali to a psychotic state. But Ali feels no compassion for Dr. Bob. He is always scheming; everything he does is to enhance his own agenda.

To hell with the promotion to Associate Professor! To hell with the raise, Ali thinks as he steps out of Dr. Bob's office. On his was out he stops at Linda's desk. "What's wrong with Dr. Bob?" he whispers.

"I don't know," she whispers back. "He is acting strange. He is under a lot of pressure. I was told the department is in deficit."

Ali starts down the corridor with a puzzled expression on his face.

A part of him again wonders how all this will affect his future, particularly his promotion with tenure. He has ruined his chances. If he had played the right tune, rather than stepping on the moral high ground, he would have made it. The money would flow in, the Saudi-Arabian Prince would make a large donation to the department, Dr. Bob would be ecstatic, everybody would be happy including the hospital administrators, and the promotion would be a shoe-in. But the Saudi-Arabian Princess is asymptomatic and well compensated. He just cannot upstage her to Category One.

Returning to Dr. Bob, he is puzzled at the rapid mood cycling. The insanity is beyond his comprehension. He returns back to Linda's desk, and leaning forward, he whispers in her ear: "What's with Dr. Bob?"

"There's a lot going on," she whispers back. "He talks to himself, and a couple of times I've even heard him scream when there was no one else in there." Ali starts down the corridor with a puzzled expression on his face. As he waits for the elevator, Linda runs up to him and tells him that she is looking to leave the place. "I don't want to talk here. Can we meet for a drink?"

Ali senses her anxiety. "Red's Vine Bar? Six-thirty?" says Ali.

When Ali enters Red's, he finds Linda sipping on a cocktail, and chatting with a man.

"Dr. Ali, this is Ricardo," says Linda. "I just ordered my second apple martini. They make them great here. What will you have?"

"A root beer will do."

"Thanks for the run-down Linda," says Ricardo. "See you."

"Boyfriend?" asks Ali.

"I wish. Good looking, right? He's gay."

The bar like a watering hole is suddenly packed with doctors, nurses, secretaries, and technicians from the hospital all quenching their thirst with beer, martinis, whiskey and wine, before they head home to their wives, girlfriends, dogs, cats, or their TV's. The music is loud. The place is getting crowded. They see a vacant divan in the far corner and rush to occupy it. "Wait, I need a refill," says Linda. "Hey, Ricardo, make it a dirty martini, but go easy on the vodka, Grey Goose, please."

"Anything for you Linda," says Ricardo. "What about you Doc'? A special mohito for the heart doctor!" Ricardo bangs on his chest, his heart.

"Thanks, but no."

Ali feels like asking for one—the occasion demands, but no. He is no hypocrite, having thrown Nancy's alcohol down the drain.

They leave for the distant corner of the bar. Two Asian women in tight Prada jeans holding round glasses of wine in one hand and clutching their Gucci purses with the other, make a run for the divan. They move close to each other to make room for Ali and Linda.

Linda takes a long sip of the dirty stuff and sucks on her fingers. She places her hand on Ali's thigh. He can feel her breath on his cheek. The place suddenly takes on an erotic quality. Her hand brushes his lips as he turns.

"So, tell me," he whispers, as he feels a hard-on coming. The two Asian women get up to leave.

"What are you looking at? What are you thinking, Dr. Ali? It's those two chicks isn't it? They turn you on, don't they, honey? Wouldn't you like to see them in the sack? It's every man's fantasy. Don't I turn you on, lover boy? You like big *culos?*" And she slaps her ample butt. Ali is amused and laughs hilariously. He is here to talk about Dr. Bob and Linda's future, but not to get seduced by Linda.

"Come on Linda, we are supposed to talk about Dr. Bob and your job."

She mouths as she sips the last remaining drops of her dirty martini: "The motherfucker gets crazy after the methamphetamines, the cocaine and the mushrooms. He needs the stimulants to keep up with the running around."

She tells him that one day when she was working late, she went into his office to give him some letters to sign, he stared at her with glazed eyes. "As I bent over the desk, he squeezed my ass. *Um punheta!*" Linda looks disgusted. "I want to leave the place, but I need the job. I have a son to support. I made a big mistake leaving your employ."

"Why don't you file a complaint?"

"Against the Big and Powerful Dr. Bob? Who's going to believe me?"

"I would gladly take you back, but I've already filled the position. I'll look around and see if there are any openings."

"Will you write a letter for me?"

"Of course! Back to Dr. Bob, what do you mean he does speed? It's impossible—the big doctor of international fame, doing speed?"

"I knew you'd say that. Maybe you won't believe what I'm about to tell you."

"Try me."

"You know Carmensita, right?

"Yes! Carmensita and her fiery red punch! Isn't she a healer or something like that?"

"She practices Santeria—it's a cult, a sort of a religion. She's the Oya, and man, she can lay the curse and make chickens drop dead. The cabrón is playing with fire."

"Who?"

"Dr. Bob. He had an affair with Carmensita."

"He wanted her herbs for the experiments," says Ali. "I wonder why he's dropped the experiments." Linda shrugs.

"Well, the affair with Carmensita has been the talk of the town since the party. But wait a second—what's this about 'had an affair' with Carmensita? Is it over?"

"I will come to that later."

Now, this was bizarre and somewhat loquacious for Ali to

believe. However, he shakes his head giving the impression of gullibility. Linda must be half-drunk and making up the whole thing: Dr. Bob doing speed? She is a real bochinchosa, that Linda, gossiping on the phone all the time: yadda, yadda, yadda. He decides to press her on it. "Come on Linda—do you expect me to believe he's doing drugs?"

"You asked me if there was something wrong with him."

"I meant psychotic—Crazy. Not an addict."

"Don't believe me? Or is it the 'doctor thing'?"

"What do you mean, Dr. Thing?"

"You doctors think you're above everybody else, right? The white coat syndrome?"

"I didn't mean it that way."

"Well, let me tell you Dr. Ali—there are rotten apples in your noble profession as well."

"Go on, I'm sorry." Ali laughs. "How do you know that Dr. Bob's doing drugs?" He looks at his watch.

"Carmensita told me. Her husband's a drug dealer. She gets the drugs for Dr. Bob."

"Now I get it: The psychosis, the paranoia, is drug related."

But Ali still has doubts about all he hears. This cannot happen to Dr. Bob—the man's too smart to get involved with drugs at the point of ruining his career, which means the world to him. But then power corrupts!

Linda relates to Ali that Carmensita and she were good friends. She had once attended the ceremony of Santeria to get her husband back. She offered candles and money to the Orishas. And it apparently worked.

"I don't know how the Jews, the Indians, and the Muslims do it, but among us Latinos, marriages don't last long. I guess it's the pork and the black beans!" They both laugh heartily at Linda's cryptic humor.

"She's a good hearted woman, that Carmensita, but very jealous and hot tempered," says Linda.

"I've got to leave. My wife will be waiting."

"You're bored of me?"

"No, not at all. I have to leave for Boston tomorrow morning."

"Did anybody tell you how sexy you look? Do you know that I fantasized with you when I was your secretary?"

"Come on Linda. Cut it out."

"And you, lover boy, you didn't even look at me. I know all about that Russian tart."

"She's my patient. She's very sick you know."

"Hmm! Anyways, I gave up on you, honey. Now where was I?" She holds on to his arm.

Ali sees Dr. Denzel enter the bar. He waves out to him. Denzel is with Jenny, a representative of a drug company. He calls Denzel over. "We can squeeze you in; anyway, I will be leaving soon." He introduces Linda Rivera to Jenny. "She's one of Dr. Bob's secretaries. You know Dr. Bob, don't you?"

"Hi, it's nice to meet you. And who doesn't know Dr. Bob," says Jenny. "He's a consultant to my company."

"A paid one?" asks Ali.

"I'm not privy to disclose that," says Jenny of Citronic Inc.

Ali can sense that Denzel is uncomfortable sitting with them. He wonders whether there is anything brewing between him and Jenny, when Jenny finishes her glass of Merlot, and gets up to leave. She has a training session at six in the morning.

"I'll walk you to your car," says Denzel.

"Did you see that?" says Linda. "The drink was just foreplay…They are going to fuck!"

"Come on Linda. You read too much into everything. Denzel is a happily married man."

"Happily married? Dr. Ali you're so naive. That's why I like you so much."

"Please, carry on with your story." Ali looks at his watch.

She tells him that Dr. Bob dumped Carmensita for that new French tart, the cheesy Dr. Claudette Pépin. "No one dumps

Carmensita, the Oya, just like that. She's a fiery Latina—a jealous one! You look very tired Dr. Ali." Ali again looks at his watch. It is almost ten o'clock.

"Where was I? Yes, yes, a cock's head was left on Dr. Bob's desk. I bet it was the cleaning lady. Carmensita must have bribed her to drop it off when she was on holiday in the Caribbean. Dr. Bob became frightened and paranoid. He began shouting and yelling: "Take it away, take it away." After he sort of calmed down, he asked me what it meant. I told him it was a curse. When he heard that he immediately left the office and called in sick.

After Carmensita returned, the threats, the blackmail began. He gave her a big fat raise—it made me very upset. She told me not to worry—soon she would see to it that I got one too."

"Where do you live, Linda? I hope you don't have to drive. You're a bit tipsy." Ali could see that she is upset now. He immediately places his arm around her and tugs her close to him.

She turns around and plants a kiss on his lips.

"I'll take a cab. I live on One Hundred Tenth Street and Fifth."

"Good night."

"Thanks for the Martinis. Ciao baby."

Linda is definitely drunk, and lonely like so many in this city of singles. Ciao baby! Ali laughs as he walks out of the bar into the hot steamy night. Whatever Linda told him about Dr. Bob sounded all so weird like a random ordering of the mind. But he begins to believe that Dr. Bob has drug related psychosis. He wonders whether he should relate it all to Nancy. She would definitely have an opinion. She had met all of them, however briefly: Linda, Carmensita and Dr. Bob. He suddenly realizes that amid the entire hullabaloo about Dr. Bob, they forgot to discuss Linda's future in any detail. When he arrives home, he finds Nancy fast asleep.

PART

IV

...a man will be careful not to be wearisome, and to keep his point, or his catastrophe, well in hand. —James Payne

CHAPTER 27

The Dawn before the Storm

When the alarm rings, Ali gently gets out of bed. It is his habit to bounce off the bed once awake, ready to take on the day, but today, he wishes he could sleep some more. Since his marriage, and unlike the bachelorhood years, sleep comes easily and effortlessly now—the pleasurable dwindling of one's consciousness like the slow flow of water in a stream. He opens the curtain ever so slightly so as not to wake Nancy. But he sees her tossing and turning in a semi-sleepy, semi-dreamy state.

He stands by the window exulting in the view, far better than the rusted fire escape he saw from his old apartment. It has become his habit to take in the East River, a sort of a compulsion in a compulsive man, to absorb the materiality of something he has paid so much for, to get his money's worth—the water still dark rhythmically laps downstream to join the Atlantic. He glances at Nancy, fully aware of her breathing, but it is her naked back he finds himself staring at, the waist still narrow, giving way to a rounded bottom all white with tinges of pink from his caresses. He wanted to make love last night, but half-asleep, she just brushed him off. Now fully formed, unencumbered, as he looks at sheaves of her tart flesh untangle in the bed sheets, he feels like taking her. He walks into the bathroom for a cold shower and sees his erection crumble like soft dough.

After the shower, he unrolls the prayer rug from the closet and facing east, he prays: "In the name of God, Most Gracious, Most Merciful. Praise be to God, Lord of the Universe..."

He comes back to the bedroom, puts on a blue suit with a matching light blue tie. As he gives Nancy a parting kiss, the phone rings. It is Anna.

"Dr. Ali, sorry to bother you this early," she whispers. "I feel a bit short of breath, but I want to go for the lunch with Mary. It means so much to me. Dr. Ali, are you there? Did I wake you up?"

"It's okay, Anna," he whispers back as he tiptoes to the living room to answer the call. "Go if you must. Take an extra water pill now. I'm on my way to Boston. If you have any problem, call Dr. Denzel."

"Who's it Ali?" Nancy asks, half-asleep. "That Russian tart again?"

He pretends he never heard, and quickly leaves for the airport.

When Ali arrived home the night before, after an exhausting day, he still had some verve left to take his laptop and go about arranging and rearranging the PowerPoint slides for his forthcoming lecture. He gave it his last ounce of energy as his enthusiasm and performance skills soared: the cadence of his words, the American accent peppered with the British, the timing, the back and forth shifting of the order of the slides, all meticulously put together and executed. At eleven-thirty he went right to sleep exhausted from his twelve-hour work schedule, while Nancy had dropped off sometime before, more from boredom than fatigue.

It is almost seven when Nancy restlessly turns her head to avoid the streaks of sunlight piercing through the half-drawn curtain in her apartment bedroom window. A little more than an hour has passed since Ali left to make the shuttle to Boston. She has plenty of time on her hands, but once awake she is not in the mood to get out of bed. She wishes she could stay in bed the whole day, but she has an important meeting with her boss that she cannot miss. She makes an effort to shower and dress up; the brown business suit she picked up from the laundry the previous evening is waiting on the hanger. The pregnancy now shows a small bulge. She hasn't even shopped for maternity dresses—perhaps in the evening if she is up to it.

During the subway ride to Downtown Manhattan she starts reading Philip Roth's *The Human Stain,* which she picked up at Barnes and Noble after her doctor, finding her blood pressure slightly elevated, had advised rest. She finds herself unable to concentrate after reading a few pages. She had mentioned the novel to Ali, but Ali has no time for novels. Fiction is not his cup of tea—he is utterly engaged and absorbed in the world of body parts, of physical reality.

As she lifts her head from the book, right in front of her there is a tall slim elegant woman with the poise of a ballerina. She wonders whether she is Russian, when Anna comes to mind. On two occasions she had prodded Ali to talk about Anna, what she looked like, what was it like to be with her. But all she encountered was a locked-up drawer. Men don't like to talk about their past sexual experiences with their wife's. Perhaps not to make them jealous or not to compromise themselves. In the beginning, she felt that Ali was honest and straightforward about the relationship: it was strictly professional—a doctor-patient relationship—and, because of Anna's illness, the affair had ended much before they met. However, she feels (call it a woman's intuition) that the ballerina still has a crush on Ali. She never wanted to interfere in Ali's professional life, but now she strongly feels that he should hand over Anna's care to Dr. Denzel. The calls were becoming more frequent and often at night. Besides, she doesn't trust these Russian tarts: heart failure or not. She doesn't want to lose Ali. He is one of a kind: intelligent, inquisitive, handsome and dedicated, but she wonders at his romanticism. He often seems so pragmatic and ambitious. Recently, however, he had revealed his vulnerability and insecurity. To her surprise, the talk she had with him about religion seems to have appeased him. She is not sure why he switched off his religiousness so easily and effortlessly, like switching off an electrical bulb. Was it a deception or a façade to get her off his back? Or was it because of her depression? After he returned from the lecture at the Mayo Clinic, he had thanked her for her wise choice of words.

As she walks out on Liberty Street, the air is fresh and crisp on a sunny, cloudless New York morning. How often has she captured such stellar mornings in New York City? She buys a tall cup of Starbucks Coffee and two large chocolate chip cookies and walks to Battery Park. Her morning sickness has now disappeared and she has a ravenous appetite. She sits on the promenade and looks towards the Statue of Liberty and beyond at Staten Island. A plane comes from the South to land at La Guardia airport. A helicopter hovers over the Statue of Liberty.

The promenade is her favorite spot. Often she sits there browsing through *The New York Times*, imagining someday moving back to her parent's house on Grymes Hill, overlooking the Verrazano Narrows Bridge. Her parents hoped that she and Ali would live there. She wished it too. But Ali was against it. "We have to make our own nest, Nan," he had said. She remains attached to Staten Island: its singing blue jays and cardinals, the changing seasons, the stellar colors of autumn around her home on the hill, and the view. Besides, it is so close to the city and yet so far, and peaceful. A graduate of business administration from NYU, she had commuted from Staten Island to Manhattan on the Staten Island ferry, often taking pictures with her Cannon F1: of the skyline during a foggy snowstorm, the sunsets, the sunrises, and the pure whiteness of the snowfall on the Hill. She would often walk on the hill during these stormy-winter evenings. When she left home, to share an apartment in the City, she felt out-of-place and out-of-rhythm missing the warmth and coziness of the house, of Grymes Hill. Someday, she would go back to live there with her children to come, and on snowy days, roast marshmallows and chestnuts in the fireplace. Her father would never sell it. It was all his life: the house, the garden, the pond; and, he would will it to her. He had told her so in a whisper on her wedding day.

Life seems almost all she wished for. Her depression is lifting; soon she may feel euphoric. There is a life growing inside her that will make its debut in few months. She touches her lower belly, barely feeling the prominence. She wonders what her son will look like: will he be tan like Ali or white like her; will he be blonde or will his hair be pitch black like his father's? She is confident he will be handsome and intelligent and perhaps he will be a doctor someday. We never know whom we bring into the world. "It's a matter of chance: which sperm meets which egg," Ali had said.

A few silly issues remain to be resolved. She is contented that Ali has shed at least for now, his newfound religious orthodoxy. They agreed that they wouldn't keep any alcohol at home, and when friends and parents visited, Nancy would make the necessary purchases of liquor. He had agreed that he would allow the baby to be baptized; however, he wanted him to be brought up as a Muslim. She objected to that. She was a churchgoer on Christmas, Easter, and once in a while on a Sunday, and would take her children with her. "When he gets of age, he can decide which religion he wants to be identified with," she had said. Ali had shaken his head. She could sense that he hadn't liked what he heard, but was in no mood to counter her point. She wanted

at least one Christian name—the first—the second could be a
Muslim one. That remained an unresolved point of contention.
"This is America," her father had said. "It is not practical to
give him a Muslim name—a Christian one will take him further
in life." She had not mentioned it to Ali. Nevertheless, she feels
that these are minor issues. Their last disagreement regarding
religion was settled amicably, or so it seems. A clinician and
scientist, he is a rational thinker; albeit, confused at times, nonetheless, his love for her will go a long way in seeking compro-
mises. They love each other, respect each other's individuality,
their love is bound to survive. She suddenly feels euphoric. The
Paxil has kicked in. Perhaps she is entering the gates of heaven:
A high-high!

And today is a different day: a day to sit and stare—a day
without a care.

A cargo ship dips below the Verrazano to disappear into the
Atlantic.

Nancy walks back past the World Financial Centers towards
Vesey Street. As her gaze shifts upwards, The World Trade Center Towers shimmer in the morning golden sunlight. She wishes
she had her camera in hand. She enters the complex and takes
the elevator to the Eighty-first floor on the North Tower. It is
8:20 AM. Sitting at her desk, she goes over the financials of device companies she has to forward to her boss, Jim Holbrooke.
She turns on her computer; logs on to the Internet and reviews
one last time the graphs and complex curves of P/E ratios, Volume, Relative Strength Index, and Stochastic of the companies
of interest, that she had prepared a couple of months back. The
fundamentals of medical device companies look good. Besides,
Ali has assured her of the booming market for implantable defibrillators. He told her that ultimately almost all patients wait-

ing for heart transplants, and those with previous heart attacks like Vice-President Cheney, would need an internal defibrillator that would instantaneously, and with the utmost certainty, shock an erratic fibrillating dying heart back into normal rhythm.

"Wow!" she had exclaimed.

"American technology at its very best," Ali said proudly. "It's like an insurance policy to prevent sudden cardiac death."

"Nan, you've got to go with Medtronic, Guidant and St. Jude. They have new devices in the pipeline."

She had prepared an impressive document before her depression had set in, and now she is confident that Jim Halbrook would be thrilled. Jim, a middle-aged man, her boss, was excited after she had changed focus from the tanking biotechnology companies to medical device companies. He suffered from angina and had stents placed in his coronary arteries. She had told him that her husband was a cardiologist, and he had opened up and discussed with her about his heart ailments. She had advised him to see her husband for a second opinion.

After copying the document from her floppy disk to the C-drive, and printing it on her laser printer, she neatly closes the folder entitled: *Medical Device Companies: The Silver Mines of the Future,* and walks over to his office.

CHAPTER 28

A Day to Forget

Ali speed-dials Anna as soon as he enters the airport. She tells him that she feels better after the water pill, but is quite anxious about the lunch meeting with Mary at Windows of the World. "Perhaps I'll feel better after a nap," she says. "You'll be fine," he says. "Enjoy yourself."

Ali takes his window seat on the plane, and watches the morning glow barely surround New York City. The air outside is clear and crisp—what a glorious day it's going to be. As Ali's flight takes off, the sky shimmers in the early morning sunrise, light blue and transparent like ice.

A stickler for order and perfection, he takes out his laptop, switches on to PowerPoint and begins to check his slides for a last-minute change. He thoroughly enjoys the newfound fame of the lecture circuit. He regrets he has no cartoon or something funny to crack the ice with the audience of serious studious doctors. Certainly, the lecture at Harvard's Mass General Hospital is a big deal. He hadn't quoted an honorarium, more than willing to lecture for free.

When he was invited to lecture at Mass General Hospital,

during their brief telephone conversation, the Chairman there had hinted an interest in recruiting him. If offered the position, he now wonders what Nancy would say about moving to Boston. He had briefly raised the issue with her. She knew he was dissatisfied with Dr. Bob, who ruled the place as if it was his own personal fiefdom. She had encouraged him to find a job with greater freedom, but not outside of New York. He'd told her that there were only two Heart Transplant Programs in New York City. Certainly, Boston would be far better than Albany. But she was reluctant to leave her family and friends behind, and she had her own career to think about. Things will sort themselves out for the best, he thought. His thoughts are abruptly interrupted by the announcement to fasten seat belts in preparation for landing.

The tall, slim, green-eyed blonde representative of Pharma Inc. is waiting for him with a large sign that reads: DR. ALI in one hand, and a cup of coffee in the other.

"Hey, Dr. Ali," she says, shaking his hand. "Would you like to go for breakfast? We have more than an hour on our hands."

"Coffee will do...perhaps a ride around the Harvard Campus, or a walk by the Charles River?"

"Sure. I'll take you around the campus," she says.

"Great."

"I read your recent paper. The cardiology staff at the Massachusetts General Hospital are eager to hear you speak," she says, as they get into her car.

"That's wonderful to hear."

"I love New York," she says, touching his shoulder. "I'm looking for a transfer. I heard that there might be an opening."

"Our Pharma. rep is getting married and might move to Colorado," he says.

"Swell. Hopefully, you'll put in a good word for me?" she says, touching his arm." Sensing the flirtation, Ali smiles.

"Dr. Ali, if you'd like to spend the night in Boston I could book you in a hotel and we could go out for dinner. You like

Italian?"

"Thanks, Valarie. Perhaps next time. I have cases scheduled for tomorrow."

He immediately senses her disappointment. He couldn't but notice her subtle coquetry; her cool sexuality amply displayed in her black business suit, red lipstick, blonde hair, long slim legs, and some cleavage. Weren't these female representatives who populate the drug and device companies hired for that specific purpose, to massage a doctor's ego? Was it easier for female reps with their respectful and proper manners, their seeming lascivious moves: the twinkle in the eye, the sudden smile, a show of leg, an inadvertent touch of the finger, the pop of a smiling face in the doorway, "I'm terribly sorry to disturb you doc"—to get to see the doctor instantly, despite his heavy schedule?

He is almost at the end of his lecture on "The Gap-Junction Protein Connexin 40 in Arrhythmic Transplanted Hearts."

"Optical mapping of deceased myocardium following a myocardial infarction," he says, "reveals significant slowing of conduction velocity and is the requisite condition for the genesis of reentrant circuits." Furthermore, he adds, "the tissue showed significant inactivation of Gap junction alpha-5 protein (Cx-40). Thus, inactivation of Cx-40 could conceivably be the cause of malignant ventricular arrhythmias and sudden death following heart attacks."

He immediately senses the enthusiasm, the awe from the audience. His singularity, the mental Eros, soars. This is Big. It could be his door to fame and fortune. He looks at his watch resting on the podium. It is 8:50 am. He is contented like a race-car driver who, after negotiating a difficult terrain, completes the race ahead of time. A stickler for punctuality, he has finished his talk in fifty minutes, and has left the last ten for the question and answer session.

As he is about to take the last question from the audience, his cellular clipped to his belt goes off. He looks at the number: It is Nancy. He waits till after the question and answer session ends.

A young doctor with a boyish face approaches. "Hi Dr. Ali. I'm Dr. Sterling, Cardiology Fellow—that was a great lecture. Do you have time for one more question?"

"Yes, certainly, but I need to make a call first." He speed dials Nancy at about 9:05 am and gets a busy tone. He turns around towards Dr. Sterling and says: "Yes, shoot!"

His return shuttle to New York is at 1:00 pm, and there is lot of time to kill. Just before the lecture, the Chairman, Dr. Rand had asked him to join him for coffee in his office. Ali senses that he is impressed with the lecture and wonders what is to come: an offer to head the Transplant Program at Harvard? He had considered the possibility when he had received the invitation to deliver Grand Rounds; after all, his original scientific article had appeared in the prestigious *Journal of Clinical Investigation*. It would be a lateral move. However, this is Harvard. Besides, he will be able to negotiate an associate professorship with tenure. If nothing else he could use the "offer" as a tactic to negotiate a raise, a promotion, and additional staff at the Medical Center. Isn't that the only way to manipulate a raise and a promotion in our capitalist culture? Or, he could tell Dr. Bob to drop dead. He is shedding his skin and learning fast.

After the lecture, as Dr. Rand's secretary, Ms. Malone, escorts Ali to Dr. Rand's office and hands him a cup of coffee, Ali speed-dials Nancy. He can hear the phone ring on the other end.

"It's me, honey. How are you feeling?" He can hear her breathing. "Is there a problem?"

"Ali, there was an accident," she says. "A plane crashed into the North Tower. I thought Jim was having a heart attack. The chest pain went away after two nitroglycerines. I gave him an aspirin and a beta-blocker he had in his pocket."

"I was almost at the end of the lecture when you called."

"We are heading for the stairway, darling—there is smoke coming through the vent. Oh my God—there is another boom. The smoke—we have to get out of here. I don't know what' going on. 'Our father who art in Heaven, hallowed is Thy name.' 'I—I love you darling. " He hears her sobbing. "Ali, say a prayer for me..."

Before he can say I love you too, the phone goes dead. When Ali enters Dr. Rand's office his face is drawn, the eyes cloudy, he stands in the middle of the room with a blank expression.

"Hey Ali, have a seat. Is something the matter? You look worried," says Dr. Rand. "You still have some time before you catch the shuttle to New York."

"Apparently there was an accident in New York. I just spoke to my wife. A plane hit the North Tower—the World Trade Center. My wife works there."

"Is she all right?"

"She was on her way down." He wants to say that he could hear her praying, and he had never heard her pray.

"Yah, these plane crashes, there have been too many these last few years. My wife always demands I call her right away when I land. She even calls the airline to find out whether the flight has landed." Ali shakes his head.

"I was impressed with your research—the slides were superb."

"Thanks."

"I am looking for a new energetic head for the Transplant Program. I would like to consider you for the position." Looking at Ali's CV that is laid out on his desk, he continues, "Hmm, your CV is impressive: a graduate of Yale, residency training and cardiology fellowship at Mount Sinai Hospital, a clinical and a research fellowship in heart failure at the Mayo Clinic, a visiting fellowship at the Hammersmith in London, Assistant Prof. at Mayo, and ten original articles in the last four years. I don't see any problem getting you an Associate Professorship. I'm sure you and your wife will love Boston. Any kids?" Ali doesn't respond.

"Ali..."

"Yes, I'm sorry. This accident in New York is on my mind. Yes, one child on the way!"

"Great. Well, Boston is no New York City, but then we have our share of museums, the arts, the Red Socks, and Harvard. You don't have to decide right now. Take your time. After you have given it a serious thought, send me a document putting down all your needs: financial, academic, staffing, etc. and we'll take it from there." Dr. Rand's words are only half-registering. He thanks Dr. Rand as Ms. Malone bursts in.

"Dr. Rand," she says, shaking all over. "There was a terrorist attack. Two planes crashed into the World Trade Center, and both the Towers are on fire."

Ali and Rand race to the patient lounge. A bunch of doctors and nurses are watching the unfolding drama on CNN. Nobody seems to know what is going on. And then they see it again and again in slow motion: the plane's sudden appearance at the edge of the screen—the crash into the North Tower, the smoke, the smoldering fire; another plane approaching and crashing into the South Tower; the towers engulfed in smoke, the falling debris—the plunging bodies. They look at each other—stone-faced, in disbelief.

Ali speed-dials Nancy. There is no dial tone.

"Why don't you come and sit in my office?" says Dr. Rand.

"I will sit here for a while and see what's going on."

Several minutes later, another bulletin: "We have a report that another plane crashed into the Pentagon. There is yet another plane hijacked, and in the air. It seems certain that this was a terrorist attack," says the CNN anchorman. "It's not clear who the perpetuators are. I repeat—it's not clear who are the perpetuators of this villainous attack—Middle Eastern terrorists are suspected."

Ali sits there crouched; his hands cover his face.

After about fifteen minutes, Dr. Rand comes by and escorts him into his office.

"Oh my God, what a disaster," says Dr. Rand. "The airports are closed. No one knows the whereabouts of the President. I'm taking you home until the situation is clear. I know you are worried about Nancy."

"No, I must leave now."

"All the flights are grounded. There is no air traffic."

"I'll rent a car. I have to leave for New York City. On second thoughts, maybe I should try to get to the airport—the flights may resume later on."

"What if New York City is closed for incoming and outgoing traffic? You could be stranded somewhere."

"I have to find Nancy."

There is a knock on the door. Ms. Malone bursts in.

"Dr. Rand, one of the Towers has collapsed," she says, in tears.

"Oh my God," says Dr. Rand.

Ali feels a sinking deep inside as if something has given way or ruptured. He wants to ask which Tower, but he cannot find the words. He dials Nancy frantically, several times, while Dr. Rand looks on with anguish. There is no dial tone. What if Nancy will not make it? And the baby? He slumps into the chair with his head in his hands. Then he asks Dr. Rand to leave the office for a few moments. He wishes to say a prayer.

Turning towards Mecca, he recites the opening Sura Fatihah:

"In the name of God, Most Gracious, Most Merciful.

Praise be to God, Lord of the Universe.

Most Gracious, Most Merciful....

"O' Merciful One, Look after Nancy and my baby."

When Ali comes out, he is calm and composed as if the prayer has allayed his fears.

CHAPTER 29

Fire and Brimstone

When Anna wakes up from her nap, at almost ten-thirty, her spirits soar; today, she is to lunch with Mary at the Windows of the World. They are to meet Mary's father and discuss the possibility of Anna starting her own ballet school after receiving a heart transplant. Mary had floated the idea during a phone conversation, assuring Anna that she and her father would do all the groundwork and the fundraising. She had arranged a car to pick up Anna at twelve o'clock.

She had asked Ali whether she could do away with the intravenous medication and the pole that went along with it. She wished to look like a woman, not an invalid. And Ali had reluctantly agreed. "Watch out, Anna—no salt whatsoever and you cannot be without the medication for more than six hours."

Mary had reassured her that she would instruct the chef not to use any salt. "You need the outing my dear, an opportunity to dress up and feel like a woman," Mary had asserted confidently. "We will have a private cubicle with a stellar view of the city."

Anna showers, turns the TV on, and opens the bedroom closet. The previous night she had settled on a pink suit and a black hat with pink lace to go with it. Anna, like her mother, loves hats: St. Petersburg hats, Moscow hats, hats from Paris, classy hats that make her look chic and European.

Placing the hat on her head and abruptly turning her head to look at herself in the mirror, her gaze spontaneously shifts to the bedroom TV. The sound from the TV is low, barely audible, when Anna sees a large skyscraper collapse. She thinks it's a movie. She puts on her pink suit, makes up her face, makes small adjustments to the hat, goes to the bathroom, looks at herself in the lighted bathroom mirror, returns to the bedroom, and sits on the chair to put her shoes on. When she lifts her head, she sees a plane in slow motion coming in from the corner of the TV screen and crashing into a skyscraper. The plane comes again and again. The anchorman is saying something that she barely hears. Another plane comes from the north, inching forward in slow motion and crashes into another skyscraper. The towers are enveloped in thick smoke. Suddenly one tower collapses like a demolition project. Then another tower collapses. It is as if one twin follows the other. Dust, debris, and smoke enshroud the area around the Towers.

She looks at herself in the mirror. She's glad she has gotten rid of the intravenous pole. She hopes she can make the lunch without getting winded. It is her first outing after a long-long time. Her gaze shifts back to the TV. It is then that she realizes that the burning collapsing towers are the World Trade Centers. On one of their dates, Ali had taken her there to the observation deck after dinner at the Windows of the World. But isn't this a movie? She presses the remote and looks at the channel—a movie on CNN? She looks at herself in the mirror making minor adjustments to the hat. She looks at the watch—it is almost 11:30. The car will be here soon. She has to hurry up. She again glances at the TV. The plane is coming again…. Is all this happening now?

Her attention span seems to be dwindling, but the images

incite her curiosity—the scenes on her TV screen begin penetrating the wall of her distraction. She takes hold of the remote and increases the volume on the TV as she sits on the bed. And then, as she listens with a sense of urgency and astonishment, the background voice announces the collapse, repeatedly. Now, the dark clay clouds and waves of dust, people running helter-skelter, and the images played over and over spells of a disaster of hellish proportions. Suddenly, it all feels so surreal, so unreal, and then so real, a raging inferno has descended on Downtown Manhattan. The end of the world is at hand. She turns up the volume another notch, when finally, and convincingly, she realizes that this is indeed no movie. This is real, and with the collapse of the two World Trade Center Towers, not only did Mary's office dissolve into the rubble, but the Windows of the World as well. Mary usually gets to work at about eight-forty five to nine o'clock in the morning. Her office was in the South Tower. Oh my God—was she there when the plane struck? Was she able to escape in time?

She looks at the icon of Christ on the sidewall and prays:

"Dear God, Eternal Father, have mercy on us, and the whole world. Jesus Christ, The Son of God, have mercy on us, and the whole world. Mary, Mother of God, have mercy on us, and the whole world."

She then collapses on the bed, hyperventilating.

I have to control myself. I cannot panic. Please Christ help me. She utters aloud. She kisses the icon, pops a double dose of Xanax, and takes in a few deep breaths. In a short while she feels composed but her breathing is somewhat labored. She gets off the bed, changes, and calls Mary at the office. What is she doing? She dials Mary's home. She calls Mary's father at the midtown offices of the Manhattan Bank. There is no dial tone. She shuts off the TV and closes her eyes.

She momentarily falls asleep.

The stage resounds with Stravinsky's music: the orchestra comes alive with its low throbbing strings and baleful trombones. Anna dances in Kastchei's garden—half bird, half-woman; her shimmering feathers taper off in orange-speckled flames. She crosses the stage in series of leaps; amber light catches her figure in various poses; the red feather glows in red and gold dust high above her head. She dances frantically across the stage in rapid successive piqué turns conjuring vivid images of flight. She spins in full force as the music attains its highest pitch, when Prince Ivan catches her about the waist. She, the Firebird, is rigid with fear. Her arms fly out and beat the air in a frantic effort to free herself.

There is loud applause as she walks off the stage. She comes back again for the bow. She is handed a bouquet of red roses. She makes her way out into the corridor. A man approaches, masked and clad in a black robe. His tiny red eyes glow like those of an albino mouse. She wants to run, but finds herself paralyzed. He has a tight grip on her waist.

She suddenly wakes up in a state of fugue, uncertain where she is, and as rapidly falls right back to sleep, and lapses into another dream: She is walking on Fifth Avenue after a shopping spree at Tiffany's. Near the Pierre Hotel, there is a man by the side of the porter staring at her. Is he KGB? She picks up the pace. Is she being followed? She turns her head to look. He is getting closer. Will they kidnap her and send her to Siberia? She runs faster and faster. As she is about to cross Sixty-fifth Street, she hears the screech of brakes.

"Miss, watch where you're going."

She wakes up agitated and winded, and immediately props herself up on her bed. She feels her heart racing, galloping away, like some uncontrollable stallion. A gray film, then darkness covers her eyes.

BAM! Her chest heaves...BAM!...BAM!

When she regains consciousness, she finds herself on the floor. She presses the Medical Alert button.

Ali remains glued to the TV witnessing the apocalyptic raging inferno, the crumbling of Twin Tower Two, followed by Twin Tower One. He feels some degree of consolation that the former had preceded the latter, and must have given Nancy enough time to escape. He continues making phone calls but there is no dial tone.

Dr. Rand coaxes Ali to join him for lunch, but he has no appetite. The announcement that all bridges and tunnels to the city are closed, that Manhattan is now a quarantined island with no access except for emergency vehicles prompts Dr. Rand to invite him to stay in Boston for the night at his home, or if he wishes, if he needs privacy, he could book him a hotel. "You could leave by bus or car in the morning if the airports remain closed," he says. "If you leave now who knows you may be stranded somewhere." Finally, Dr. Rand books him a room at the Airport Hilton and drops him at Hertz. Ali leaves for the airport.

Overtaken by a feeling of doom, the end of many chapters, or the tattered fiery end of a book, of life itself, perhaps Mary's life and her own, in the ambulance, Anna restlessly trashes about.

"Turn off the defibrillator—let me die," she says.

"Give her some Versed," a paramedic says.

With the world on the brink of disaster, she yearns for the presence of loved ones. She sees Mary's face again, as she had approached her on Sixty-fifth Street, many years ago.

"Mama, Katya," she calls out as she suddenly wakes up from her twilight sleep, as the speeding ambulance goes over a bump.

Anna is carried on a stretcher into the madness of the ER: the moans, the screams, the beeps, the overhead pages, stretchers all over the place, doors crashing, trolleys clanging, doctors and nurses running amok...

"We are waiting for the injured from the World Trade Center. Please clear the area," orders the triage nurse.

"We have a cardiac patient with shocks from the defibrillator," says the paramedic. An intern immediately arrives.

"Do you have a doctor, Miss?" she asks.

"Dr. Ali and Dr. Grimes," Anna utters aloud.

"Page Dr. Grimes," says the nurse.

"What happened Ms.?" asks Dr. Sanchez, the medical intern.

"I had shocks from the defibrillator. Please call Dr. Grimes. Please turn it off." The intern confused and perplexed stares at her.

"Place the magnet over here on the defibrillator. Dr. Grimes told me so—get the magnet, please, before it goes off again."

Dr. Grimes promptly answers. The nurse locates the doughnut magnet on the crash cart.

"Yes, that's it," says Anna. The nurse tapes it on her chest over the defibrillator. The defibrillator is turned off. Anna calms down.

When Dr. Denzel hurriedly makes his appearance in the ER, he finds Anna confused, her breathing labored, the color ashen, the veins in the neck engorged, and the blood pressure hovering in the mid-seventies. He immediately admits her to the CCU where she is administered a host of intravenous medications, and a catheter is introduced to measure the pressures inside the heart.

"Where is Dr. Ali?" she asks.

"I don't know. He's probably still in Boston, and likely stranded there. Anna, I'm upgrading you to the highest category IA for heart transplantation," says Dr. Denzel, confidently.

"Shouldn't you check with Dr. Ali?"

"I can't reach him. I'm sure he will agree."

She understands that things look bleak, that she may not last long. The expression on Denzel's countenance spells it all, her time is up. she must receive a heart or to take her leave. She had prepared herself for this, even rehearsed it several times in her mind, but now, she finds herself at a loss. There is no one around to reassure her. Her mother is in Russia with Katya, and Mary perhaps lying under mounds of rubble. Who should she say goodbye to?

Her mind is in a constant state of flux from the low blood pressure and heart failure. Lucid moments are interspersed with a gray fogginess; and, there are moments filled with restlessness—the restlessness that comes from knowing that death is near, just around the corner. "Am I going to die?" she keeps asking the nurse. "My chest hurts, and my breathing is getting worse."

The nurse calls Dr. Sanchez, whom Anna had met in the ER, and who was unsure what to do when she asked for the magnet to turn of the defibrillator. She decides to increase the dose of the drug Primacor, a heart stimulant. Within fifteen minutes or so, Anna goes again into a rapid heartbeat. The bedside alarm goes off. The nurses and resident doctors surrounded her. "I'm afraid of the shocks," she cries.

They page Dr. Grimes. Anna trembles. Her body stiffens. She clenches her fists.

"Turn it off—the magnet, the magnet. Please, let me die in peace," she barely whispers.

The nurse injects a sedative. Dr. Sanchez places the magnet on her chest over the defibrillator. Dr. Grimes arrives on the double, and reprograms the internal defibrillator with an external programmer, and begins administering another intravenous drug after he diagnoses her rhythm disturbance as atrial fibrillation—an irregular rhythm from the upper chamber of the heart seen invariably in patients with heart failure.

She hears faint voices in the background: "She's very sick—I doubt whether she will make it without a new heart. I hope she gets one within the next forty-eight hours."

"If she doesn't come out of this, she should have an assist device to help her heart pump the blood," Dr. Grimes advises. Dr. Denzel concurs.

The intravenous medication stops the irregular heart rhythm. The interns and residents feel reassured—Dr. Grimes is a cool, collected genius. He goes over the tracings from the interrogation of the defibrillator and the management of the heart rhythm abnormality. At least for now the crisis is over.

CHAPTER 30

The Terrorist

Uncertain what to do or how to proceed, Ali checks into the hotel after being turned away from the airport. He crashes on the bed, dialing, dialing, his apartment, his parents, Nancy's parents, and the hospital, over and over. He switches on the TV: the news, the images of the loaded planes crashing into the towers, watching death and fire on a large scale, a catastrophe beyond comprehension, of innocent people taken to their death slices like a knife through his very bones, his shattered sensorium. And then he sees bodies, human figures, contorted images jumping out of windows from the raging inferno into the emptiness, perhaps momentarily believing that there is some cloud, some flying machine, or a spaceship sent by the gods safe enough to land upon? Or is it just a fear-flight reaction to the encroaching, scorching fire? Had Nancy jumped out of the window from the scorching fire? No, she was on her way down. He wraps her image on the descending elevator like a warm blanket around his chest. He remembers the words from the Surah 101: al Qarieh.

Oh, the striking of the Last Hour!
The sudden calamity!

And what could make you conceive what that sudden
   calamity will be?
On the Day when men will be like moths swarming in
   confusion,
and the mountains will be like fluffy tufts of wool. . .
And then, he whose weight of good deeds is heavy in
   the balance,
shall find himself in a happy' state of life;
whereas he whose weight is light in the balance,
shall be engulfed by an abyss.
And what could make you conceive what that abyss
   will be?
A fire hotly burning.

He hurriedly checks out of the hotel eager to drive back to
New York City to find his wife. In the car, he cannot get her off
his mind. What if the elevators or the stairs were obstructed by
fire or by smoke? His intention is to keep on calling from his
cellular but he decides against it, afraid to know the worst. But
Ali is an optimist. He assures himself she's well; after all, she
was on her way down the Tower. Again, he holds on tightly
to that thought. He puts on the car radio and dials on to NPR
News. The radio announcer wonders what the world is coming
to. This was an awesome feat of terrorism unlike any other in
history targeted at the economic and military might of America—the only Super-Power. The unknown whereabouts' of the
President and the grounding of all flights in the continental USA
is of profound symbolic, economic, and military significance.
The most powerful country in the World is under siege. The pre-
cision, the secretiveness, the meticulous execution is mind-bog-
gling. How could the intelligent services have missed it all? Who
are these people, and what is their ultimate objective?
   There is hardly any traffic on I-95 and Ali covers the distance from Boston through Rhode Island into Connecticut in a

little more than one hour. As he approaches I-84 in Connecticut, he sees a police check point up ahead. They stop him.

"Where are you going, man?" the police officer asks. There is another by his side.

"To New York City."

"Where are you coming from?"

"Boston."

"Boston?"

"That's where two of the flights originated," one of the officer's remarks to the other.

"Where do you live?"

"New York City."

"Show me your driver's license."

"Here."

"You Muslim?"

"Yah, I'm a doctor. I was in Boston to lecture."

"Is this your car?"

"No, it's rented. I was supposed to take the shuttle back. It was grounded."

As he fumbles in his shirt pocket for the hospital ID, the officer pulls out his gun and asks him to get out of the car.

"I'm a doctor. My wife was in the World Trade Center. I must get to New York," Ali protests.

"World Trade Center?"

"Yes, World Trade Center," says Ali

The policeman pushes him hard onto the car, kicks him and pins his face on the side glass of the car. Ali's legs buckle. They prop him up and handcuff him. Two more officers arrive and hold him down. He is pushed inside a police car and taken to the station. One of the police officers is on his cellular. "We have a suspicious looking Muslim here on his way from Boston to NY in a rented car. He says his wife was in the World Trade Center."

"Hold him there, we'll come and question him."

Ali pleads with the police officers when he comes out of his daze. "You don't understand. My wife was in the World Trade Center. I must find her." His supplications are ignored.

His head hurts. He feels the taste of blood in his mouth. He swallows hard. He asks them to call the hospital in New York City. They tell him to shut up, and shove him into a cell. He again pleads with the police officer, but is ignored. He sits on the floor, his hands covering his face, hot tears running down his cheeks. Finally, within an hour or so, two FBI agents arrive and he is taken out of the cell for questioning. By then Ali is composed. He explains everything: the slides on the CD-ROM, Dr. Rand's invitation and then accidentally, in his jacket pocket, he finds his doctor's ID—that precious piece of plastic that makes all the difference. The ID finally convinces them; however, they insist on dialing the Medical Center.

"You do understand, we can't take anything for granted," one of the FBI agents remarks.

The operator confirms Dr. Ali's identity and connects the FBI officer to the OR where the Chief of Transplant Surgery, Dr. Cohen, who had just finished operating on a bleeding aorta, picks up the phone. He confirms Ali's identity, and after speaking to Ali, requests to speak to the police officer in-charge.

They let Ali go. He asks for some peroxide and a bandage and places it on the cut on his forehead. The arresting officer, now visibly apologetic, tells him that he shouldn't have resisted arrest. Ali hadn't resisted arrest; but Ali now knows he best not argue.

"We could book you—Doc or no Doc," says the cop who accosted him. Ali stares at him with an intense angry look. The cop looks down, avoiding his piercing eyes.

"Two of the hijackings originated in Boston. You were on your way from Boston to New York in a rented car. This is War, man," he says, looking out of the window.

Ali doesn't answer. His civil rights were violated, but it

doesn't matter for now. He has to get the hell out of there.

There were disappointments, minor personal disappointments that Ali had encountered in his life, but now Ali feels a
profound sense of devastation as he steps into the car and takes
off on I-84. The aura of self-confidence, the hubris that surrounded him since his childhood, into adolescence and adult-
hood, is shattered. Tears cloud his vision, tears he sheds for
Nancy and for himself, as he drives on the highway in a daze.
As an American Muslim, he had felt free in a country that shel-
tered everyone, and New York City was the best the world had
to offer. Suddenly, his sensitivities are acutely awakened. How
will he explain himself? Indeed, in the past, he had been saved
by being a doctor, a brilliant academic cardiologist. He wonders
now how far the medical attributes he possesses will go in the
new world. He doesn't know the moment he will reach home.

There is another roadblock on the Third Avenue Bridge.
Anxiety now surges like an overflowing bucket of hot water. He
feels butterflies in his stomach. He flashes his doctor's ID. No
questions asked; they let him through. He speed-dials Nancy.
There is no dial tone. The FDR Drive south is deserted; yet he
drives slowly and cautiously. A shroud of despair descends over
him as he exits on Ninety-sixth Street and proceeds south on
Second Avenue to Seventy-fifth Street. The streets are an empty
wasteland. It is as if all the inhabitants of this great city disappeared, pulverized into nothingness or floated away into outer
space. As he unlocks the door to his apartment, he feels cold and
clammy; sweat pours down his face and chest. He feels exhausted, his legs buckle, and he can barely keep his eyes open. He
goes to the fridge and snaps open a can of Coca-Cola. He drinks
its contents in one single long gulp. *Where is Nancy? Could she
have gone to her parents in Staten Island?* He speed-dials her

mother; there is no dial tone. The Brooklyn Battery Tunnel and
the Verrazano Bridge are closed; there is no way he can make
it there. He will have to wait for the phone-lines to be restored.
As he stretches on the sofa, his eyes close involuntarily. He feels
the dimming away of his consciousness, as a dark film descends
upon hm.

Ali finds himself walking into a canyon—an uneven mud
road, the asphalt melted and piled up in heaps. Around him is
a world of fire: the skyscrapers with their fiery walls and sag-
ging windows like curtains of crimson flames. Men, women,
and children—human fire balls dance around him. They beckon
him as their burnt flesh oozes in rivers of molten flames. He runs
away, eyes shut, wherever his feet will carry him.

When he opens his eyes, he sees buildings all burnt out and
melted away, resembling trees of metal skewed. The roadside
electrical poles are twisted into balls like tread reels. The cars all
misshaped, half dissolved, caked with ash and dust—the dust
of a bright orange color. The sky is overcast; a light film of fog
moves along the canyon lit by a strange orange glow. There is
no sign of life anywhere. He walks quickly in this burned out
canyon looking on all sides for a trace of life. Where have all the
people gone? Where am I? He enters what remains of a burnt
out building beside a fallen cracked statue of what looks like
the face of Christopher Columbus. Is this Columbus Circle near
the New York Coliseum? He carefully avoids the grey pools of
melted glass as he clambers through the ruins. He enters a large
space, perhaps a solarium. He sees mangled cars and boats; piles
of twisted metal are all over and in the middle, a large mass of
what looks like flesh with tinges of orange and purple color
as if preserved or poisoned by some lethal chemical. The smell
is acrid—the smell of liquefying bone. Frightened, he rapidly

exits the building and begins to run. He feels thirsty and cold. Orange flakes of snow keep falling and burning like acid. He takes shelter on the sidewalk of a burned-out building. Where am I? What has happened here? Suddenly, an animal passes by—a strange animal, its face macerated, dripping thick saliva, like gel. The body that of a dog; its frightened bright eyes move rapidly like ball bearings in its empty skull. The animal runs at a rapid, galloping pace, like a horse, startled at something it saw. Ali feels a shiver.

He wakes up startled, and in a sweat, the dream still vivid in his mind. He looks around grappling with his surroundings. Gradually, the landscape draws him in, and rapidly claims him as its own.

He is in his apartment, safe and secure. He runs to the window and looks out at the East River. He is in New York, on the East side; the world around him still stands—he is not in a post-apocalyptic world, a world illuminated by a strange yellow light with shades of orange without any remnants of human life.

He then realizes what has happened.

He looks around for the phone. There is a message from a Dr. King, which simply says: "Dr. Ali, your wife Nancy is in the Intensive Care Unit at the Downtown Medical Center. When you get this message please come down immediately." The dream now fades away entirely, as dreams often do—bagged and hidden away like some useless treasure. He feels a sense of relief. His fatigue suddenly dissipates. He even feels upbeat.

Nancy is alive!

He leaves immediately for the hospital.

Nancy is unconscious, with head and neck injuries and a broken leg. She is maintained on a respirator. Dr. King informs Ali that she was brought to the hospital at about eleven o'clock.

"We really don't know what happened. She was probably hit by falling debris from the crashing South Tower."

"No!" Ali bites his lip and shuts his eyes.

"I'm very sorry, Dr. Ali," he says. "The MRI showed massive brain contusion. There is a small collection of blood in the brain and a subdural hematoma, which we could evacuate."

"I see," says Ali, hesitatingly.

"I honestly don't know if it will help. But if you agree, it's worth a try." Ali pensively shakes his head.

"Can I see the MRI?"

"Sure. Go to the basement and look for Radiology. Ask for Dr. Chen."

"Oh yes, I almost forgot. I called the OB service—the baby—she lost the baby, and by the way, if it means anything to you, her heart is fine." He places his arm around Ali. "There was kidney shutdown from the muscle destruction; however, she has started making urine, and should tolerate the surgery fine."

Ali kisses Nancy. He holds her hand then slumps on the chair with his head in the palm of his hands. As Dr. King is about to leave, Ali tells him that he will consent to the surgery, and asks him to do all he can.

He calls his in-laws on Staten Island and his parents on Long Island (somewhat contented that finally, the phone lines have been restored), and relays to them what has transpired. He proceeds to Radiology to look at the MRI.

CHAPTER 31

At the Bakhchysarai Fountain

For the first twenty-four hours Anna waxes and wanes in the Coronary Care Unit. At times she registers her small quadrangular world of monitors and intravenous poles and defibrillators where white coats appear and disappear; at other times she is oblivious, dozing off, her attention span playing hide and seek.

The following day, her doctors confirm some improvement in her condition, and the need for an assist device is deferred. A little more than twenty-four hours have passed and the rapid heartbeat hasn't recurred.

The events of the last forty-eight hours have temporarily faded from Anna's mind. By evening however, she is more attentive, and is able to watch and listen to the TV. She sees the replays of the World Trade Center collapse and the reaction of the other nations. When her own Russia isues a statement, she is overtaken by homesickness for her country in her half-awake lethargy. She notices a sense of gloom permeating among the nurses and doctors who glance at the TV screen while monitoring her heart rhythm and blood pressure. A nurse comes with some pills and a small little cup with water. "Just a sip to swallow the pills," she says.

Soon, Anna falls asleep. The gift of flight is being restored again, as she becomes woven of radiant air.

In a lamé pink dress with speckles of silver, Anna, enters a garden surrounded by columns with statues of female gods and kings. Hiding behind a column, she scans the scene. In the center, a fountain spews liquid fire. On the right side sit the queen and king; ladies in waiting stroll with their cavaliers.

A sudden rushing cadenza bursts from a harp. Anna enters the garden and dances joyfully. Four handsome Princes approach carrying gifts. She is flattered, but continues dancing. A prince rushes to present her with a single red rose. The music slows. She does a pirouette, and accepts the rose and moves to the next Prince. He gives her a purple rose. Again, she turns and dives into arabesque. The third Prince presents his pink rose, and she pirouettes and holds her arabesque. The fourth prince presents his yellow rose.

She tosses the roses in the air.

The petals fall all around her transforming into multicolored iridescent butterflies that cling to her body.

Anna, the butterfly queen dances a pas de bourrées in a diagonal line and then circles the garden in accelerating chaîné turns. As the tempo of the music builds up, the butterfly queen returns to the garden and makes another circle in accelerating chaîné turns. A young girl appears out of nowhere, and stands right in front of her. Anna stops dancing and stares. The young one's cheeks are red, and her chest is hollow and wide open. Anna sees the girl's heart: red and beating. The girl points to her heart. "Take it, my butterfly queen, it's yours, I have no use for it," the girl whispers. "Your heart is weak, take it. It's a gift; it's yours for keeps."

Anna is perplexed. She circles near the girl mesmerized by the red beating heart. The girl takes Anna's hand and places it in the hollow of her chest, on her heart. Anna takes hold of the heart and pulls it. It gives away like an apple from a tree. She looks for the girl to thank her, but the girl disappears. Anna dances with the gift of the heart, but when she looks at it again, the heart has transformed into a spindle. She pricks her finger on its needle-like tip and blood droplets fall on the white marble floor.

Anna screams. She collapses.

The princes, the queen and king, quickly surrounded her. Anna is pale and her eyes are foggy. In the distance, the sound of a trumpet, and the sweet soft strings of a harp.

Anna's hands and legs jerk and twitch.

"Are you all right, miss?" the nurse just come for the night shift, asks.

"Where am I?" Anna says.

"You are in the Medical Center, in New York City."

"What happened here?"

"You don't know Miss? You must be confused with all the drugs. There was a terrorist attack on the World Trade Center. Thousands of innocent people have died."

It now hits her hard like metal on a raw wound: This City, her adopted city, the City of Freedom—New York City—lies bleeding and shattered, much like her.

CHAPTER 32

In the Intensive Care Unit

*I*t is almost morning when Nancy's parents leave for Manhattan with Ali's father who was kind enough to drive from Long Island to Staten Island to pick them up. The MD license plates allow them to use the Brooklyn Battery Tunnel and the FDR Drive. The drive across the tunnel feels eerie; they are the only ones zipping through. As they enter Manhattan, they are stopped by National Guardsmen with machine guns. Ali's father slows down the car to a mere crawl as he approaches the light. He stops the car and steps out, and is asked to get back in. To the right is the West Side Highway—the World Trade Center disaster barely two blocks away. He is ordered to lower the window, hand over the driver's license and the registration, and explain the purpose of his visit to Manhattan.

An acrid smell of burning bone enters the car; the air feels heavy, foggy and polluted. A cloud of dust hangs over the Hudson River extending over Battery Park City like a creature jutting out of the water. After thoroughly searching the car, the Guardsmen let them go.

The FDR Drive is deserted. There is not a car in sight. They are in a bombed-out zone where the people of this vibrant city, have suddenly melted away. Staten Island and Long Island seem far off distant lands, different Continents.

Ali waits for them in the surgical waiting lounge, pacing up and down. He thinks of the baby that is lost. They can always have another, but it is Nancy who concerns him. What if she doesn't make it? What will he do without her? His plans and his dreams for the future mean nothing now. She is so much a part of it all. It all seems so meaningless, so senseless.

Ali explains her condition to his in-laws, and tells them that surgery is in progress. Her seventy-year old father looks old, tremulous, and devastated. He can barely speak. Her mother maintains her poise and demeanor. She is the pillar of the family as mothers often are. Ali takes his own parents to the side and explains: "the pupillary reaction to light, and the results of the MRI scan are all disconcerting." They are both doctors, they understand, and they console each other. A television set is on, the sound is high, and images appear repeatedly on the screen of the World Trade Center collapse. They watch as if blindly, the planes crashing on the Towers, the ensuing inferno, the shapes of people jumping from the Towers; the fear, the fright on people's faces as they turn and run. Nancy's father gets agitated. "Somebody turn that thing off," he suddenly shouts. Ali walks up to the screen. "May I?" he asks an old man watching, and turns the TV off. The old man doesn't seem to mind. There are few others who sporadically raise their eyes, who perhaps realizing what caused such a repulsive reaction in Nancy's father, don't protest. Ali cannot sit in the bright sterile waiting room any longer. He takes off abruptly, walking several deserted blocks at a fast numbed pace like an aimless robot, and then returns. They sit again in the waiting room in stark silence.

When Dr. King makes his appearance in the visitors lounge in his green scrubs, he carries a broad smile on his face that is reassuring to the elders.

"We drained the hematoma—now we will have to wait and see," he says to Ali. "She is doing as well as expected. The next twenty four hours are critical."

"My daughter is a fighter," her father says. "Don't give up on her."

They all go to the Surgical-ICU, where Nancy's mother Pat, takes out a devotional scapular of St. Anne, and a picture of Saint Jude. She places both objects on Nancy's pillow. Her head is covered with a circular bandage. Her eyes are closed and taped. What little of her face shows is bruised and swollen. She has a brace on her neck and a cast on her leg. Intravenous tubing disappear into her arm; a tube in her gullet is connected to the respirator that hisses twenty times a minute. The only reassuring sound is her heart, which beeps its regular rhythm. "Nancy, Nancy, my baby," her mother and father call out, as if she is fast asleep and will wake up any moment and hug them all. Ali's mother stands behind and silently weeps her tears. A long uncomfortable silence ensues, broken by the sounds of the heart beeps and the sighs of the respirator.

Pat asks for the priest and requests the last rites of the Catholic Church. Perhaps she senses hopelessness, as only mothers can. They defer to her judgment. When the priest has finished, Ali convinces them to go home or better still, stay in his apartment. They go back to the waiting room and sit there. Somebody has put on the TV, and on and on and on it replays the World Trade Center collapse. They leave the waiting room and make phone calls, then come back to tell Ali that they have found two rooms at the New York Hilton. Ali understands; they don't want to impinge on his privacy.

Ali and Pat stay with Nancy.

He feels impotent, something he has never felt before. He has faced many difficult decisions with his patients over his career, but he has never dealt with a life and death situation that involved his own family, where someone he loves is at risk of dying. There was his mother, who had a heart attack, but he had acted promptly, it was his area of expertise; the intervention was quick and fast and successful. Life and death have their own dynamic in a doctor's life, but when it comes to a family member, all defenses break down; the walls of detachment, which usually assure clarity of thought, collapse, and panic sets in. A doctor's knowledge can be beneficial in some situations and detrimental in others. Ali is well aware that medical complications occur more often in doctor's families, for at times too much is done, at other times too little. Often, there is an artificial optimism; at times a skeptical pessimism. He wants to avoid getting involved in Nancy's care. He senses hopelessness on Dr. King's face and worse still, the neuro-radiologist who was unaware that Ali was a doctor. He had spelled it out in no uncertain terms, later realizing his folly when Ali identified himself. But Ali also knows that there are cases and situations when people wake up, when miracles do happen.

He stays by Nancy's side, managing to doze off from sheer exhaustion. In the morning, he opens her eyes to test her pupillary reaction to light. Soon, he realizes that there are decisions to make and wonders whether he has to involve his in-laws in the process. He briefly discusses Nancy's condition with Dr. King who orders an electroencephalogram to measure brain electrical activity.

As Ali walks out of the ICU, Brad walks in. They look at each other briefly, when Ali hears a voice from behind: "Dr. Ali, I don't know whether you remember me, but I'm a friend of Anna."

"Yes, yes, I remember," he says, turning around.

"My wife, Mary, and I, met you at the hospital and at Anna's apartment. Are you here to help out?"

Ali hesitates.

"Mary was at the WTC—they just operated to remove a blood clot in her leg," says Brad. "The doctor says the surgery went well. Could you please take a look at her?"

"My wife too…She…she was seriously injured in the World Trade Center—she's in the Neuro—ICU."

"Oh my God, I'm so sorry, Dr. Ali," says Brad. "Mary arrived at the World Trade Center just as the plane hit the South Tower. "She stayed around to help out. I don't know what really happened. The doctor says she had an asthmatic attack from all the dust and debris, followed by a respiratory arrest."

"I need to make a phone call and do an errand," says Ali. "But when I return, I'll gladly see Mary. I'm not a pulmonologist however, or a vascular doctor—I'm not qualified to give an opinion."

"I understand," says Brad.

Ali returns to the ICU in the afternoon. When he goes to Nancy's bedside, she is undergoing an electroencephalogram. He decides to visit Mary at the other end of the ICU. By now everyone knows Ali, and show him deference. As he approaches Mary's bed, he finds the curtains drawn, and hears faint moaning sounds coming from around the bed. A silhouette of a stooped man with feathered headgear hops around the bed uttering indecipherable incantations while brandishing a feathered pole. As Ali so slightly opens the curtain, he sees a Native American—perhaps a medicine-man doing his thing. Brad, in jeans and a T- shirt, stands beside Mary as if in a trance. They don't notice Ali's presence. Ali steps out and waits in the sitting room. In about fifteen minutes, Brad and the American Indian, headgear in his hand, emerge. Brad approaches Ali.

"My friend's a Navajo Hatahi—Jim Twowings," says Brad. "I'm a Native American. I believe in the power of the spirits. After this is over, I will go back to the reservation in Arizona, and to the Grand Canyon where my people came from, and there I will play the sax in the wilderness. In these moments when the world is torn apart, we need to commune with nature—to seek spirituality, to find ourselves."

Ali listens, but barely.

"We'll all go there," Brad continues, tapping him on the back. "You, your wife, Mary and me and Anna, and there in the canyon of my forefathers, I will play the sax and beat the drums to thank the spirits. Promise me, you'll come." Ali nods his head.

"So much hatred in this world... Growing up on the reservation I felt hatred for the white man, for all they had done to my people. But Mary melted my hatred away. She is my angel." Brad points to the scar on his cheek.

"You see this scar? It reminds me of the gangster life I lived— the drugs, the alcohol, the mescal, and the speed. I was high, psychotic, and mad at the world. I knifed a man without any provocation. I played a crazy horn then—I was a mean man." He goes silent for a while as if in contemplation, as if he has lost his trend of thought. After a coughing spell, he continues: "In prison, I discovered the music of Stan Getz, but when I got out of prison, I went back to the same life of empty beer cans, sleeping with coyotes or in friend's mobile home. One day, as I sat near an ancient burial site, blowing my sax into the sunset, Mary heard the sad tones. My music lead her to me. She was working as a volunteer on the reservation. She was the rising Sun. She recognized my talent and brought me to New York. The sax gave me a living and Mary gave me life. It was Mary who persuaded Anna to go along with the heart transplant."

Ali quietly listens. He wonders what is left for him to say. Until this, he had hardly seen Brad speak, and now he opened up like a gushing fountain. It is what tragedy does to us all— opens us in many different ways. Ali is silent, drained; he has no shamans to turn to. His mind is in a state of siege. At this time, at this moment, the only god he can worship is the god of science. He hopes that this god will come to Nancy's aid.

"Yes, I don't know what this world is coming to," Ali finally says. "There is too much hatred and vengeance, and it all seems to be going around. There is no end in sight to the violence. History repeats itself, it speaks badly of the human race, and innocent people, wonderful people, like your wife and mine, have to suffer."

"Yeah, you said it all man," says Brad.

While Ali is on the phone with his father in-law and his parents, Dr. King approaches and they discuss the findings of Nancy's brain electrical activity.

Soon thereafter, Dr. Wang rushes into the waiting room. "The surgery went well," he tells Brad. "Mary has regained blood supply to the limb. All the signs are positive."

Brad hugs Dr. Wang.

CHAPTER 33

Anguish and Solitude

It is almost five o'clock in the evening when Ali steps out of the hospital and walks towards his apartment. Outside, the air is foggy; a peculiar smell of smoldering fire and bone permeates the air. The sky is overcast. There are hardly any pedestrians on the street. An old woman in a full-length dress, somewhat grand in her silver-white hair, pushes a grocery cart full of trash bags and Pepsi cans. The yellow cabs plough up and down the Avenue, looking for customers.

Ali walks slowly, then fast, and then, he is overtaken by a desire to run. He starts sprinting and finds the bag lady staring at him.

Was he running from something? Were they after him? There are no more criminals left—only terrorists!

He abruptly enters a Deli and picks up a tuna sandwich and a can of Coca-Cola. Once outside, he takes a bite of the sandwich. It chokes him; he throws it in the trash. As soon as he steps in his apartment he feels weighed down by a profound solitude. Nancy's photographs line the corridor: the Staten Island Harbor, the Staten Island Ferry, the Manhattan skyline, the two of them together laughing, and innumerable pictures of Vermont and Grymes Hill fall foliage. He sits on the couch overtaken by a strange emptiness, as if his chest is hollowed, as if his heart is missing. He feels the need to talk to someone—not his mother, not his father or his in-laws. He calls Dr. Grimes on his cell, but he doesn't answer. He then pages Dr. Nalini at Memorial Sloan Kettering Hospital, and when she responds, he tells her that Nancy is brain-dead. He begins sobbing, and hears Nalini sob. She promises to come over right away.

"I knew it when I saw her, when I tested her pupillary reaction to light, but then, you always wish for a miracle," he says to her seated in his living room, his head bowed, his eyes hot with tears. "She's brain dead Nalini—the EEG showed no activity." Ali pauses to wipe his eyes, collect his breath. Nalini listens quietly, her hand caressing his shoulder and back, like the soothing hand of an older, wiser sister.

Finally, she breaks in. "Have you considered donating her heart?" He lifts up his face to hers.

"I think she would have wanted it. We often talked about it, not at a personal level, but in a general way. She was aware of the paucity of donor organs. She even wanted to start a drive for donors. My Nancy—she was so human, so giving." Ali cannot continue. He starts sobbing.

"I will miss her so, Ali."

"I was not deserving of her, Nalini. I'm a selfish man, and perhaps, I'm expressing my own selfishness, of wanting to see her buried in one piece."

"When it's someone you love, it's heart-wrenching whether you are a doctor or not."

"And I have a feeling that both my father and hers will oppose the idea."

"Look Ali, it's a noble thing to do—but so very personal. If they refuse, it will finally be left to you. Just try to put yourself in Nancy's shoes, and it will all become clear. Besides, she could languish on the respirator for a long time."

Ali meets with his parents to discuss Nancy's condition and the donation of her heart. His father vehemently objects. "Nancy will have a proper burial. You will not carve her up. I don't want to hear any more about it," he says, and abruptly walks away. Ali's mother sobs and embraces him. "It's your decision," she says. They cry in each other's arms.

He then takes Pat aside and they talk. She is sympathetic, and says she had a premonition of her death. "Sean," she pauses. "He will not hear of donating her heart." She begins to cry. Ali loses his composure; he feels distressed and wonders why he had even brought up the issue.

Amid sobs, Pat continues: "She is my baby, Ali; but she is his life. I will go along with whatever you decide."

Then unexpectedly, she asks him how long Nancy will last on the respirator. Ali wonders if she's struck with doubts, with guilt, if she wants to hang on to Nancy a bit longer. As Ali is about to answer, she asks, "Is it that hopeless Ali?" She sobs. "I'm—I'm, sorry....."

He is dismayed, dumbfounded, and overwhelmed. He is used to crying: his patients, their wives, husbands, lovers, and children, sobbing hysterically on the phone. But this is different. And yet for a moment, a short moment, these familiar motions of death were so much a part of his daily routine. Now his lips tremble and tears again start pouring from his eyes. He is overwhelmed with fear and insecurity, feels an utter loss of control of his faculties, and an unyielding paralysis of his thought process.

Talking to his father and Nancy's mother has brought him no consolation. If anything, it weakened his resolve; amplified his doubts.

Death was and is, so much a part of his doctoring, so much a part of his professional milieu; and yet, death, with which he has dealt deftly and somewhat impersonally, has now come close to home.

He made the calls, like doctors do, come rain or shine; all but one remains. This last call to Dr. Denzel, who is working tirelessly in this shattered world. When he calls him, Dr. Denzel immediately tells Ali of Anna's precarious condition, and that he has moved her to the top of the list for a heart transplant.

When Ali doesn't respond, Denzel expresses his sympathy and asks him to take off as many days as he wants.

"One more thing," he says. "Dr. Bob was on United Airlines flight 93 that crashed in Pennsylvania. He was on his way to San Francisco to lecture."

CHAPTER 34
The Organ Donation

Ali paces his living room and methodically reviews his options like a good doctor, but finds his concentration shifting time and again. "I cannot accept this," he utters aloud.

Maybe Nancy should have another electroencephalogram. Perhaps he should seek an outside opinion. He cannot give her up to the morgue. He chokes. He is unable to think like a doctor any longer.

For the first time he faces the dilemma that relatives of so many donors struggle with. He thinks of his own father's opposition and the doubts Nancy's mother expressed. Should he permit removal of Nancy's heart? Should he call Nancy's mother and enforce the fact that she should discuss the issue with her father? But isn't all of this irrelevant?

He is Nancy's husband. He is her closest kin.

He thinks of Anna, too, now upstaged to Category IA. Would she be the one to get Nancy's heart? There were other patients waiting: there was Nick and Stanley and Mrs. Martinez and Miss Brown and Princess Fatima—the list was long. He doesn't even know what Nancy's blood group is, and never bothered to find out. Removing her heart, and willing it to Anna—is it murder? Is it? He cannot go through with it—he could be guilt-ridden for the rest of his life. Maybe he should request that Nancy's heart be donated to someone in New York; after all it was New York City that was the site of the catastrophe. And maybe with serendipity Anna would get Nancy's heart. It is not as if he is murdering Nancy for Anna's sake.

Am I losing my mind? This is not the Ali, the Ali he knew—that Ali is summarily destroyed. This Ali cannot think straight. This Ali cannot pray. He sobs uncontrollably. He puts on the TV for distraction and keeps on shifting channels to avoid the replay of the World Trade Center disaster. He pops a Xanax to calm his nerves, and before he realizes, falls asleep on the couch.

He wakes up startled and confused not knowing where he is, and is overtaken by a strange foreboding, a premonition of death. He looks for Nancy on the couch by his side. When he comes to his senses, he feels an emptiness overtake him, as if he is traveling in a void, in a canopied world with nothing to hold on to. Slices of despair accumulate one on top of the other, the superimposition of dark shadows on a grey landscape.

He is so alone.

It is 9:00 PM. He shakes himself. He showers. Hot water massages his wounded self; he turns the tap to ice-cold. He dresses and leaves for the hospital. There is a big commotion going on at the entrance to the ICU. Brad is there with his horn demanding that he be let in. "I want to play a tune for Mary. It will wake her up," he says. He promises to play soft.

"I will not disturb the other patients," he pleads with the head nurse.

"The visiting hours are over, you must leave now, or I will call security."

"Mary is unconscious on a respirator," says Brad to Ali. "I signed the papers anyway. She wouldn't want to live on a respirator. If she goes, I want her to go flying like the eagle. *I signed the papers donating her heart to Anna—Mary wanted it that way."*

Ali loses his balance and is struck by what Brad said. Mary had willed her heart to Anna.

Here is courage above all else.

Here is love. Here is religion. Here is God. Right here!

Ali goes to the ICU and talks to the resident staff. He returns to the waiting room and explains to Brad that Mary had a cardiac arrest due to a low potassium level, which has now been restored. She is back on the respirator, and her unconsciousness is related to the sedation she is on, so that she doesn't fight the respirator.

"There is nothing for you to do," he says. "You may as well go home."

Then Ali goes to Nancy's bedside. He kisses her lips one last time. He then meets with Dr. King and signs the papers permitting Nancy's heart to be removed.

Nancy is pronounced dead at 12:20 AM.

CHAPTER 35

A Heart for Anna

The dawn arrives with a gray haze over New York City. The city itself is half-deserted, and those still doing their chores do them in a daze, somewhat lost, not sure what the future will bring. The traffic remains sparse, the FDR Drive and the Brooklyn Battery Tunnel remain closed except for emergency vehicles and police cars and the black SUV's of FBI agents that speed by, sirens blazing. The nurses in the Coronary Care Unit have a distant disconnected look on their long faces. It is as if all joy has been drained and people go about performing their tasks in a robotic way. It is what happens when death comes suddenly and unexpectedly on a massive scale.

Anna wakes up late, at almost ten in the morning. She had fallen asleep at one o'clock, still glued to the television set. She is better and the rapid heartbeat is under control. It is as if, again, she has been given a new lease on life, however short that might be. The resident doctors after their examinations discuss transferring her out of the CCU to the Cardiac Center. Anna likes the idea however both Dr. Denzel and Dr. Grimes exercise their veto power. "No way," they say, "let's observe her for another twenty-four hours."

Anna had arrived in the Emergency Room with a small suitcase packed with a couple of night gowns, a tooth brush and
tooth paste, several CDs, a photograph of Katya and her mother, and a second photograph of Mary and Brad. She was well-
aware of her precarious condition and for more than a year she
had her suitcase ready, like women about to deliver do. She had
already used the suitcase two times in the past year. She now
asks the nurse to hand over a CD, and she listens to Rostropo-
vich when her phone rings. She wonders whether it is her mother. It turns out to be Brad. He tells her that he had called her but
there was no answer; and subsequently, he had called the super
and come to know that she was in the hospital. He tells her
that Mary was injured at the World Trade Center, and that she
is in the Downtown Medical Center. He assures her that she'll
be fine, and after wishing her good luck with the transplant, he
abruptly ends the conversation. Anna wants to question Brad at
length, but her own precarious physical and mental state traps
her in fear; besides she hears trepidation in Brad's voice. Then
again, Brad is a man of a few words.

She badly wants to talk to someone—her mother, even little
Katya deftly—about all that has happened. And then, a profound exhaustion overtakes her, perhaps from the lack of sleep
and the heart failure, or perhaps from not knowing what to expect, how much longer she must take this wait for a heart. Two
years seems a century when one is hanging by a thread. Her
blood type O is the most common and has the highest demand.
Perhaps her reclassification in the most urgent Category, IA,
will make all the difference?

Late that evening, a bed is needed in the CCU, and Anna is
transferred to the Cardiac Center. She is fast asleep with a sleeping pill, when Jackie wakes her up, and excitedly, gives her the
news: "Anna, we have a heart for you. I just got a call from the
National Organ Procurement Center."

She turns around and goes back to sleep, but the words "a heart" keeps repeating in her mind. Is she dreaming? Suddenly she realizes that it's not a dream. There is a heart for her. She props up in bed in disbelief.

Somewhere, a person was lying on a hospital bed with a beating heart and a comatose body. Somewhere, a person was pronounced brain dead. Somewhere, a person was taken to the operating room, anaesthetized, the chest was sawed open, and the heart was removed. Somewhere, someone's blood type, and antibody profile was matched with that of several hundreds or thousands of would-be recipients. The lucky recipient was notified, like the winner of a lottery—the winner of life—and that someone is Anna.

Now Anna is wide-awake. Stunned. She wonders where the heart is coming from. For a moment she thinks of Mary. A sudden chill overtakes her. She manages to cork the memory of the fresh bleeding wound, the constant TV replays of the towers going up in smoke, the falling bodies, the crumbling of one-hundred and ten stories one after the other, one twin following the other, and the cloud of debris moving like a tsunami wave engulfing all. Her mind goes blank the way it used to for the curtain calls, or when she went on the stage and performed.

Like someone perennially waiting for the numbers of the winning lottery, she has waited for this news for so long. Sometimes she even heard the phone in her sleep, and picked up the receiver only to find that there was nobody on the other end. "They are only phantom calls," Ali had said. The wait has drained her of the little energy she has—a slow agonizing death. Often she felt it was not worth the effort. Her mother would care for Katya, and Katya would survive as so many orphans do. Mary and Brad would adopt Katya.

The news of the available heart seems strange, almost unwanted like a long overdue marriage proposal. Could the donor be someone from the World Trade Center? Could someone by dying in this awful catastrophe, save her? Or was it someone brain-dead from a car accident? Aren't all accidents—car accidents, gunshot deaths—disasters after all? The World Trade Center attack was no accident.

She thinks of the woman whose heart she will receive. Did she have a family: a husband, perhaps a child? What kind of a person was she? Would this stranger's heart change her? She thinks of Mary and wonders how she is doing. There was a tremor in Brad's voice. Was he putting her on? She wishes she could go and see Mary. What if they couldn't save her? What if the heart…Oh God, no—she mustn't think this way!

She calls her mother in Russia to give her the news. The call doesn't go through. She calls her newfound friend Margarita in Staten Island. "Udache, good luck," the friend says. "The bridges and tunnels are all closed Anna, or I would be with you."

Jackie walks in and out of Anna's room, giving orders, making sure all goes well. But now it is Ali that Anna wants to see. In these moments when her life is on the edge, perhaps to survive like a refueled flame, or to die like the wick of a candle at its very last end, she longs to see the ones she loves. Will Ali come? She needs him now more than ever. The near-death experience has brought her closer to Christ. She has been given the gift of flight. It has changed her dramatically: her vanity, the anger, and the tantrums have all dissipated. She has turned into a new person with a new life, however tragic, however sad. The love she feels for Ali is a selfless love, a love to simply want to love, for the sake of love, a love devoid of carnal pleasure, like the love of Christ. Perhaps it is the only way she can rationalize her love.

She has never stood a chance—the mirror, yes the mirror—that wall, that world, that friend of a ballerina, now her foe, has constantly revealed her pale, bluish, and emaciated face, the swollen legs, the sparseness and flimsiness of her pubic hair. The long-line physique, of long, lean, willowy limbs, is long gone.

And her sex drive is in ruins, like an abandoned dance hall.

"Cardiac cachexia—the general physical wasting as a result of heart failure," the cardiology fellow had explained to the medical students. She remembers one of the young female doctors, a resident whispering to another female resident: "At one time she was a ballerina—look at her now..."

She looks at the album from Russia that has a catalogue of pictures since she was a baby. How beautiful, how shapely and tall, like a swan she had grown to be. Her body, tall and lithe, her long-reaching legs, like those of gazelle, were made for dance, to soar up in the air; and her long neck held her head high, like a solitary star. Her leanness, extreme flexibility, and far-reaching extensions were close to, if not identical to that of the prima ballerina Pavlova. Her face was stunning then: somewhat oval, with high cheek bones, a nose that was straight with a slight upward tilt at the end that gave her an aura of self-importance, an aristocratic flare; hair that was black, and her eyebrows extended to the edge of her eyes; eyes that were pale brown. That seems so long ago. The face now looks long and gaunt, the cheekbones excessive, and the hollows under her eyes, dark gray. Will it all change after the heart transplant? Will she get robust and strong and be able to dance and glide in the air?

"Will Dr. Ali come to the OR during the transplant?" she asks. Jackie is distraught at the question. "He is grounded in Boston," she says. "I haven't heard from him. I couldn't get hold of his wife either. My God—to think of it, she worked in the World Trade Center. I hope she's all right. Dr. Denzel will be harvesting your heart for some research."

She had briefly met the transplant surgeon Dr. Steven Cohen, and was told he was damn good despite his youthful appearance. What if something goes wrong? She trusts Ali—he would go all the way for her.

"Finally, Anna—you have waited so long, consider yourself

lucky," Jackie says, squeezing her hand, and summarily ending her anxieties. "There was one other, with your blood type and body habitus—the Saudi Arabian Princess. There was a rumor that her father was willing to donate millions to the Heart Center. She was called to be ready. She couldn't be located. Apparently she and her family flew out of the country."

PART

V

It is infinitely better to transplant a heart than to bury it. —Christian Bernard

CHAPTER 36
The Prep

In the Heart Center, in the one-bedded room that had often been her home, Anna has a couple more hours left. She thinks of her ordeal, the repeated cardiac arrests—the shocks from the defibrillator—with some relief that all this is about to end. She remembers the dwindling of her life, her detaching and deserting her body, and gazing at her lifeless carcass from a distance; the doctors and nurses ceaselessly working, pumping, and shocking repeatedly with electricity. She wonders whether that floating away feeling, the peeling away from her body, would come again when they put her under general anesthesia. And what if she never returns this time? What if she dies? What will happen to Katya? She had done well by meeting with her lawyer and willing her daughter's adoption to Mary and Brad, if she were to die. She had also signed a living will instructing that she should be removed from the respirator if brain dead.

But where is Mary? Perhaps she's already dead? And if she were dead, what would happen to Katya? She had to go on living for Katya's sake. Oh God, please, let the transplant take—let my body not reject it. Let it accept as its own.

A knock on the door interrupts her prayer. "May I come in?" The entourage of doctor visits begins in preparation for the transplant: Dr. Kim, the cardio-thoracic Fellow, enters her room with a broad smile on his face.

"Are you ready for the Big One, Miss Anna?"

They ask the same questions and she answers them—it is a ritual in teaching hospitals. He hands her the consent form, which she signs without bothering to read it. And then it is the anesthesiologist—the man who would put her to sleep. He asks her when she last ate, not once, but three times.

"Did you drink any water, tea, orange juice? Any dentures?"

For Christ's sake, get on with it, she feels like telling him. He examines her mouth; places a stethoscope on her chest—they all do. Why? Her heart is going to come out anyway. What does it matter how it sounds: Lub-dub or lub-dub-dub or doesn't sound at all? She is alive isn't she?

Her chest and groins cleanly shaven, Anna, is swaddled in intravenous tubing and very dopey after a sedative. She is now alone with nobody to hold her hand. It is one o'clock in the morning.

She hears a faint voice: "Is it you, Mama?"

"Come, come here Anushka. There, there he is, Anush-ka—your father is on television marching in Red Square on the Great May Day Parade. Come soon—there, he is saluting the Politburo—they are focusing the camera on him. Do you see him, Anna? There, there, on the podium reviewing the military parade is General Secretary Brezhnev."

"Is that Papa? Will he come home soon?"

"Nyet! We will not see him for a long time, not until he gets drunk and she kicks him out. Why do we need him, Anna? We are better off without him. When you grow up, when you become a ballerina, I will send you to America, where gold grows like apples. And you will be rich and famous, my Anushka. Come, come, my Anushka, come lie in my lap."

"Where is America, Mama?"

"Far away."

"I want golden apples...I want golden apples..." she sings.

"Anna, honey, you dreamin' again? Wake up, honey. Come, help me get you on the stretcher," says the Jamaican orderly.

"Where are you taking me?"

"To the OR—you is getting a brand new heart."

The spotlights are blinding in the white and light blue of the Operating Room. The surgeons, anesthesiologists, nurses and technicians, all masked in their sterile gowns, like faceless-robots, move around, talking among themselves, all doing their thing to keep alive Anna's broken machine.

"Just a small prick, Anna...let me know if it hurts," says Dr. Klein, the anesthesiologist. She feels a burning sensation going up her arm as if her vein is a lit fuse of a bomb. "It's the anesthetic Anna. It will pass away." He begins inserting a tube though a vein in her neck, which snakes into the heart to measure pressures inside her heart. She barely senses the tube going down her throat into her lungs; another into her gullet, to look at her heart—the transesophageal echo, the one she had so many times before.

"Take a look at this, her heart barely moves. It amazes me how these people survive at all," Dr. Klein explains to the resident. He stops to catch a glimpse of Anna's forehead, closes her eyes and tapes them. She wants to tell him to stop, but she cannot move her lips. She feels sad. Alone. She longs for her mother like when she was a little child. "Mama, Mama," she whispers. "Come Mama, please sing me a lullaby. Please Mama, soon, I may die......sing me a poem, a partying lullaby." She has no sensation left. She is floating away on a cloud. It's so wonderful, so painless; all her troubles are coming to an end.

The machines do their work: monitor the rhythm of her heart. Blip—blip; the blood pressure in her heart, her body temperature.

She hovers over her body. She sees her gown taken off and straps secured across her legs. She is naked under the floodlights. A faint antiseptic whiff of Iodine fills the air. Like wet sticky paint, they scrub her whole body with Betadine. Sterile blue drapes cover her. Her face is placed under a tent. She could be in a grave. Will Ali come, like he had when she had the defibrillator? Will he open the drape and put his face inside the tent? Will he look inside the grave, to take a peek at her?

"Is the donor heart here?" asks the transplant surgeon, Dr. Cohen.

"The ambulance is on its way. It should be here in another ten minutes," says Elena, the OR nurse. "There's no traffic. The streets are empty."

"Great, I will scrub then."

Dr. Cohen, well known for his speed, his diligence, his creativity, and his calm under pressure, stands beside the sink just outside the OR, all masked and hatted, and stretches out his hands under the gushing tap as he rubs them vigorously with a sponge full of antiseptic, over and over again for five minutes until his arms and hands are pale, almost purplish. He enters the operating room with his hands apart like a priest about to give a benediction. He wipes his hands with a sterile towel when Elena hands him the sterile gown the color of the sky. She opens the gloves with her hands and he inserts his own, and the gloves snap around his fingers, first the right hand, then the left. He looks at his hands, the hands of a master craftsman, as if to confirm that they are still there, his perfect hands, all intact. He remembers his school days when his friends compared their hand size and he never made the big hand boy club. His were delicate, sensitive, the way he made circles with a pen, the way he moved them like a virtuoso on the keyboard. Those steady sensitive hands serve him well when he performs surgery on the heart, the minute sutures for the coronary anastomosis, and the heart valve repairs. Only recently, on the advice of his brother, an investment analyst, he had insured those delicate master hands. He never boasts of his skills, but in his own mind, he is no less than Michelangelo or Picasso.

"Dr. Cohen, we are waiting for your orders," says Elena.

"I was a bit distracted there. We have some time on our hands."

CHAPTER 37

The Heart Transplant

"Can I proceed? Is the donor heart here?" Dr. Cohen asks.

"It's on its way. Anytime now," says Elena. He has some time on his hands.

"Did you guys see the replays on TV?" he says. They nod their masked heads.

"Only yesterday I had a chance to see what went on. I was in the OR the whole day of the eleventh. Oh my God, the raging inferno—it was unreal. Hollywood stuff. I couldn't imagine anything like it in my wildest imagination."

"My neighbor, a twenty-five year old mother, a commodities broker, perished in the North Tower," says Elena.

"I know a firefighter, a friend from Staten Island. He's gone, leaving a young three-month pregnant wife," says Lopez.

A sudden disquiet settles in the operating room, followed by a spontaneous moment of silence, unplanned, uncalled for, as if in respect.

"What happened to our CIA and FBI? This is the second time around with the Twin Towers," says Dr. Cohen.

"I'm sure there will be a lot of questions when the dust settles," adds Lopez.

"It's here. The donor heart is here," Elena announces, and for a moment the OR is stilled with expectation like during the curtain call of a stellar ballerina. And it arrives in a portable cooler.

Anna hovers over the cooler.

In a cooler? Anna ponders. What if there was a mistake and somebody exchanged the cooler and all that it contains are cans of Budweiser? What would happen to me? Would they just close my empty chest and announce that I died of heart failure? Doctors do these things at times, don't they? Do one thing and say another?

Elena opens the cooler. It is packed with ice. A plastic tie sticks out. Elena pulls on the tie. It's a plastic bag that Elena unties. Ice cubes fall, chilled water drains, and another plastic bag. She unties the second one.

There it is, pale-purple—the heart frozen at four degrees centigrade.

Will it ever beat? Anna wonders.

Dr. Cohen holds it in his hand. Examines it closely like someone examining the ripeness, the firmness, the tautness of a mango. "It looks great," he says, the ultimate connoisseur of hearts. "Did she die in the World Trade Center?" Dr. Cohen asks.

"I don't know. Why do you ask?" says Elena.

"I wonder whether there are any others. We have several people waiting—donors are hard to come by. It's sad it takes a disaster."

At that moment, Jackie comes rushing to the OR.

"Dr. Cohen, you've got to hurry. There are plenty of more

donors. I just got a call from the National Organ Procurement Center. They have donated their hearts to New York City."

"Who?"

"Connecticut, Texas, Cincinnati, Oregon, California, Washington... There are two chartered planes with military escorts taking off. I have called all our patients on the list to stand by."

"Wow, I can't believe what I am hearing. It takes an immense disaster such as this: to Give A Heart—to Have A Heart."

Dr. Cohen injects a cold cardioplegic solution in the vein of the donor heart. The veins engorge like leeches after sucking blood. He places the heart in Anna's empty chest. "A perfect fit," he says. "I'm certain it was a woman with her body build, probably her age as well."

To Anna, it looks brand new, slim and taut.

An electric saw rips open Anna's breastbone. A retractor keeps it apart exposing the heart. The knife cuts through the outer lining of the heart.

"Look at that—it's like a wobbly leather bag engorged with blood," explains Dr. Cohen to the surgical residents in training.

Large tubes are connected to the big artery—the aorta, which arises from the heart and pumps blood to the body. Tubes are also connected to two large veins, one coming from the upper part of the body, and one coming from the lower. These tubes, like rivers, are connected to the heart-lung machine. The aorta is cross-clamped. Blood ceases to circulate around the body. Dr. Cohen nods at the perfusionist, Mr. Lopez. "Let's go Loopy," he says.

Anna is placed on the heart-lung machine: the surrogate pump-purifier. Her disconnected heart, now irrelevant, beats its slow, weak, stumbling pace like a wounded soldier tracking up an icy hill. Her body temperature is lowered to twenty-five degrees centigrade. Her heart quivers like a dying jellyfish and then stops, puckers, and collapses like an empty wine leather sac. Ready to cut out Anna's heart, Dr. Cohen asks for the knife.

Hovering above her draped body, like she had during her cardiac arrest, Anna watches Dr. Cohen cutting her heart out, neatly, cleanly, like slicing an overripe melon about to implode. He hands the crumpled lifeless bag to Elena, who hands it to the waiting Dr. Denzel, all gowned and gloved who takes it in his two hands like a discarded piece of steak, plops it into a jar and rushes out.

"Hah, hah, hah, there it goes," Anna laughs, "my poor lousy, and good-for-nothing heart. I hope they hack it to pieces and look it over under the microscope for the benefit of science, and grind it like minced meat and make pies out of it—heart pies to be distributed in my poor old Russia."

She feels free—*a free-floating atmospheric spirit.*

"Do you have any news of Ali?" asks Dr. Cohen, as Denzel makes for the door. "Is he back in the hospital?"

"I just saw him walk into the hospital… His wife was in the World Trade Center."

"Oh my God, yes, I know. The poor guy—he went through some ordeal on his way back from Boston. Well I don't want to talk about it now. Let's proceed." Dr. Cohen collaborated with Ali on his research protocols and has a fondness for him. They were childhood friends, and it was he who had raised doubts in Ali's mind about God.

CHAPTER 38

The Agony and the Ecstasy

After signing the papers, Ali briskly walks out of the hospital. As he hails a passing cab, he is overwhelmed by that despairing moment when he weighed the unnatural death of his wife against a mindless life maintained by a machine. The next moment she was gone. Soon her body will be cold and rigid, felled by his decision to disconnect the life support, or the other way around, the holding-death support. To lose all things of grace and beauty that one loves and holds to heart has a common denomination: of pain and lingering sorrow, of shearing apart one's very existence, of disrupting the very flow of blood. She is dead, and the idea of it, he has to place on the altar, like a sacrament to worship hereafter.

As the taxi approaches his apartment building, he finds himself reluctant to go home. The feeling of emptiness overtakes him, as the weight of his decision takes hold of him again. He asks the taxi driver to take him to the Medical Center instead. It is perhaps only there, in the environment he knows best, that he can seek refuge. The memory of Nancy is too fresh and raw in the apartment; and the memory of the son, his son, whom

he will never know, his room is there—a monument to the Unknown, to the Unborn.

He feels a strong desire, an inner call, whatever its meaning,
its symbolism, to bring her back for one last moment, to feel
her beating heart, to say one last word, to see that smile one last
time, to tell her how much he loves her. He feels an irresistible
longing to begin life all over again with her, so that they can say
and do everything right. But he has to give in to the finality of
death. Death: with its unrelenting power to extinguish life; to
be alive, lively one moment, to be gone, the next. He remembers
the brief conversation they had as she was about to come down
the Tower. She would have made it, but luck was not on her
side, for an instant, things just went wrong. She had waited for
her boss, had helped him with the chest pain. What happened
to him? And Dr. Bob, yes, Dr. Bob, he's gone too. Demons were
let loose. The world has gone mad.

He walks into the hospital, which is desolate like the City
itself. His footsteps echo through the emptiness, as he hastens
towards his office.

Ali sits in his office, his head resting in his hands, contemplating. She was so wonderful, so kind and caring and understanding. It is people like her who bring some degree of sanity
to this insane world. Overwhelmed with guilt that he is alive,
while she and his son are dead, he feels unworthy of them. He
remembers the incident on the Ashura day, the mourning for
the Imam's martyrdom, when he held the blood-splattered body
of the dying young martyr. Nancy was a martyr, an unwilling
martyr, a sacrificial lamb killed randomly at the hands of the
jihadis.

Sinking deeper and deeper into this collage of interrelated
thoughts, he bangs on his desk, cursing in sheer desperation.
He throws the books against the wall, the porcelain ballerina
that Anna had given him, the Swarovski crystal watch, a gift
from one of his fellows; he tears at his hair, he bangs his fists

on his chest and slumps into the chair. He looks at the shreds of glass, the fragments of porcelain on the floor like slices of his shattered life.

Exhausted, he leans on his empty desktop with his head in his hands, numbed. All his dreams, his accomplishments, have gone up in the furnace of the WTC. He wishes to join these flames, to be charred, like the widows in India in the ritual of *sati* who sacrificed themselves, and went up in the crimson buttered flames with their husband's remains on the funeral pyre. He sees Nancy's image in the ICU, hooked up on all those machines. In her, he sees the fragility of life—its greatness, its hopes and promises one moment, its hopelessness the other. When he most wanted Medicine to succeed, that element of science that lived in his very bones, his own faculties, had betrayed him; and so it seems that even God, the merciful God, has abandoned him in many different ways. And in all this he sees himself deserted, immersed in the lost reality, unprepared to embark on a new journey, to go it alone, to tread the extra mile.

"Ithaka gave you the marvelous journey.

"Without her you would not have set out.

"She has nothing left to give you now."

Nancy's picture stands on the bookshelf. He holds it in the palm of his hand tracing her smile with his eyes. He sobs uncontrollably. *Why, God, why?* Is all he can ask and hear himself say, bobbing his head. The image of the bleeding young man in his arms, of Nancy swollen, immobile, lifeless on the respirator, the image of the burning Towers, the image of death, of martyrdom, of self-sacrifice, a lost ideal—this juxtaposition of images and ideas keep recurring in his mind.

"*It is hopeless. I don't want to live anymore,*" he finally utters aloud.

The thought, the very idea now takes hold of him, that the ultimate sacrifice demands he take his own life for the cause. If he dies for the cause, he will be a martyr, no matter how he takes his own life. But here his mind enters the realm of the irrational, as he tries to define the cause, the sacrifice. His mind goes blank, suspended in space like an aimlessly, lifeless floating balloon, and then, unexpectedly, it suddenly strikes a chord. He sees the cause, the ideal, staring straight at him, and the ultimate sacrifice he has to make: the donation of his organs, like the donation of Nancy's heart.

Yes, I have it now, potassium chloride, easy and slow, and I will write a note to donate my organs. One man's death is another man's life. It is the only way I can redeem myself, to follow in her footsteps.

While Dr. Cohen is busy suturing the donor heart, Anna hovers over it and stares. It looks pale and puckered; she wonders if it will beat, if it will come alive.

She realizes there is an important errand left. She has to go find Mary, before she has to get back into her body. Brad had told her she was at the Downtown Medical Center. She knows where it is; once, many years ago, she was taken there herself when she felt dizzy and nearly fainted.

She finds Brad sitting in the waiting lounge with a blank expression on his face, as if he is wearing death's mask. Another long-haired man sits by his side. He consoles Brad, his hand resting on his shoulder. The man has peculiar features, rugged and old, as if he is an ancient, a recycled spirit from another world. Anna senses that something is wrong—that Mary isn't well. She enters the ICU, her spirit unseen. She goes to Mary's bedside and strokes her face; Mary momentarily opens her eyes. She calls out to her: "Mary, Mary!" And Mary opens her eyes again.

Mary fights the respirator. The alarm goes off. A nurse comes running.

"She's awake—it must have been the sedation. Let me page the resident doctor. I think we can take her off the respirator."

Dr. Smith appears. He pinches her arm. Hard. She responds by moving it.

"Hi Mary?" he says. She opens her eyes, and moves her hand gesticulating that she wants the tube out.

"Let's extubate her," Dr. Smith orders. He leaves the ICU to tell Brad that all is well. Mary is awake. She is going to make it. Brad hugs the old man. The old man stands up and does a circular dance.

"It's the spirits of my ancestors, Doctor," Brad utters, shaking the doctor's hand.

Anna is happy for Mary. She is happy for Katya. She is no longer needed. She will be a hindrance to herself and to her daughter. She feels alone, crushed by the sheer weight of her sadness.

"Is life worth living?" she asks. The pain and suffering she had endured, the constant separation from her daughter, and now, with the new heart, the examinations she would have to constantly submit to: the biopsies, the echoes, the scans, the infections and the immunosuppressive drugs. Another five years or so, at most—that is, if she is lucky. The life of a transplant recipient is fraught with unknowns—it is weathered and soiled. She feels drained to go it all alone. And her suffering will be her daughter's suffering. Mary will make a wonderful mother, and Katya loves her. It is best for all.

Now, at this very moment, she has to take her leave.

Anna goes to the lakeside in Central Park. The swan maidens crowd around her. They sense her distress. The small black swans flutter their wings creating tiny wavelets. The full moon reflects on the lake and bounces off its ripples like silver pearls.

"He will come," the swans tell her. But Anna shakes her head. There is no Prince any longer. This is not the script of the last scene of *Swan Lake*. It hasn't played the way it was supposed to play. The sorcerer died a long while ago. They are all free to go. Come morning, they have to leave the lake. For her, it is different. Her Prince married another. There is nothing left for her now. Tchaikovsky's music cries out for her grief, as she runs towards the edge of the lake. The swans intercept and implore her to wait.

"Your Prince is only human. He didn't know the sorcerer's cruel power."

"No," she shakes her head. "This is not the last scene of Swan Lake." She crouches in agony, like a dying swan, and sobs. "Only in death there is redemption for me."

The swans gasp, bewildered.

In the Operating Room, Dr. Cohen completes attaching the donor heart into Anna's chest. It is now the moment of truth. He asks Loopy to warm her up. He waits for the donor heart to start beating.

The heart engorges with blood.

There is a bluish hue to the heart.

Dr. Cohen holds the heart in his fist and squeezes it like squeezing a lemon.

It puckers, fills up, and distends like a fat plum.

He squeezes it again, and again, giving open heart massage.

The donor heart doesn't beat on its own: no lab-dab....lab-dab.

"Give her some calcium," he orders. He seems at a loss. Droplets of sweat gather on his exposed forehead. He signals Elena to wipe them off.

"Page Ali," he says, and in desperation. "Cool her down."

Suddenly, Anna and her sister swans see two masked figures: a woman and a man at the lakeside. The couple commence dancing a pas de deux. The woman wears a white flimsy gown that shimmers in the moonlight. A misty radiance emanates from her. She casts a glow on the lake water. It is as if she is disengaged from space and time. The man is tall, dark, decked in black, and masked. His lean body casts a long sinuous shadow like that of a weeping willow on the silvery lake; his eyes reflect a profound sadness, as if he is mourning a loved one's death.

The swan princesses stare in awe.

The man holds his partner around the waist and lifts her high above his head. She executes supported arabesques followed by pirouettes that terminate with an open pointing of her leg. The man then stands behind her. She leans back softly against him. He opens his arms, as she opens hers, and they turn around and embrace. She turns a final series of small pirouettes in his arms, moves slightly away, rises on pointe and lifts both arms up. He holds her by the waist and moves her toward him. They remain in embrace, as if oblivious to the world around them. Anna and her sister swans watch mesmerized and dazzled at the two masked figures, now almost one in the showering moonlight. For an instant, the moon hides behind a curtain of clouds as a large shadow covers the lake. The swans flutter their wings, thinking it is the evil sorcerer.

There is a sudden crash of cymbals.

The lovers remain embraced, undisturbed, like two loving ice statues.

Two Spanish couples appear and dance a quick divertissement to the sound of Flamenco guitars. Then Five Hungarian couples line up and commence a czardas that gathers in frenzy to end in a swift whirling finish. The Spanish and the Hungarian couples leave the lakeside. The lovers seem unaware of the celebration of their love around them.

There is another crash of cymbals.

The swans flutter their wings in fear and crowd around Anna, their Swan Queen. Anna pushes them away urging them to shed their fear.

The woman's body suddenly trembles as if helplessly, as she disengages from her man. He wakes up from his trance-like state to watch her leave. He stretches his hand toward her, as she glides further and further away, like an ore-less boat carried by a swift current. He runs after her in great strides; she runs faster overpowered by a blazing energy. She stops for a moment in front of Anna, a single-short moment when she stretches her hand, barely touching Anna's, as she looks at her and smiles.

She continues running, now almost at the edge of the lake. He runs after her. "Wait! Wait!" he cries. His voice echoes far beyond the lake, through the pines and birch trees.

She suddenly transforms into a white Swan with wide wings, and takes flight. She circles around the buildings around the park, and slowly rises beyond, far beyond the moonlit horizon.

As Ali contemplates how to obtain vials of potassium chloride from the Coronary Unit, his beeper goes off; at the same time his phone rings. Responding to the beeping sounds like a Pavlovian dog as all doctors do, awake or asleep, in sickness and in health, ready to charge, to save a life—at least that's what they try—he looks at the number. It is the operating room. He reflexively dials the number.

"Dr. Ali, you are wanted here. They have an emergency with Anna." He changes into the OR scrubs and charges ahead, forgetting about himself, about the insanity that took hold of him of taking his own life just a few moments ago. He bursts into the Operating Room.

"Thanks for coming, Ali—we cannot get the donor heart going. I don't understand it," says Dr. Cohen. "I had to place Anna back on the heart lung-machine. There is no bleeding. The coronaries are well connected and superbly perfused. It is as if this Anna doesn't want to come back to life."

"Maybe it's the donor heart," says Dr. Kim.

"The donor heart looks fine to me," responds Dr. Cohen. "It's mysterious."

"Well, let's try again," says Ali.

"Warm her up!" Dr. Cohen orders.

"Let's inject epinephrine and calcium," Ali suggests.

"Done."

"The heart's fibrillating."

"Shock it."

"Hand me the paddles. Set the current to maximum."

"Here Dr. Cohen."

"No dice."

"Let's try again."

"Any suggestions, Ali?"

"Give her one-hundred and fifty milligrams of Amiodarone."

"Done."

"Let's shock it again."

"No dice."

"Give her another one-hundred and fifty milligrams of Amiodarone and ten milligrams of Bretylium."

"Done."

"Let's shock it again."

"Flat line." Everyone expectantly waits.

"Another ampoule of calcium."

"Flat line."

"Pace the heart at 110 beats/minute."

"Done."

"She's generating blood pressure."

"Another ampoule of epinephrine."

"The blood pressure is coming up."

"Stop the pacing. Let's see if she has any rhythm," says Ali.

"She's in junctional rhythm. Great, we got it working."

"Two milligrams of Atropine."

"She's in sinus rhythm."

"Let's pace her heart at a rate of 110 beats per minute."

"Done."

"The blood pressure is 110/70," says the anesthesiologist.

"Let's take her off bypass," orders Dr. Cohen.

"She's off bypass," says Loopy.

"Great, we got this one going. I am dying for a cup of coffee and a chocolate glazed donut. I'm done here. Will you guys close her up?"

"Will do," says Dr. Kim.

"You want to join me, Ali? We have a lot to talk about," says Dr. Cohen. As they cross the Avenue to go to the nearby Deli, the early morning sun rises over the East River. The cross streets are empty. There is no one in sight. A yellow taxicab with a bearded, skull-capped driver ploughs slowly, anxiously, on Madison Avenue.

Dr. Cohen places his hand on Ali's shoulder as they enter the Deli.

"You have a brave heart, Ali," he says.

We only part to meet again. —John Gay

EPILOGUE

After Nancy's funeral, Ali moves in with his parents. Pat boxes all of Nancy's stuff. Some of her belongings, including clothes, and some relics of childhood and adolescence, she carts away to her home. Only three pictures line the naked corridor: the snowfall on Grymes Hill, Nancy and Ali embracing each other with the Vermont fall foliage in the background, and the downtown New York skyline in black and white—the World Trade Center's two silhouettes in the distance. These, Ali keeps in his possession. The crib and toys in the baby's room are donated to the Salvation Army. The apartment is bare, empty and silent. The walls speak of nothingness, as empty walls often do. The end of one cycle; perhaps the beginning of another.

Into this apartment, Ali makes his appearance four weeks after Nancy's death, barely recovered from the acedia that consumes him. He sits on the couch, watching the shades of amber enter the living room as dusk gives way to night. He listens quietly to the hum of sporadic traffic piercing the perfect silence. Outside, life is back to normal, or so it seems, but the strain of 9/11 is visible on the faces of pedestrians, unclear, unsure, wondering whether it will happen again.

Ali stands up and closes the window to shut out the world. He unfolds the closeted prayer rug, placing it in the living room. He kneels, bends down, facing the East, the Land of the Crescent Moon, his head touching the silken treads, smelling the damp-stale odor of the rug, as if commiserating with an odor of reassurance, an odor of belonging, an odor of a different time, an endless time... In the distance, it is as if he hears a voice, a shrill raspy cry from atop a minaret, invoking the greatness of God, Allah u' Akbar.

He weeps...

He prays: O *my Lord! Grant me that I may be grateful for Thy favor, which Thou hast bestowed upon me, and upon both my parents and that I may work righteousness such as Thou may approve; and be gracious to me in my issue. Truly have I turned to Thee and truly do I bow to Thee in Islam (Surah 46:15).*

He folds the prayer rug, places it in the empty closet, picks up the text book on tropical medicine, opens its pages and absorbs himself in the diagnosis and management of malnutrition and infestations: of hookworms, roundworms, and malaria. He is eager to enter an old world, of old diseases, diseases of the far East, of refugee camps, of war-torn countries, of displaced bodies, ravaged minds who want nothing but a morsel of food, some water to drink, a piece of land, and a place to sleep. On and on he reads, until a shroud of fatigue settles over him, and he succumbs to a deep, dreamless, and undisturbed sleep. When he gets up at six in the morning, he realizes that he is due to resume work—the heart mending at the Medical Center. However, his career doesn't matter to him any longer; the high-tech world he lived in, of heart transplants, of mechanical devices, of heart biopsies, have lost their appeal, their brassy shine. Perhaps, all this is temporary, a sort of a numbing feeling, a reaction to Nancy's death, as if it has placed him under some anesthesia, spinal perhaps, awake and yet insensitive from head to toe.

He researches on the Internet about the organization *Médicins Sans Frontières/Doctors without Borders,* and the work they are doing in Africa and Asia among the refugees and the displaced of the world, and the idea of joining the organization begins taking shape in his mind. He simply wants to move away from the world he lives in, a world of personal achievement, of a constant urge to climb the ladder, so to speak. His position in New York, the offer in Boston—all that has lost its charm, its testosterone hauteur. All dissipated, evaporated into thin air. He has retreated into a solitude that has grown day by day, but gradually, he is ready to shed it all, to vanquish the shadow of the man, to conquer the man within.

Anna recovers from the surgery; the new heart gallops in her chest steadily and confidently. She is rapidly taken off the respirator, and in just two weeks she is up and about the Cardiac Center. Her mother and her daughter return from Russia to an emotional reunion. Her body accepts the new heart as if it is its own; there is no sign of rejection.

When Ali enters her room, on the very day he returns to work, Anna is asleep after a heart biopsy performed at eight in the morning by Dr. Denzel. Standing at the foot of the bed, Ali stares at her. She is smiling in her sleep, as if contended. He notices the radiance in her cheeks, the hair done up in a bun. He remembers her as he had seen her for the first time dancing briefly—the Swan Queen at the Lincoln Center. He wonders whether she will dance again.

She wakes up from her sleep to see him standing at the foot of the bed.

"I'm so sorry, Ali," she says. They embrace each other.

"Don't you want to listen to my new heart?" she finally asks, as he pulls away. He fumbles in his white coat pocket and finds his stethoscope missing.

"I forgot, or maybe I lost my stethoscope."

She undoes her hospital gown exposing the scar on her chest. He places his hand on her chest, below her breast, and feels the apical impulse of her heart. He is overtaken by a sudden desire to listen to it with his bare ear.

"May I?" he asks, as he lowers his head and places it on her chest to hear a consistent *lab-dab*—a rhythm he was too familiar with, a rhythm he had known many times before. He withdraws, flushed with tears.

"It's beautiful, your new heart," he says, as he chokes.

"I wish you were there to see it."

"I was there, Anna, when it struggled to beat."

"What do you mean?"

"Never mind—it's all too technical. What's important is that the donor heart is working fine, and there are no signs of rejection."

"Yes, it feels beautiful, and warm and so alive," she says.

"What a difference—the new heart; I'm going home tomorrow to a new life."

They sit on the bed side by side in silence, fingers briefly touching like the moment on the Staten Island ferry years ago, each of them unclear where they would ultimately land, each of them struggling to retain the faith, *as if holding on to the heart that now belongs to both of them.*

War looms over Afghanistan. Soon, smart bombs, bunker busters, and daisy cutters will rain over the mountainous landscape. The newspapers report that American Special Forces and the CIA have already infiltrated the country, preparing the ground for the coming invasion. Refugees crowd on the border between Pakistan and Afghanistan. The United Nations relief agency predicts a catastrophe. Ali finally receives the call from Doctors without Borders in response to his application. "You are assigned to the refugee camp in Afghanistan, at the border, near the Pakistani town of Peshawar," says the voice on the other end. "You will receive a letter spelling all the details, the training, the preparation, the immunizations, etc.

At Kennedy airport Ali's parents and Anna are there to say their goodbyes.

"Will you promise me to write?" Anna says.

"Yes, I'll write, Anna, I'll write."

"Promise me," she insists. "I cannot understand it. You are just running away."

He smiles and shakes his head; words are stuck on his immobile lips.

"Please stay, Khokon," says his mother, her face flushed with tears. "If not New York, then Boston."

"I'll return in a few months, Ma."

His father embraces him, and wishes him well. "May Allah be with you," he says.

In London, as he finally boards the flight to Pakistan, he feels a rising uncertainty, as he remembers his last flight to Boston. His world has never been the same since. For a moment he wonders what lies ahead for him without Nancy. Where is she? He ponders. She's here he thinks, and pounds on his chest, his heart.

As the plane takes off, Ali imagines Anna jumping high up in the air, her new heart pounding and pumping. Her ground seems solid, while his is riddled with cracks and crevices.

When the plane crosses into Afghanistan, toward Pakistan, the sun slowly rises in the East, the stars disappear, but they are still there, unseen, like the human faces that vanish from sight, but remain alive in the crevices of one's mind, frozen in time.

Ali looks out of the window. Below, the sun casts a glow on large snow-capped mountain ranges in a desolate arid land, a no man's land that has seen constant invasions before, and history is about to repeat itself. His concern is for the ordinary people, the powerless people, the refugees, the innocent women and children who will get caught up in the mess. A sudden sadness tears at him. He sees the world at the brink of war, and asks himself how it could all have happened. How optimistic he had been after the end of the Cold War, the downfall of Communism, and the roaring late nineties and America's positive engagement in the World. It all seemed the makings of a peaceful new century. And suddenly, the world has catapulted backward, into another time, of fundamentalism, of religious wars, crusades and jihads.

As the plane begins its descent, an eagle soars and banks towards the distant mountains. For an instant he hears a voice, a whisper:

"Ali, listen to your heart...listen..."

GLOSSARY

Arabesque: a posture in which the body is supported on one leg, with the other leg extended horizontally backward.

Bharatnatyan: is a major form of Indian classical dance that originated in the state of Tamil Nadu.

Blackout spell: is a temporary loss of consciousness and muscle tone caused by a precipitous fall in blood flow to the brain.

Burqas: a long, loose garment covering the whole body from head to feet, worn in public by many Muslim women.

Catheterization Laboratory: is an examination room in a hospital or clinic with diagnostic imaging equipment used to visualize the arteries of the heart and the chambers of the heart and treat any stenosis or abnormality found.

Cardiac Unit: is a step-down unit where the heart rhythm is monitored constantly.

Calcium signaling: is the use of calcium ions (Ca^{2+}) to communicate and drive intercellular processes often as a step in signal transduction. Ca^{2+} is important for cellular signaling, and once it enters the cytoplasm it exerts regulatory effects on many enzymes and proteins.

Cardiomyopathy: is a disease of the heart muscle that makes it harder for the heart to pump blood to the rest of your body. It can lead to heart failure

Coronary Care Unit: is a specialized hospital ward dedicated to caring for people with serious or acute heart problems.

Chaotic electrical storm: a rapid heart rhythm known as ventricular tachycardia/ventricular fibrillation that can result in a black out spell and sudden death.

Chaîné turns: is when a dancer is performing a series of turns on both feet, picking up each foot back and forth in order to keep moving in a line or circle. It could easily be considered one of the most basic turning step or exercise because chaînés or "chaîné turns" don't rely balancing on one leg.

Conscious sedation: is a combination of medicines (sedatives) to help relaxation (a sedative) and to block pain (an anesthetic) during a medical or dental procedure. The subject will probably stay awake, but may not be able to speak.

Curandeira: is a traditional native healer/shaman found in Latin America, the United States and Southern Europe. ... Many curanderos emphasize their native spirituality in healing while being practicing Roman Catholics.

Czardas: a Hungarian dance with a slow introduction and a fast, wild finish.

Divertissement: a short dance within a ballet that displays a dancer's technical skill without advancing the plot or character development.

Echocardiogram/Ultrasound: An echocardiogram checks how the heart›s chambers and valves are pumping blood through the heart. It uses ultrasound technology to see how blood moves through the heart. An echocardiogram can help your doctor diagnose heart conditions.

Electroencephalogram: a test to record brain electrical activity.

Electrophysiologic stimulation study: is a test used to evaluate your heart's electrical system and to check for abnormal heart rhythms. ... Electrical signals are also sent through the electrodes to stimulate the heart tissue to try to cause the abnormal heart rhythm.

External programmer: computer that programs the pulse generator of a pacemaker and internal defibrillator. It can detect the heart's rhythm and transmit this information to the pulse generator in the body.

Familial cardiomyopathy: is a genetic form of heart disease.

Fellow: a doctor specializing or subspecializing in a specific area in medicine after finishing his residence training.

Grand Rounds: A formal meeting at which physicians discuss the clinical case of one or more patients. During Grand Rounds the case is presented to a senior faculty member, usually a Professor of Medicine or Surgery.

Heart biopsy: is a procedure wherein a heart specialist inserts a device into the heart to take tiny pieces of the heart muscle for pathologic examination.

Heart function: measures the pumping action of the heart and is measured as the ejection fraction (EF) expressed as the percentage of the blood the heart pumps with each beat. The normal EF is more than or equal to 55%.

Heart failure: is a condition in which the **heart** cannot pump enough blood to meet the body›s needs. The presence of heart failure can cause shortness of breath, heart irregularity and ultimately result in death.

Internal defibrillator: is a small battery-powered device placed in the chest connected to electrodes placed in the hearts chambers to monitor the heart rhythm and detect irregular heartbeats. It can deliver electric shocks via one or more wires connected to your heart to fix an abnormal heart rhythm.

Jêté: a jump in which a dancer springs from one foot to land on the other with one leg extended outward from the body while in the air.

Mariinsky Theatre: it is a historic theatre of opera and ballet in Saint Petersburg, Russia. Opened in 1860, it is the preeminent music theatre of late nineteenth-century Russia, where many of the stage masterpieces of Tchaikovsky, Mussorgsky, and Rimsky-Korsakov were premiered.

Mass General Hospital: stands for Massachusetts General Hospital, a prominent institution in Boston, a major affiliate of Harvard University.

Mutations: is a change in a DNA sequence. Mutations can result from DNA copying mistakes made during cell division, exposure to ionizing radiation, and exposure to chemicals called mutagens, or infection by viruses.

National Institutes of Health: is one of the world's foremost medical research centers. An agency of the U.S. Department of Health that confers research grants to individuals and institutions.

Neurotransmitters: are chemical substances that are released at the end of a nerve fibers by the arrival of a nerve impulse in nerve synapse or junction in the brain. The neurotransmitters serotonin, dopamine, norepinephrine, and gamma-aminobutyric acid (GABA) are thought to be linked to mood and anxiety disorders. Neurotransmitters are in charge of regulating various body functions and emotions.

Nenuphar: A European white water lily (Nymphaea alba) or the yellow water lily (Nuphar lutea).

Nuclear membrane: is the **membrane** that encloses the nucleus. This bilayer **membrane** is made of lipids, and encases the genetic material in eukaryotic cells. The **nuclear membrane** is made up of a double lipid bilayer.

Ob/Gyn: Obstetrics and Gynecology

Pas de bourrées: a transitional movement in ballet in which the dancer transfers body weight quickly from foot to foot in three small steps.

Pas de deux: a ballet dance for two people, typically a man and a woman.

Paxil: a psychotropic drug, used for depression.

Pericardial tap: a needle is inserted in the sac lining the heart to remove fluid or blood.

REM-dream state: Is characterized by rapid eye movement sleep and vivid dreams.

Rounds, Rounding: When an attending or consultant doctor

sees a patient in the hospital either by himself or with his residents and fellows in training it is referred to as making rounds or rounding.

Sarcomere: a structural unit of a myofibril in striated muscle, consisting of a dark band and the nearer half of each adjacent pale band.

Synapses: a junction between two nerve cells, consisting of a minute gap across which impulses pass by diffusion of a neurotransmitter.

Sudden cardiac death: sudden unexpected death within one hour of the onset of symptoms

Subdural hematoma: is a type of bleeding in which a collection of blood—usually associated with a traumatic brain injury—gathers between the inner layer of the dura mater and the arachnoid mater of the meninges surrounding the brain. It usually results from tears in bridging veins that cross the subdural space

Ventricular fibrillation: is a heart rhythm problem that occurs when the heart beats with rapid, erratic electrical impulses. This causes the pumping chambers in the heart (the ventricles) to quiver uselessly, instead of pumping blood.

Well-compensated heart-failure: means your heart works well enough that you either do not notice any problems or the symptoms are easy to manage. You do not have fluid buildup in your legs and feet, and you can breathe without trouble.

Ya tebya lyublyu: *I love you*

ACKNOWLEDGMENTS

To my wife Margarita Suren Mikhno for being the source of inspiration for this novel; to my editor, publisher and friend, Walter Cummins; and to the Two Bridges Writers Workshop members for their revision advice.

ABOUT THE AUTHOR

António Gomes, also known as J. Anthony Gomes, is a Professor of Medicine at The Mount Sinai Medical Center, NYC. He has published extensively in Medicine including two textbooks of Cardiology, *Signal Averaged Electrocardiography: Basic Concepts Methods and Application* (Kluwer Academic Press, London/Amsterdam, 1993) and *Heart Rhythm Disorders: History, Mechanisms and Management Perspectives* (Springer-Nature, 2020). He has also published articles in the humanities in anthologies, books, newspapers, and magazines; two books of poetry entitled *Visions from Grymes Hill* (Turn of River Press, Stanford, Connecticut, USA, 1994) and *Mirrored Reflections* (GOA 1556 and Fundacão Oriente, 2013); and a novel, *The Sting of Peppercorns* (GOA, 1556 & Broadway Books, 2010); 2nd edition, Amaryllis, New Delhi, India, 2017) and *Nas Garras Do Destino*, published in Portugal and Brazil in May 2019 by Chiado Editora, Brake Media, Lisbon, Portugal.